THE

MINOR PROTECTION ACT

A NOVEL

"The wicked freely strut about when
what is vile is honored among men."

PSALMS 12:8 (NIV)

Jodi Cowles

ISBN 1-933204-11-7
Library of Congress Control Number: 2005935221

for my family: here with me, and there with Him.

CHAPTER 1

If the politically correct set was searching for a poster couple, they would need to look no further than Erik and Roselyn Jessup. In college they lit up doobies while attending passionate speeches about legalizing marijuana and freeing Tibet. Erik was even arrested once for helping break into an animal research center. Roselyn bailed him out. After five years of dating they decided to tie the knot. Seven years later, after Roselyn had enough time to get established in her career, she gave birth to their pride and joy, Jayla Lynn Jessup.

Both had satisfying full-time jobs that left them only enough time to pour themselves into Jayla. They attended every event at school, even if it meant working overtime and paying the after school program for a few extra hours. When Jayla made the principal's list or won a spelling bee, they were cheering, and filming, from the front row.

Jayla began junior high at a brand new school with a brand new curriculum. It was being called "progressive" in the papers; the first program of its kind implemented in California with plans for a nationwide rollout over the next 10 years. Praise poured in from around the country, applauding the straight talk about sexuality and focus on tolerance.

Erik and Roselyn were thrilled to have their daughter in this groundbreaking program. Granted, it took several phone calls to district authorities to accomplish the transfer and Roselyn had to drive an extra 30 minutes each morning to drop off Jayla, but it was quite a coup to brag about in their circle of friends.

Jayla turned 13 two years into junior high. For her birthday she told her parents she wanted to order pizza and hang around the house – there was something she needed to tell them. Over pepperoni and Coke, Jayla calmly informed them that she'd been discussing it with her friends and teachers and had decided she was gay.

Though she had never had a girlfriend, or a boyfriend for that matter, Erik and Roselyn were quick to affirm her decision and let her know she had their full support. Roselyn applauded her daughter's honest, courageous move and told Jayla how proud she was. Erik was also supportive and went so far as to tease Jayla about her best friend Sara.

There weren't too many lesbians in her junior high and Jayla had a pretty average experience, but she attracted attention when she entered high school wearing the rainbow buttons specially purchased by her mother. Soon she was 15 and seriously involved with Carla, the 17-year-old senior who was President of the Gay Pride Club. When Erik and Roselyn saw the relationship deepening they sat Jayla down and had a heart to heart "sex talk," encouraging her to be responsible and safe, and only to have sex if she was truly in love.

She was. However, when the year ended Carla left for college on the east coast and broke off the relationship in a letter.

Jayla was heartbroken. Erik and Roselyn were quick to comfort, as any loving parents of a shattered teenager, but their answers seemed hollow to Jayla, their comfort cold. At 16 she began dabbling in drugs - a first for her.

By the time her senior year began the family bond that was once so strong had disintegrated to the degree that she seldom spoke to her parents unless it was to strike out in anger. She had not entered into another dating relationship, as much as they encouraged her in that direction. Rather, she seemed withdrawn from the world and spent endless hours either locked in her room or suspiciously absent. Finally, Roselyn had enough and took her to a doctor who prescribed an anti-depressant for teenagers that had just been released on the market.

By Christmas the medication seemed to be working. Jayla was coming around, spending more time at home. She seemed calmer and more at peace. They were even beginning to talk about college. But New Year's morning they found her dead, her anti-depressant bottle and a quart of vodka laying empty in the trash and a mass of journals and letters scattered around her in the bed.

Erik and Roselyn were devastated. Jayla had been their whole life. They dove into the letters and journals, trying to make sense of it all. What they found only served to inflame their anger. Some boy named Nick had been telling their daughter that she was a sinner, quoting Bible verses that said her sexual preference was an abomination before God. Jayla's journal was full of self-loathing, page after page about her relationship with Carla, page after page of rambling, agonizing pain.

Why was she made like this if homosexuality was a sin? Why would her parents have supported her if it were an abomination? Why had she listened to the seventh grade teacher who told her experimentation was the best way to determine her sexuality? What was wrong with her?

They could hardly stand to finish it but they read every word. In the end their grief found relief, as it so often does, in bitterness and hatred. The day after Jayla's funeral, attended by hundreds of students from Jayla's school, Erik and Roselyn met with the District Attorney. A year later, bitterness not yet assuaged, they went to see a lawyer. In the culture of America, where there is rarely tragedy unaccompanied by litigation, they found a willing law firm. Someone would pay.

CHAPTER 2

SUPERIOR COURT OF CALIFORNIA COUNTY OF
VENTURA
HALL OF JUSTICE, COURTROOM 22
JULY 30

The courtroom was still, the only sound coming from the podium where a tall, relatively handsome man stood shuffling papers. He gave the impression that he wasn't looking for anything, just making sure all eyes were on him. He need not have worried on that account.

"Ladies and gentlemen of the jury, it is a great honor for me to be standing before you today. It is a privilege, not only to appear in this court of justice, but to be allowed to present closing arguments for such a just cause. The case before you deals with matters at the heart of what is tearing our great country apart. In the past 20 years we have observed a considerable escalation of violence in our cities and schools. There has also been an intolerable rise of teen suicide in that same time frame. Why? What is causing our children to act toward themselves and others in such violent terms?

"Ladies and gentlemen, I want to tell you a story. It's the story of a family. A family just like yours and mine. "Jayla Jessup was a 17-year-old senior in high school. Her parents, Erik and Roselyn, had high hopes that she would attend their alma mater, Stanford the next fall. There had been a fair amount of problems in this family - they were by no means perfect. Jayla had a relationship that ended badly and reacted like teenagers all over the world by withdrawing from her parents and writing bad poetry. However, toward the middle of her senior year she began to come out of her shell and rejoin her family and school society. Her parents were spending weekends helping her write college application essays. Then, on New Year's morning, Erik and Roselyn found Jayla dead. She'd committed suicide and they were left with no explanation other than the journals and letters surrounding her which served to form an extensive suicide note.

"Those journals told an awful tale - a secret she'd been hiding from her parents and friends. Jayla was being brutally harassed by students at school; particularly one student, 17-year-old Nick Rodman. Nick and his gang of friends who called themselves a 'prayer group' had been attacking Jayla and her lifestyle choices for nearly a year. The letters from Nick were filled with hateful remarks calling her a sinner, telling her that she would go to hell because she was a lesbian. Her journals grew increasingly desperate, full of more and more doubt, more and more self-hatred. She wrote in despair that maybe she should just end it all - maybe that's what God required of her.

"The evidence before you is undeniable. Nick Rodman and his gang terrorized Jayla Jessup into committing suicide. Those are the clear, hard facts. Whether they believed themselves well intentioned, or were acting out their own self-hatred, the resulting outcome is the same. Left alone to pursue her own happiness she would never have committed such a drastic act. You have heard hours of testimony from experts in the field testifying about the effect peer pressure has on teenagers; the effect such gang tactics would have on a girl who had never before faced such bigotry, intolerance, and I believe I may say, hatred."

The man had remained behind the podium up to this point, but now he paused and slowly walked over to stand in front of the jury box. Every eye in the courtroom followed his movement, including the electronic one in the corner.

"May I remind you, Nick Rodman's guilt is not the issue before you today. Last year he was convicted under the National Hate Crimes Bill and is currently serving a 15-year term in the California prison system.

"Seeing their daughter's murderer behind bars was not enough for the Jessups. Not because they were consumed with thoughts of vengeance, but because Jayla's parents couldn't live with the thought that this might happen again. After Nick's conviction they sought legal counsel to determine what could be done to ensure that no other parents would ever have to go through the hell they'd endured. Erik and Roselyn Jessup decided to sue Steve and Ellen Rodman, believing that this was as clear a case of parental responsibility as you can get. If they could highlight the legal connection between hate-mongering parents and the acts of their children, they believed Jayla's death would not have been in vain.

"The National Hate Crimes Bill is clear on the subject of parental responsibility - if their children are researching and ordering bomb materials on the Internet, parents are responsible. If parents are too caught up at work to notice their son is hoarding firearms in his room, they are responsible. The Supreme Court has upheld that law in two separate rulings since its passage.

"I ask you now, how much more responsible is a parent who shows his child how to make a bomb? How much more responsible is a parent who buys his child a firearm and takes him out for target practice, then buys bullets and helps the child load them in his backpack before driving him to school?

"You might say I'm being dramatic, that such a thing would never happen. Members of the jury, I stand before you today as the representative of one family who felt the repercussions of the very situation I've described. Steve and Ellen Rodman provided their son the weapon that killed Jayla Jessup. They showed him how to load it and helped him practice firing.

"You have heard witness after witness testify that the Rodman's taught Nick their intolerant belief system and ingrained in his mind from early childhood that it was superior to all others. Not just superior, but the only correct belief system. They taught him the intolerance he wielded like a battering ram every day. They quizzed him on the Bible verses that he used as bullets to pierce Jayla's psyche.

"Ellen Rodman was arrested ten years ago for blocking entrance to a reproductive freedom clinic. She taught her son a very powerful lesson at a very young age. She showed him through her actions that it was okay to break the law and infringe on other people's rights, as long as you felt strongly enough that you were right and they were wrong. Steve was no better as a role model. When he went to bail his wife out of jail he had Nick bring along balloons and turned the whole episode into a celebration. During the last six months of her life Jayla spent increasing amounts of time at the Rodman residence. Not only did Steve and Ellen witness their son's behavior and do nothing to stop it, but Jayla's journals indicate they added to her despair. She wrote about thinking of Ellen as another mother, feeling welcomed into the warmth of their home. But at the same time, Steve and Ellen were approving and supportive of Nick's agenda. Jayla was getting beaten down from every side."

Once again the man paused. He slowly walked back to the podium from where he'd been pacing in front of the jury. After taking a small sip of water from the glass near his notes he continued in a more subdued tone of voice.

"The worst thing about this case, the thing that makes me physically ill when I can't sleep for thinking about it, is that we have no clue how Nick Rodman might have turned out had his parents not systematically poisoned his mind from birth. We have no idea what a fine young man he could have been, perhaps getting ready for college with his best friend Jayla, rather than facing 14 more years in a prison cell as her killer. We'll never know what he could have become because his life has been destroyed no less dramatically than Jayla's.

"I have asked you one question again and again over the course of this trial and today I will ask it a final time. When does a person, expressing their own beliefs in accordance with our Constitution's right to freedom of religion, go too far? When does that expression cross the line into infringement of another person's Constitutional right to the pursuit of happiness?

"The case before you today will make history, ladies and gentlemen. You hold in your hands the very future of America. Your decision will shape the climate of our country for the next century. I beg you, don't allow this tragedy to be replayed over and over again. This is your chance to change the dangerous road we're on. Your decision at this moment will be remembered by your children's children. Send the message that parents will no longer be allowed to brainwash their children with bigotry and intolerance. Send the message that acting out in religiously-motivated hatred will no longer be tolerated in our great society.

"I want you to look at the Jessups, parents just like most of you. I want you to look at them and think about why they're here. They are not bitterly angry, nor out for vengeance. They didn't sue the school system that allowed Nick and his gang to flourish, despite being in clear violation of the Constitutional mandate regarding separation of church and state. They didn't sue anyone else in the so-called prayer group. No teachers, churches or youth pastors that were involved. They don't want blood, they only want justice. The Jessups have not banked a dime of profit out of their tragedy, funneling all monies into Jayla's Fund, a non-profit they set up to help schools deal with the repercussions of hate crime. Look at them, think of their motivation, and think of their loss."

He picked a battered journal off the podium and flipped to the back. "In closing I'd like to read Jayla's words, written less than a month before her death. I ask you to listen carefully and let your conscience guide you:

'Why would Nick say such hateful things? How can he be so kind and funny and caring in so many ways, but so hard and cruel on this issue? How can he say he loves me but not accept that I'm gay? And Steve and Ellen - they treat me like another daughter and pour out so much love that I want to move in sometimes, yet I see in their eyes that they agree with Nick. Are they right? Am I an abomination? Am I a sinner who's going to burn in hell because I'm a lesbian? I'm tired of being told I'm damaged goods. I'm tired of these questions and accusations going around and around in my brain. I don't think they'll ever stop. I know Nick will never stop. I don't know what to do anymore. Maybe if I just get it over with and kill myself God will accept that as just punishment and not make me go to hell. If not, at least I'd find oblivion. At least this awful pain would end.'"

When he finished reading there was absolute silence in the courtroom, as if time paused, giving humanity a moment to decide which path it would take.

SUPERIOR COURT OF CALIFORNIA COUNTY OF VENTURA
AUGUST 2

It was a madhouse outside, with the kind of media presence usually reserved for the more infamous Malibu courthouse nearby where yet another celebrity was being arraigned on charges relating to drugs, drunk driving, shoplifting, or whatever else could be counted on for a good 6 o'clock story. However, the difference was clearly painted on the sides of the vans now filling the parking lot. If this had been just another celebrity slip-up they would be the local channels like KTLA and Fox 11. Instead, the vans parked nose to nose boldly proclaimed the interest of Fox News, NBC, ABC and CNN. This was a major story and the line-up of easily recognizable, nationally known faces speaking with the courthouse as a backdrop reminded Jack of the frenetic energy surrounding the 2000 election. He had been a senior in high school at the time and hadn't paid much attention. His only real memory was that the news kept preempting his favorite TV shows and he hadn't been able to watch anything else for a week. The reporters appeared now as they had then, falling over one another in an effort to get the best position for their dramatic LIVE reports.

Jack took a deep breath, pausing just a moment before they caught his scent. Obviously the usual moles hadn't yet passed on the information that the verdict was in, otherwise they'd have spotted him already and would be tripping each other in the rush to jam a microphone in his face. The jury returning after only three days of deliberation was quicker than he'd expected and sooner than he'd hoped. He was a practical man and knew he had asked quite a bit more than the average American sitting on a jury was willing to give.

Of course, this jury couldn't exactly be labeled a group of average Americans, or even a jury of the defendant's peers. Jack had been able to convince the judge that anyone with a conservative Christian background would be biased so they were cut automatically. The judge even cut a few moderately religious prospective jurors just to be safe. Jack then used his challenges to cut as many philosophical conservatives as he could. The fact that he was pulling jurors from one of the more liberal counties in Southern California helped considerably. Overall he'd done well, effectively smearing the opposing lawyer before the opening arguments when his prize juror was chosen as forewoman, a Berkeley educated single parent whose college age daughter was gay.

Jack felt that this was the perfect case to change the future and he had high hopes for his handpicked jury. Those hopes kept him awake the entire three days and nights of deliberation, pacing the hall of his apartment when he wasn't busy avoiding phone calls from industrious reporters who thought the idea of a judicial gag order didn't apply to them.

His eyes lingered briefly on the figure of Beth Billings, NBC's newest golden girl, before scanning for the easiest approach. Just as he reached for the door of the car he'd borrowed from his brother to sneak in unnoticed a man came bursting out of the huge double doors and announced, "They're back."

Jack groaned, "Too late," and quickly stepped out with his head down, preparing to run the gauntlet. Cameras and microphones immediately materialized and managed to record him as he stumbled over a cord haphazardly lying on the red brick sidewalk. For a man so eloquent in the courtroom, Jack was known for being accident prone in front of the press and had tripped on no less than 13 cords during the two-month trial.

Finally he made it through the unruly herd and was greeted by strong-armed guards who let him pass unmolested while, at the same time, managing to stop the crowd behind him at the metal detectors.

Entering Courtroom 22 Jack barely glanced at the Rodmans, huddling with their bargain basement lawyer in the same position they'd occupied throughout the duration of the trial. The same friends and family, all looking slightly shell-shocked, sat behind them. The first few weeks he couldn't stop glaring at them. Every time he caught Ellen's eyes he saw something that, if he hadn't known better, he might have described as pity. That, along with her calm demeanor, infuriated him. Whenever he paused in questioning or note taking he would glance at his open briefcase and the side-by-side pictures of Jayla and Nick and it would start the burn in his stomach all over again. Twin tragedies.

After the first month of the trial Jack realized with some consternation that he didn't exactly blame the Rodmans. Seeing their obvious devastation day after day, he couldn't help but feel a little sorry for both of them. He began to look at them the same way he looked at an alcoholic or a drug addict on the street. Someone who couldn't help themselves, granted, but also someone who shouldn't be allowed to make major decisions that influenced young lives.

He nodded to the Jessups already seated at the plaintiff table. They had arrived before him, as per usual. Erik's stone face betrayed the cold fury burning in the pit of his soul, while Roselyn's radiated bone-deep anguish. Jack sat down quickly, opened his briefcase and positioned the pictures one last time. He stood as the judge walked in, sat for the jury, and tried to keep his legs from twitching while he waited for the bailiff to make the long walk between forewoman and judge, and then back again. He held his breath as the forewoman stood and read the verdict.

"We, the jury, in the matter of case #423J7 Jessup v. Rodman, find in favor of the plaintiff and award compensatory damages in the amount of 200 million dollars and punitive damages in the amount of 300 million dollars."

The uproar was surely loud, but Jack couldn't hear it over the buzzing in his ears. He'd won. He'd actually won. The announcement was made to the press in front of the courthouse at exactly 4:45pm. It was August the 2nd, a day America would never forget.

MOORPARK, CALIFORNIA
AUGUST 23
7:45AM, FRIDAY

Jack was relieved to be returning to work. It had been three weeks since the ruling and he'd spent nearly the entire time doing phone interviews with reporters from across the globe, as well as on-camera interviews with Larry King Live and the Today Show. When he'd gotten home the night before there was even a message from someone claiming to represent the Oprah Winfrey Show. Unfortunately, the caller sounded remarkably like his youngest brother plugging his nose.

The trial itself had gained so much national attention he thought he'd be prepared for the verdict, but the media blitz mushroomed and the past three weeks had been incredibly draining for a man accustomed to a quiet private life.

This would be his first day back in the office. Matt had told him to take the weekend but Jack was too excited about the prospect of normal life, although he wasn't sure how normal his life would ever be again. Time and Newsweek had both run cover pictures from his closing argument and he was sharing the center billing of next week's People with the Jessups. For most of his life Jack had dreamed of being a moral crusader, but a celebrity lawyer? Never! He found the attention that accompanied his role disconcerting and was a little worried about how his 15 minutes of fame seemed to be expanding with no end in sight. Going into work seemed like the only normal thing to do.

A black limo flanked by two sedans pulled up just as Jack stepped out of his apartment. Piling out were serious young men in suits looking a lot like all other serious young men who surround people of power. As Jack reached the bottom step he nearly stumbled at the incongruous sight of Benjamin Henry's gray head making an appearance in his small neighborhood.

"Jack! Wonderful to finally meet you," he said, extending a hand as he smoothly completed his exit.

"Sir...Mr. Attorney General, sir, I…yes, the pleasure is mine..." stuttered the usually unflappable Jack.

"Jack, I'm just on my way back to DC but I was wondering if I might have a word with you. If you wouldn't mind forgoing the traffic this morning I could drop you at work on my way to the airport." Anticipating the answer, he was already sliding back into the limo.

Jack took just a moment to wonder how the Attorney General had known what time he'd be going to work this morning before sputtering, "Uh, yes sir, that would be an honor..."

"Jack, forget this sir business, call me Ben." Jack barely got an affirmative "hmmm" out before Ben launched into his speech.

"I'll be straight with you, Jack. This trip was already planned because I had to meet with some folks, but after that verdict came down Tony and I decided I needed to make a point of meeting you." Jack blanched at this casual reference to arguably the most popular President in the last 100 years, but luckily the AG had glanced out the window so Jack had time to quickly compose himself.

"We're both just tickled pink with the job you did. That summation will go down in history. You should have seen the VNs!"

Jack actually had seen his VoteNow numbers, but he didn't put as much stock in them as the White House did. "Well, thank you, sir, I was just speaking from my heart…"

"And that's what we appreciate about you, Jack, your firm stand against bigotry and hatred; your idealism, believing what you do can make a difference. I don't think I have to tell you Jack, that kind of shooting from the hip is sorely needed in our country, especially in the viper's nest where I work."

Jack was having trouble keeping up with the Texan's quick pace, but he managed to slip a "No, no, sir, you don't," between energetic sentences.

"That's why I stopped by this morning. Tony and I have been tossing an idea around for a couple years now, but the timing has never been right. We'd like to share it with you because we think you're the man for the job. I've got a box of reports here and I'd like you to review them over the weekend. No big preparation or memorizing necessary, just read them and get the gist. Do you think you could fly out Sunday and meet with Tony and me Monday morning?"

"It would be an honor, sir." Though sincere, it came out just a little stilted to Jack's ear, but suddenly seeing his exit coming up he decided to screw on his courage and jump for it. "Can I just say, you've been a hero of mine - watching your career and the impact you've made has always been an inspiration to me."

He probably would have continued rambling platitudes as the Attorney General nodded and smiled, but the limo came to a stop and it was time to get off the merry-go-round.

"Monday morning, Jack. You should find all your travel information in that box."

"Yes sir, certainly sir. I'm the man for you..." to a closing door and an accelerating limo. Jack stood in a daze for a minute, clutching the box tightly before slowly turning to climb the stairs.

It took an hour to get out of the office. After explaining to Matt why he'd decided to take the day off after all and why, in fact, he wanted to take the next week as well; he had to repeat the story 14 times to get out the door. Without the benefit of police sirens clearing the way it took another 45 minutes in the wretched traffic to get from his office in Westlake Village back home. Matt insisted on having the office driver take Jack home so he spent the time staring dazedly out the window, running the scene over and over in his mind. Finally he made it home, changed into shorts, and stared at the box on the table before him.

"Let's see what we have here, Charlie," he spoke more to himself than to the golden retriever whose head was flopped in his lap. Taking the lid off the box another surprise was waiting for him on the very top of the stack, a handwritten note with the Presidential seal signed simply "Tony."

He unconsciously sat a little straighter and read: "Jack, I'm glad you agreed to take a look. Familiarize yourself and we'll discuss it all Monday morning. I believe we've finally found the man for the job. Tony. P.S. Don't cheat!"

It would have been a simple note, but for the fact that it was penned by the leader of the free world. It was that fact alone that kept Jack from ignoring the postscript, skipping the thick stack of reports and ripping right into the sealed envelope he'd found at the bottom after methodically taking everything out of the box and arranging it on his scuffed coffee table. The bold lettering scrawled on the outside stated: "Don't open this until you're done with everything else!"

Dutifully, he picked up the first item, a 150-page report that covered governmental findings regarding school violence during the last 20 years. A few hours later he flipped it closed. Watching each of those events on television had been difficult enough one at a time, but putting them all together was really depressing.

Charlie woke up when the leather from the ancient couch squeaked with Jack's upward movement. The dog knew the routine and settled back down for another segment of napping while Jack took a five-minute jog through the rooms of his small apartment definitely an acquired skill.

Five minutes, precisely, and Jack sank back into the couch with a Mountain Dew and grabbed the second report. This 256-page effort was the result of another governmental commission and included criminal actions involving reproductive freedom clinics.

It also covered the last 20 years, but most of the information appeared to relate to the last five years since President Farmer got his Reproductive Freedom Act passed. It took Jack over three hours to wade through that report.

Another five minute jog, bathroom break and second Mountain Dew along with a delivered pepperoni pizza helped Jack through the third report. The most massive so far at 497 pages, it contained the usual hate crime statistics released to the public, but also had a detailed summary documenting each occurrence that looked to include classified FBI case file information. Jack found himself wishing he'd eaten the pizza with a different report. It was full of personality profiles, notes from teachers and family members, school report cards. Each optimistic batch followed by the details of some horrific crime accomplished by the person everyone thought was "quiet" and "kept to himself."

The most disturbing was the fourth report. In a simple accounting format, clean columns clearly organized, the author had set forth some startling statistics. According to the research, which looked like it included every crime he'd just spent all day reading about, individuals who perpetrated 50.2% of school violence, 74.7% of hate crimes and 96.9% of the violations of the Reproductive Freedom Act were raised in what had been classified as fundamental religious homes. The implication of these statistics was beyond his imagining.

Report five, the final chapter of his assigned reading, appeared to be another government study ominously labeled "The Roots of Terrorism," each page stamped with a bold "Classified." Jack stacked it against all the other reports and found it came out ahead. He continued anyway, stubbornly, as it was nearing the tenth hour of intense reading and he was tired of all the bad news.

Around midnight he rubbed his eyes and stood slowly to stretch. This had been the worst to stomach. It was a study all right, but one the likes of which he had never seen. The report recounted the lives of 500 different terrorists active in the past 20 years. Through detailed analysis that went on for page after page, the authors accounted for every factor that could have created and/or fed into the terrorist's psychological state. The last section was a summary of 10 key indicators, what they called early warning signs of cultures and households that were breeding terrorists. For some reason Jack was struck with the similarities he saw between the indicators and Nick's upbringing.

The final sealed envelope that had looked so tempting to him this morning was just too much. Even for the President Jack couldn't read any more bad news. Besides, he had all weekend.

Saturday the envelope called to Jack as he walked by, but he ignored it and headed out the door. The previous day's effort had taken too much out of him. Being confronted in clear black ink with everything he'd been fighting against, every wrong he was trying to right brought to light the frustration and helplessness he'd felt all his life. He just couldn't bear to deal with it.

It didn't happen often, but sometimes the task Jack had set for himself seemed too big and he wasn't up to the fight. Whenever he was overwhelmed like this he'd get in his beat-up old Honda and drive up the coast until he found a quiet beach. Sometimes he rode his bike and sometimes he just sat and stared out at the ocean for hours, not moving a muscle until the last rays of the sun sank away. Then he would shake himself awake and drive home to fight the battles in front of him.

He'd spent many evenings at the beach when he was working on his closing argument for the Jessup case. Whenever he found himself getting worked up about Nick's ruined life he would automatically head for the car. Pacing back and forth in the sand he worked his way through several versions until he came upon the one he'd delivered. He wasn't sure what it was about the ocean that was so soothing; he just knew that it managed to calm his nerves. It was rejuvenating and reminded him that there was something bigger out there that he was fighting for - justice. And it encouraged him in his belief that justice could be accomplished if he worked hard enough, one day at a time.

On his way home Jack buzzed the Taco Bell drive-thru for the dinner of champions and then slept a long, dreamless sleep. Sunday morning was a leisurely gift for him, reading the Times and drinking a whole pot of coffee. A little before noon he went for a run beneath the peaceful trees of Tierra Rejada, then came back and showered before finishing his packing.

When everything was ready and he sat outside waiting for the airport shuttle he carefully opened the envelope and pulled out the final document. Considering the topics of the others, Jack was expecting another summary of criminal activity, or perhaps more psyche reports. Instead he found an internal report from Children's Protective Services. It was rather short, a mere four pages. There was a page of statistics and three pages highlighting the normal criterion required and procedures to be followed when removing a child from parental custody.

Jack finished and sat back against the steps, fairly well lost as to the meaning of this final report and how it related to the others. Thinking there must be something more to it he looked in the envelope and found a single sheet of paper that he'd accidentally left inside. He read along very calmly until he reached the last section, when he launched himself off the steps. Jack was still wildly pacing 20 minutes later when the shuttle arrived.

THE MINOR PROTECTION ACT

Americans believe in freedom. Ask anyone. We have spent our money and spilled our blood on fields of battle all over the world fighting for that belief.

We allow our journalists to criticize, investigate and condemn the government when other countries would kill them for the least of those offenses. Freedom of speech.

America gives a home to followers from every world religion. 90% of Americans believe in God and live their lives however that works for them. We even allow expression of beliefs 90% of Americans can't stomach. Freedom of worship.

Our citizens have come from every other nation on earth to realize the great American dream. Hard work, integrity and perseverance will not only feed, but prosper your family. Our poor eat better than 70% of the world. Freedom from want.

Americans spend billions of dollars a year in defense, both internal and external. Our Armed Forces work tirelessly to keep our country and many others protected. Freedom from fear.

Freedom. It is every man's desire and America's ideal. But even in America there are limits to freedom. A man does not have the freedom to murder another man. A woman does not have the freedom to steal from another woman. We must all live together, and living together means we give up different portions of our freedom for peace and harmony.

In the last 20 years we have experienced increasing turmoil that threatens to shatter our nation into a billion fragments. Freedom has been expressed and attacked in ways our founding fathers could never have imagined. They could never have envisioned one man shooting another in cold blood, claiming religion as a valid defense. Nor could they have envisioned terrorists toppling the monuments of one of our greatest cities in the name of religion.

In our 200+ years as a nation we have evolved in many ways. Now it is time for our idea of freedom to evolve as well. No longer can we allow one man's freedom of worship to infringe upon another man's freedom from fear. No longer can we accept the expression of bigotry, hatred and intolerance in the name of religious freedom.

Some parents are raising their children in a hostile environment filled with intolerant hate speech. The government has an obligation to protect the interests of these innocent children. Possibly more so, as children from these homes tend to learn from their parents and become intolerant, hate-filled bigots themselves. Raising children in this type of environment poses as much a threat to a child's healthy development as raising them in a household filled with crack cocaine. It encourages violence and bigotry, hatred and intolerance.

We have spent trillions of dollars fighting terrorism bred and fostered by religious zealotry overseas while ignoring disturbing signs among our own citizenry. No longer. We cannot keep our heads in the sand about our own breeding grounds. We cannot allow this to keep passing from generation to generation in our own country while lecturing the rest of the world from our supposed moral high ground. Religious extremism is cropping up in more and more places around our nation. Not just radical militia groups stockpiling weapons in remote corners, but average teens in middle-class suburbia expressing violent hatred for those who are different.

Never in our history have we held a child accountable for the sins of the father. Children are good and innocent; only by systematic instruction can they become mouthpieces of bigotry, hatred and intolerance. We've seen this again and again in terrorist states, young men and women brainwashed by religious zealotry that demands their lives. It is the responsibility of the parent to bring up a child who will live respectfully and tolerantly in our society. The government's responsibility is to protect its citizens from harm. If a parent cannot or will not take their responsibility seriously, the government must intervene as we have been intervening for almost 75 years with Children's Protective Services.

CPS takes children out of hostile environments and places them with more suitable foster families. CPS has always tried to keep custody with the parents, but in the event parents are harming their children there is no choice but to intervene for the safety of the child. If a parent cannot get their alcoholism or drug addiction under control, their child must be removed. If a parent is physically or sexually abusing their child, the child must be removed.

The Minor Protection Act expands the boundaries of current CPS standards to classify homes where parents teach bigotry, hatred and intolerance as hostile environments from which children may be removed for their own protection if no positive reforms are undertaken by the parents.

CHAPTER 3

FLIGHT 3006

To say it was a long plane ride, Jack felt, would be an understatement along the lines of "Tiger Woods was an ok golfer." Even though he was in first class and hypothetically could get away with almost anything, the flight attendant finally had to ask him to sit down. His pacing was getting on her nerves, as well as getting in the way of the free drink service.

He spent several hours sightlessly watching the heartland of America slide along beneath him as his mind traveled in another dimension altogether. Finally Washington came into view, monuments passing by his window one after another as the plane settled into the narrow corridor assigned to Reagan. Jack had flown into the city this way before but he was again struck by the airport's proximity to some of America's most recognizable landmarks.

Following the directions outlined in his travel plans, Jack picked up his luggage and looked around for his name on a stick. Within a minute he spotted it, attached to a young man in a chauffeur uniform. Wow! he thought. This kind of service definitely rates last year's tax increase...or maybe not.

Jack's driver introduced himself, picked up his one bag and led him out to the curb where a limo was waiting. The White House sticker prominently displayed was the only reason the parking cop wasn't writing a ticket, or worse, having the limo towed. Instead, he just stood there glaring at Jack and the driver, thinking somewhat inappropriate thoughts about the rich and powerful as they drove off.

Since it wasn't too late Jack asked his driver to take the scenic route. He loved Washington D.C., the sights, the smells, the pace. Everything rolled into a perfect ball of energy and influence. As the limo rolled over the streets it was received with the same nonchalance he gave limos in Los Angeles. Had it appeared in

Boise, Idaho it might have caused more of a stir but Jack would still not have noticed; he was caught up in childhood remembrances of the first time he'd experienced this city.

Jack fell in love with D.C. at the tender age of 13 on a family trip the summer before his parents split up. The beauty and history of the city had combined with relief that his parents had finally stopped their constant fighting to form a golden haze in his memory that lasted into adulthood. At the time he was too naïve to realize detente didn't signify peace, but rather the irrevocable dissolution of the relationship. His dad moved out a week after their return to California and Jack became the man of the house, surrogate father to his two younger brothers.

His disgust with Christians began the weekend after his dad's departure. The family had attended church semi-regularly as long as Jack could remember but it didn't have much effect on their lives other than increasing business. His dad volunteered as an usher and liked to joke that he passed out more business cards at church than at his monthly networking meeting. The Sunday after his dad moved into a new apartment Jack and his brothers accompanied their mother to church. He went to the youth group, as per usual, but when it got out early he snuck into the main service in time to hear the pastor announce his parents' divorce from the pulpit. The pastor asked anyone who knew the couple to stay after the service and Jack would never forget the look of shock and humiliation on his mother's face as the whole room full of people bowed to pray for her crumbled marriage. The fractured family never returned to church and Jack continued to harbor ill will toward what he thought of as "hypocrite Christians."

Over the years the strength of those childhood emotions faded, but Jack still maintained a healthy disgust toward all things religious. After high school he headed across the country to attend NYU at the end of August 2001. It was in the following month that his feelings about religious zealotry broke out again full force and he spent a good portion of his first semester volunteering at Ground Zero. He had been unsure of a direction when he went to college, but the hot and sweaty hours crystallized his thinking and he made the decision to attend law school. Jack knew he could do nothing for his mother, or for the victims of September 11, but he made it his goal to fight religious zealotry on the small scale wherever he found it.

The tiny firm Jack joined after law school gave him that chance. He spent four long years slugging out small battles and winning even smaller victories, but he gained a reputation in the area and when Erik and Roselyn Jessup were looking for a lawyer his name was mentioned. Erik felt very strongly that their best chance would come with an unknown lawyer, as opposed to using the ACLU or the other various and sundry celebrity lawyers salivating at the opportunity. He knew their case would not be helped by someone who sought fame as much as justice. There was just too much riding on it to prejudice the jury against them because of a slick law team. They weren't looking for a show; they just wanted someone who genuinely believed in their case.

After six months of legal wrangling Jack had managed to get the Palmdale Unified School District to overturn their policy of allowing student-led prayer at graduation. He was riding high from that victory when Erik called and asked for a meeting. Of course Jack knew who the Jessups were and he had sweaty palms when they walked into his office. The rest was history – the David and Goliath kind. Jack won a battle no one in America thought he had a chance to win.

Shaking himself from the bumpy trip down memory lane, Jack took a look at his watch. He could have stayed out as it was still relatively early but he decided an hour of touring was long enough and asked the driver to head to the hotel. Once there he ordered room service, flipped through the reports briefly one final time and turned in by 10. The driver said he'd be back at 8 and Jack wanted to be well rested. He might just as well have gone out and painted the town because he tossed and turned all night.

The Jessup trial had been Jack's first big case. He couldn't believe his luck when Erik and Roselyn showed up and told their tale in his small office that looked more like a supply closet. To catch a case like this, four years out of law school, was unheard of. He'd gotten quite a few calls and endured a lot of ribbing from old classmates in the early days of the trial, but once it got going strong and the media attention came to bear he'd returned fewer and fewer calls. The exposure had been great, but he'd been a bundle of nerves for months. He was just getting used to the level of energy in the trial when the verdict came down, thrusting him into a higher plane of attention with its accompanying anxiety.

The only reason Jack felt he had prevailed and come across at all articulately was the passionate belief he had in his cause. No matter the nerves, no matter the anxiety, as soon as he began speaking to the judge and jury, or even at rare intervals in front of the press, his nerves calmed, his intestines unclenched and his knees went rock solid. Seeing him make the transformation from fumbling everyman to jaw-clenched hero every day had captured the country's attention and been one of the reasons he rocketed from novelty to stardom. It also seemed to help his popularity that he didn't immediately ink a book deal and sign on as a network legal correspondent. He was sincere in an age of slick celebrity lawyers and that made him all the more likable to the public.

Jack was a novice who'd been in the right place at the right time. He hadn't been prepared, but he'd been swept up in the whirlwind and, consequent of his exceptional performance, had been reborn.

Nevertheless, as he lay that night between rented sheets, a few short hours from the biggest meeting of his life with the most powerful man in the world, he couldn't sleep. He could only toss and turn and toss and turn. Around two he finally dropped off and slept fitfully, dreaming of making one presidential faux pas after another.

1600 PENNSYLVANIA AVENUE
AUGUST 26
8:32AM, MONDAY

Jack's knees were wobbling.

For all the times he'd been a silent voyeur in this room through
the magic of television he thought he would be a little calmer, or at
least be able to look around without dragging his chin on the
ground. Sadly, he could not, and nearly got a rug burn before
locking his jaw back into position. Lucky for Jack the President
was running three minutes behind. The Attorney General had
effusively greeted Jack in the hallway and escorted him into the
Oval Office, then disappeared upon hearing of the free three
minutes.

Jack wondered at the implicit trust of leaving him alone in this
place, even for three minutes. He knew there were people who
would kill for a mere 30 seconds in which to do some secret
damage. Technically, yes, he wasn't alone since the door was open
and a stone-faced secret serviceman stood in the corner, but Jack
was fairly certain the man hadn't blinked once since the AG had
left the room. He wasn't sure that the man saw or heard anything,
though he did wonder what would happen if he tried to make a
prank phone call.

Snickering at his own joke calmed Jack's heart rate down a few
beats. At least now he could hear the clock behind the President's
desk ticking. Before his heart had been drumming too quickly and
the blood rushing in his ears had deafened him. He was abruptly
startled from his thoughts when the door opened again and the AG
entered.

"Jack, Tony is right behind me. He's just getting a picture taken
with some Girl Scout troop or other. You know how it is."

Not really, Jack thought but he nodded anyway.

"Did you get a chance to look over the material?"

"Yes sir," Jack quickly said, wondering if there was a lunatic
living who would come unprepared to a meeting like this.

And suddenly, he was there. President Anthony Farmer strode through the door mid-sentence, "And send up a sandwich for me, will you?" Normally those last two words would constitute a question, but Jack thought, in this instance they appeared rhetorical.

"Jack! So good to finally meet you." At least, that's what Jack thought he said. Since his heart rate was speeding up again Jack had to rely on reading lips. The President strode across the most famous rug in the world with his arm extended and they shook hands.

Jack had time to feel like a schoolboy standing at attention, but not much. The President offered a seat and began.

"Jack, I'd like to start right in if that's alright with you."

Similar to his first meeting with the Attorney General, Jack barely got in a nod before the President continued. "Like Ben told you, we've been tossing around the idea of this bill for a few years now. I'm sure you read the reports that we've been privy to so you know what we're up against."

Jack nodded again and the President continued, "What am I saying – you watch the news, of course you know what we're up against! The amount of hate crime and religiously motivated violence has skyrocketed in the last 20 years! We've got to do something before out society self-destructs! I believe it's incredibly short-sighted of us to watch the signs that parallel the Arab-Israeli conflict and not do something about it!"

The President's voice, normally the perfection of pitch and pace, always eloquent but rarely passionate, was receiving quite a workout as it reached repeatedly for the heights of exclamation. "I have to tell you, Jack, I can't believe I'm sitting here talking to you. When I heard about the Jessup case months ago I thought it was more than a long shot – I didn't think you had a snowball's chance. But I followed the case, getting daily reports of your progress. And I watched that summation three times. You have accomplished something that our lawyers told us wasn't possible for another ten years. I just want to congratulate you."

The President paused expectantly, ostensibly waiting for Jack to say something intelligent. He had to wait a few extra seconds for Jack to catch on, whereupon he mumbled out a, "Thank you, Mr. President." Jack was starting to feel a little better now that he could hear something besides the thrumming of his blood.

"Well, now we come to the part of the meeting where you tell me what you think of our little bill. Do you think you could sell it?"

After a slightly longer pause than necessary Jack began slowly, "Well sir, first of all I have to say, whoever thought of this may have created the document that will mold a new America as much as the Constitution and the Bill of Rights."

The President smirked in the Attorney General's direction as Jack picked up some steam. "Honestly, Mr. President, I never would have thought we'd come to a place like this as Americans. I'm a big believer in the goodness and, more importantly, the reasonableness of mankind. I would think that we could talk people out of this kind of reckless, illogical behavior; that all we had to do was keep reasoning until we saw a substantial philosophical shift. But reading all those reports, especially that final study caused me to do a lot of thinking. Perhaps we have come to the point in our history where we need to evolve." Jack spoke that last bit purposefully, calling to mind the wording he had read.

"Sir, I believe this bill could revolutionize the way Americans treat one another. We could finally have the kind of society our founding fathers dreamed of so many years ago. Realistically I think it will be a hard sell, but it is a cause that is completely worthwhile. I would love if you would consider putting me on your team."

After getting his pitch out Jack paused to take a breath. His passion had overtaken him and before he could get a hold of himself he'd spouted out in one long breath the entire speech he'd carefully prepared the previous night during his bout with insomnia.

The President looked at him for several seconds in utter silence, which seemed to Jack like a full hour. "I knew you were the man for the job. It's fortuitous that you have offered your services because that is just what Ben and I discussed before he met with you. We want you to present this bill to America. We both agreed that we don't have what you have right now. You have the skill, you have public opinion in your favor and incredible VN numbers. And most importantly you have the passion to educate the American people and turn the tide of opinion. Your summation was unbelievably supported by the public. Apparently you hit a nerve because your VN numbers were through the roof across the board. We believe you are the man and this is the time to enact legislation that will chop off attacks like the poor Jessup situation at the root. On a future note, when this bill gets passed as I believe it will, I want you to move onto our team here and help us nail down the rules of enforcement."

FOUR SEASONS HOTEL WASHINGTON DC

9:43PM Jack sat on his bed, gazing out at Rock Creek Park, peaceful in the darkness. More than twelve hours after the meeting destined to change his life and still he couldn't believe it. Six months ago he was pegging along at a semi-profitable law practice and was unknown to all but a small circle of friends. Six days ago he was relaxing from a victory in the biggest case in a generation and was fairly well known throughout the civilized world. And now, at the relatively young age of 31 he was getting ready to help start a revolution.

The President had concluded their eight minute meeting with some genuine back-patting along the lines of "I know you're the man for the job," and etc. Jack spent another 20 minutes in the Attorney General's office and the rest of the afternoon with several other lawyers who brought him up to speed on all the aspects the White House considered important. The Brooks Brothers lawyers weren't exactly pleased with the upstart newcomer but they remained professional to the end. Only as he walked out the door did he hear a snide remark about the heritage of his tie.

The plan, as outlined by the Attorney General, would be for the President to capitalize on Jack's current popularity level by introducing him in the next television address, one week hence. Jack had that time to prepare his initial speech of no less than six and no more than six and a half minutes. On that point Ben had been very clear. He would then be scheduled on a round of all the political talk shows during the next month. More if the VNs didn't go up quickly enough, but Ben assured Jack that both he and the President had a firm belief that Jack wouldn't need extra time to convince America.

The only thing that surprised Jack about the plan was when Ben casually mentioned his intention to remove the first child within a few days of the bill's passage. He hadn't expected such quick action but Ben convinced him it was necessary to make a few clear examples right away so that the rest would fall in line post haste.

Jack rode back to his hotel in almost complete silence, only speaking to instruct his driver to meet him at 10 the next morning for a trip to the beach. That was now twelve hours away and Jack knew he needed some sleep if he was going to come up with a killer speech appropriate to the occasion. He'd had quite a bit more than a week to prepare his Jessup summation and he knew the President expected nothing less than his best. With such a crucial bill hanging in the balance, Jack expected the same.

WASHINGTON MALL
ONE WEEK LATER
3:01PM

"Jack," the driver's voice carried across the wind. Jack had asked for the "wake-up" call at 3. Not that he was sleeping, but he was so caught up in practicing his speech that he couldn't break concentration for a simple thing like checking his watch. There wasn't time to make it out to the beach today so he'd been wandering the Mall all morning, absently noticing the scenery as he mumbled aloud.

In his California Casual attire he could easily pass as a participant in one of the many flag football games perpetually underway at the base of the Washington monument. It was incongruous, to say the least, for any first time visitor to see athletes racing around under that white monolith. They seemed out of place; too common for such historic ground. Nonetheless, all but those first time visitors had grown used to the sight and Jack passed unnoticed all morning, only garnering attention when his mumbling got out of hand.

The first Monday of every month President Farmer addressed the nation in a half hour program he'd instituted during the first year of his first term. Called simply "Talk," it was a forum for the President's pet issues, as well as his chance to respond to whatever was going on in the country and the world. It was important, Farmer said, to get a feel for what the country thought and he always took at least three polls during the program.

It had been fortuitous, perhaps, that the networks rolled out their new VoteNow rating system in the first year of Farmer's presidency. Some grumbled that it had been ready the year before but Hollywood had kept it from Farmer's conservative predecessor whose hand-picked candidate lost the election to Farmer by a small margin. Regardless of when it was created, the rollout happened at a perfect time to be utilized by Farmer.

His movie star good looks didn't hurt. Neither did the Hollywood image consultant brought along by his B-list actress wife. His political clout and her celebrity status, combined with the instant polling of his new program and liberals in the White House again for the first time in eight years helped to make him tremendously popular. His second election the previous year had been a blowout and there were perpetual rumors about overturning the Presidential term limits amendment.

For years networks had been pouring millions into replacing the Nielsen rating system and finally found something that would work. It cost several more millions to institute, but an inexpensive chip was placed in 95% of American television sets within a year of the rollout. The second phase was a new remote control for every American. There were only three buttons: red; white; and blue. Whatever was being measured, a small menu appeared at the bottom of the screen instructing which button to press for what vote. That data was sent to a central processing center whose computers then spit the results to anyone with clearance. All networks funded the center but it was independently run for the sake of data integrity. Within two years television was revolutionized by the instant viewer feedback. Of course, there were always the detractors who said television had completed its downward spiral toward pleasing the lowest common denominator, but those detractors had deplorable VNs so no one listened to them.

The system also spawned a whole new popularity scale that let everyone know who was in the country's good graces. VoteNow Popularity (VN-P) became the official ranking system for television shows and movies and the unofficial ranking system for celebrities and politicians. A good VN-P got you far; a great VN-P got you anything.

Another index of importance was the VN-S. VoteNow Satisfaction. This rather vague indicator was used to rate the public mood at any given time. How satisfied are you with... It was the most frustrating of all VNs for those in power to deal with. Everything could be going fine and then VN-S would take a dip merely because the weather was too cold for too long, or the Yankees lost a crucial game. Farmer's policy was that as long as VN-S was above 50%, everything was fine. As long as at least 50% of America was satisfied with how things were going in their lives he had nothing to worry about.

The last liberal President had often been accused of governing by focus group. Farmer got a great deal of satisfaction over perfecting that arcane system. His first issue had been a campaign promise to reverse the dangerous path his conservative predecessor had begun – eroding a woman's Constitutional right to choice. He began with what he called the unconscionable 2003 Supreme Court ruling that said abortion protestors could no longer be charged under federal racketeering statutes. Within the first year of his administration he signed into law a bill called the Reproductive Freedom Act that addressed physically blocking access to clinics. First strike, misdemeanor and $100 fine. Second strike, one night in prison and $1000 fine. Third strike, down for the count with a mandatory three-year prison term. Farmer was a little ticked at the leniency he perceived by giving two chances before the hammer fell, but it was necessary to get the majority vote.

He'd received a big boost when the ancient swing vote on the Supreme Court announced his resignation the day Farmer was sworn into office. Many cried foul at the blatant politicizing, but after he appointed a new justice who believed in the living Constitution Farmer was assured a majority vote for any legislation he favored.

The best part of the VN system from President Farmer's point of view was that he could get immediate feedback on any idea he introduced. His "Talk" show was among the highest rated programs on television because everyone in America tuned in to make their opinions heard. Farmer returned the feeling that voting mattered, and not just the passing feeling that the 2000 election had incurred - voting percentages had gone down again right after the spike for the 2004 election. Now everyone voted because everyone had a say, true governance by the majority. Some called it mob rule, but they rarely made it on the air.

The most compelling evidence that "Talk" was a hit was that the biggest night for pizza delivery switched from Must-See-TV Thursdays for the first time in almost 15 years. In truth, the release of that statistic was a lead story that had more to do with Farmer's unprecedented Congressional cooperation than anything he could have said. He had complete control over which guests he picked and politicians did whatever was necessary to garner a spot. Anyone who appeared had an immediate jump in their VN-P which always went over well back home.

There were times when Farmer's ideas weren't received very well. It was at those points that he brought out his big guns who went on the campaign trail. He would discuss the topic again the next month, and again the month after until he had the percentage he wanted, or until six months had passed, in which case he gave a brief talk about how he'd tried, but the public had spoken. It was the only time Farmer was known to be maudlin.

Jack shook himself and hustled to the limo. As close as he was he still needed to leave the Mall by 3:00 to get back to the hotel, change and arrive at the White House in time for the 6:30 taping. No one was late for "Talk" time.

CHAPTER 4

WHITE HOUSE STUDIOS
SEPTEMBER 2
6:27PM, MONDAY

Beth Billings had fought long and hard for the exalted media persona she now enjoyed. Driven since childhood, she'd pursued the top slot at NBC to the detriment of social life, family and anything else that might distract her from her goal. At age 32, she was within jumping distance of that goal. She appeared on the Nightly News at least twice a week and had a steadily climbing VN-P to remind her producer of every time a plum assignment came around.

The recent four point jump she'd gained from an investigative report on Welfare fraud put her two points ahead of every other correspondent at the network besides the aging anchor, whose VN-P was untouchable. That two-point lead was the reason she was sitting in the front row of the very small, very select "Talk" gallery, waiting for what the rumor mill promised would be a major announcement. It was also the reason no one was talking to her. She pretended not to notice, or care, as greetings and smart remarks swirled around her. The buzz abruptly stopped when the On Air light flickered. Beth glanced quickly at the President through the sound proof window to her right, then focused on the big screen in front of her.

The screen flickered with the familiar "Talk" logo, then faded to the smiling face of Anthony Farmer and his standard greeting, "Hello America." Early on he had been roundly panned in the media for that cliché greeting, as well as his boring show title, but the media quickly hushed when the ratings started coming in.

President Farmer's grinning face met the camera as he did his version of an opening monologue for several minutes, commenting on the state of various programs, before introducing Jack. "It's my distinct pleasure to introduce a man most of you are already familiar with. Jack Stone has been in the public eye nearly every day from his opening statement three months ago to his outstanding summation last month. We feel quite lucky here that we were able to pull him away from his busy schedule of TV interviews to speak with us today." Everyone in the gallery chuckled. Though Jack couldn't hear them through the sound proof window, he noticed the laughs and ducked his head.

"Jack is going to explain to you the particulars of a new plan of which I am very proud. I've been keeping close tabs on him these past months and I can assure you, he is what he appears to be. A man who believes in personal liberty and the right of every individual to practice his or her beliefs and lifestyle choices without fear of harm. I trust him and I know you do too - his VN-P being 15 points higher than mine right now. The reason I've asked Jack to speak to you will soon be clear, but I ask that you pay close attention to what he has to say. I'm devoting a good portion of the program tonight to this topic because it is an issue of incredible importance. But before I steal his thunder, I'll let him explain. Jack…"

Beth noticed once again how smooth the President was in front of the camera, introducing the next segment as deftly as a professional anchor. The camera angle switched and 62.3% of the television screens in America showed a picture of Jack Stone from the waist up, standing behind a simple podium. From Beth's viewpoint he looked much like he had during the Jessup summation, wearing his best suit, tie slightly askew, hair partly damp, hands gripping the sides of the podium. It was, Beth had heard, the same kind of podium he'd used in California, brought in specially to complete the picture of the strength, passion and integrity for which Jack was known. His posture also happened to match the cover photo that had sold out issues of both Time and Newsweek.

"The President has asked me to present a new bill to you tonight, but I feel I must begin with some history. If you will bear with me, I have a few statistics to share." At this Jack leaned over and lifted the huge FBI report in range of the camera. "Don't worry, I'm not going to read this whole thing…"

Beth thought he looked a little self-conscious at that point, looking around for a jury to laugh at his little joke. He pulled himself together pretty quickly and began again.

"In the past 20 years there have been 2,352 school shootings, bombings or attempts of the same, 50.2% of which were perpetrated by students with a fundamental religious background. In the past 20 years there have been 343,492 documented hate crimes, 74.7% of which were perpetrated by individuals with a fundamental religious background. And in the past 20 years there have been 413,243 documented criminal incidents involving reproductive freedom clinics, 96.9% of which were perpetrated by individuals with a fundamental religious background."

Jack paused for a full three seconds before continuing. "A conservative estimate of the lives of friends and family directly affected by these events is 140 million people. That's 50% of America. I'm talking about directly affected, not including those affected by simply seeing such violence and hatred reported on their local news, which would raise the number to 100%. 50% of American lives forever altered by the acts of approximately 750,000 individuals."

Jack paused again, but this time he couldn't make it to his full pre-determined three seconds because he was on a roll. "Those 750,000 individuals were born to 1.5 million parents. For those keeping track, 1.5 million is a little over one half of one percent of America. Those 1.5 million parents raised 750,000 individuals who were so filled with hatred, intolerance and bigotry that they could not function in our society. So filled with hatred, intolerance and bigotry that they forever altered the lives of half our country.

"I don't know about you, but when I read this information from the FBI last week I was completely floored. I have felt that things were sliding out of control in our country, but seeing the cold hard statistics has made it difficult for me to sleep the past few nights."

Another pause, this time to get his breathing under control. "I believe we have come to a point in our history where we cannot allow the reckless and irresponsible behavior of one half of one percent of Americans to destroy the lives of the rest of us. I call it reckless and irresponsible because, just as I can't imagine Steve and Ellen Rodman intended to raise a killer, I can't imagine that this half percent realized that they were perpetuating the tear that is ripping our country apart."

"I know I've gone on for a good bit about numbers and that can be a little dry, but now I'd like to give you a small history lesson that depends on those numbers." He paused for a moment to shuffle through his papers, before pulling out another thick report and holding it up for the camera.

"This is a 20-year study entitled 'The Roots of Terror' that was just completed and submitted to the President by a governmental think tank. They assigned 20 PhDs in various fields to study the roots of terror in the Arab-Israeli conflict. They spent time living in the Gaza Strip and the West Bank, as well as studying the early childhood and family lives of many of the most infamous terrorists of our day. The study was commissioned to specifically focus on the factors and characteristics of terror-breeding families and societies.

"You might ask what this has to do with my topic. I bring it up to highlight two comparisons. One, we are all more than familiar with the major details of the Arab-Israeli conflict. The reason I belabored the numbers a few minutes ago was because our percentage of terrorists in the population has now reached the level of being comparable to that of both the Palestinians and the Israelis. Second, the study shows startling similarities in religious zealotry across the board."

Jack raised a piece of paper from his podium and continued. "The bill the President will be presenting to Congress next month is called the Minor Protection Act. This bill seeks to put an end to both the moral slide America has taken in the past 20 years and the reign of hatred, intolerance and bigotry that is ripping our freedom to shreds. The President will present this bill not as an emotional or political response, but because it is the right thing to do. We must act now and hold each American accountable for their parenting. We must stand as one, united to say our children must be protected. Our children must be raised to respect the freedom of each American. It is time that the half percent be held responsible for the repercussions of its actions on the rest of us. If this half percent cannot accept the responsibility of raising peace loving and tolerant children, that responsibility needs to be taken from them."

Beth found herself wishing she had a pin on her, the audience was still enough to try out the old cliché. Everyone had been half listening while busily scratching notes throughout the numbers lesson, herself included, but when Jack mentioned taking away parental responsibility even the most seasoned reporters surrounding her looked up with slack jaws.

Beth felt like she was watching a tennis match, eager to see Jack's every word, but also captivated by the look on the President's face while Jack was talking. She'd never seen that exact expression on his face before, but if she had to describe it she'd say it looked a little like glee.

Jack paused one final time, looking as sincere as if he was speaking personally with each American in their living room. "I know it seems harsh to take children away – but the truth of the matter is that extremist beliefs lead to extremist behavior. We have seen the world erupt time after time with this truth, whole countries set ablaze with the flames of so-called martyrs. In this country we have always valued freedom above all else, but now is the time to take a stand and say healthy children are an even higher goal. Now we must value the freedom of the majority against the freedom of the tiny minority spreading this cancerous poison. We must get children out of these hostile environments before the history of the next 50 years is set in stone. I expect most of these people will just take the warning that we're serious and we will not accept this kind of hateful, bigoted intolerance to continue to the next generation. If we take the courageous step to stop this now and save these children we can change our destiny and eradicate hatred, intolerance and bigotry in our great country in one generation."

The screen held Jack's image a few seconds more before breaking for a commercial. Viewers collectively let out their breath and forsook the usual commercial activities to wait stock still in their seats for the President to return. Beth and her colleagues were no exception.

During the single highly lucrative commercial break they watched the President get up and shake Jack's hand before returning to his anchor chair.

"Jack has done an admirable job presenting to you just what the Minor Protection Act is, and why it needs to be implemented. What I would like to discuss with you is why it is so imperative that we do this now."

Farmer spoke directly to the camera, no looking down at his notes, no eyes flickering back and forth. He spoke from his heart and with a passion rarely used. He was so eloquent that Beth forgot for a moment that he was reading from a teleprompter. "You know that I received a Master's degree in Middle Eastern Studies from Harvard and that, in the course of my studies, I spent a year and a half living in Jerusalem. I have spoken of that time often because it had such a great impact on the development of my consciousness of the world and my responsibilities therein. I have also continued that learning process in my meetings with the Prime Minister of Israel and the Palestinian Authority. It is a very personal issue to me because of these connections, which is why I have continued to pursue peace when everything points to continued violence in the region. I appreciated my predecessor's meritorious efforts on that score, though they failed.

"What I would like to say publicly tonight, for the first time, is that I see amazing parallels between the hostility of the environment in Israel and the hatred fomenting in our own streets. Everyone, including myself, is horrified every time there is a new suicide attack by Hamas and their ilk, and by Israel's harsh responses. But what is not generally thought of is the fact that, comparing populations, we have more religiously based terror attacks than Israel. I know it is hard to grasp numbers and statistics whizzing by the first time around, so I trust that you all will carefully study what Jack just presented to you to determine for yourself that the information is correct. Everything that he and I discussed and referenced tonight will be up on the Internet within the hour by following the MPA link on whitehouse.gov. I can only tell you tonight, as your President, that I have seen the numbers and it horrifies me.

"My record on fighting terrorism, both at home and abroad, is well documented. I was in the Senate on September 11, 2001 and strongly supported my predecessor's moves thereafter. I voted with him on the subjects of Homeland Security, the campaign in Afghanistan and the war with Iraq. It is also well known that I disagreed, at first, with his doctrine of pre-emption."

Beth's eyes glazed over as they usually did when Farmer started being blatantly political. He rambled on about how much he had supported his predecessor. How freedom had moved forward and the world was a better place. All that was true of course, but Beth remembered quite clearly how critical Farmer had been at the time. He started running for President two years out and spent most of his airtime badmouthing the administration's policies. Of course that wasn't his current line – now the story was that he couldn't have been more supportive.

"...today our country is in the process of becoming like the very countries we've just spent billions of dollars helping. We stand in the peculiar position of watching the development of fledgling democracies in Afghanistan and Iraq while our own religious extremists are growing further and further out of control. I understand why my predecessor was unwilling to broach this subject, but I am now in a similar position to that which he found himself in September 11, 2001 at 8:30am. I see flames – different than his, but flames nonetheless. And they are threatening our way of life once again.

"You will remember that I ran my first campaign with the slogan 'Home First.' I made you five promises as I stood on the steps of the Capitol building and swore that oath. So far I've managed to keep four of them."

Beth had heard the four promises so many times she could write them out herself. One, firm up abortion with the Reproductive Freedom Act. Two, Protection of Marriage Act which was the opposite of every PoMA in the country in that it made marriage available for any two people. Three, cut the defense budget drastically and funnel it to education. Four, National Hate Crimes Bill. Then he would wrap-up by saying the country loved him because they'd put more Democrats in office. Yep, there he goes.

"I know that these important issues resonated with you because you voted me in again last year and increased the Democrat majority in both the House and Senate.

"Tonight I am making a move that goes along with my final campaign promise to keep America as safe as she was given to me. Toward that end I bring you the Minor Protection Act. I believe that the time has come to turn the focus of our war against terror internally. I believe we should learn from history and not allow our great country to dissolve into the kind of madness and widespread terror shaking the Middle East as we speak. Specifically, we need to learn the lesson of the Arab-Israeli conflict. The reason Hamas is able to continue its terror campaign is that they begin poisoning the minds of their children from birth. I know you all have been as horrified as I to see small boys brandishing AK-47s in the streets and shouting 'Death to the Jews.' If only we could rescue one generation of those children, we would have that peace in the Middle East that we have been pursuing in vain for so long.

"It is that very thought that has kept me up late at night for the past several years. Every time a new report came to me about religiously motivated terror in our own country, the thought prodded my conscience again. My fellow Americans, I feel the weight of my oath very strongly. My promise to protect this great nation of ours was made with full knowledge and consent, and fuller devotion to fulfilling it. I believe history will judge me if I do not do everything possible to protect our country and our children.

"I believe the Minor Protection Act is an extension of our broader war on terror. A pre-emptive plan to avoid our society disintegrating and following the path of every other great society that has fallen into ruin and exists now only in history books. Upon passage of the MPA, I will commission an MPA Advisory Council to dissect the study Jack referenced and come up with a formula we can apply for screening terror-breeding families in our own society here and now.

"The weight of my oath is a powerful motivator. I believe this is the right course for our country and I hope you will both trust and come to agree with me. History will judge us all by the decisions we make on this issue. Either we will hijack this homegrown terror movement and head into an unparalleled time of peace and prosperity, or we will continue to descend into the madness that threatens our very existence as a beacon of light and freedom in this world. We must act now before we have a full scale West Bank in our own country.

"Thank you and goodnight." Jack slept peacefully that night. The President had been whisked away right after the camera flickered off to broker a deal with striking airplane workers, but the Attorney General stuck around the necessary 30 minutes to receive poll results. At the end of the program the President had asked simply, "Do you agree that now is the time to institute this bill?" In a classic split, 35% agreed, 30% were undecided and 35% disagreed. That was enough to put the Attorney General in a great mood since the yes's were 5% higher than his people had optimistically predicted.

"All we need to do is convince 15% of the undecideds to change their mind and Congress will pass the bill. That'll be a walk in the park for you Jack."

Jack didn't think getting 15% of Americans to change their minds in a month would be a walk in the park, but he did believe strongly in the cause so he felt up to the challenge.

After a week of furious campaigning on every talk show he could fit in, both political and otherwise, Jack talked 5% of the undecideds into agreement. The second week brought another 2%, but 4% went from undecided to disagreement.

In the third week, Jack movingly presented his case on the Oprah Winfrey Show, the tape of which he sent to his youngest brother, and when she endorsed the bill 2% more swung his direction. Another point came from a perfectly timed appearance in People's "50 Most Intriguing People" issue that included a carefully worded statement about what had happened in his life that caused him to believe so strongly.

Still, he was five points short and when the Sunday before his final week came along Jack was wracking his brain for a new strategy. He never came up with anything, but he was in luck. Monday morning a 16-year-old boy walked into a suburban school in California and shot up a lunchtime prayer meeting. He killed 15 and wounded another 25 with the spray from an AK-47 purchased on the street. The cameras were rolling as he was taken away, microphones close enough to catch him as he shouted about how those kids had been attacking him for years, bullying him until he couldn't take it anymore. The cameras caught the whole thing and broadcast it repeatedly, up to and including the final desperate breakdown when he saw his parents.

The President gave a special address that evening with somber words. He only spoke briefly, but managed to share his feelings about the students killed, as well as the young man who was driven to commit such a horrible crime. It was a long week of replayed footage and endless interviews with parents and friends while the country mourned both the students killed and the young killer. Jack was on Larry King Live that Friday.

LARRY KING LIVE
SEPTEMBER 27
9:50PM, FRIDAY

The program started out a little rocky with Larry having to fend off callers with dating questions about his guest, but after the first break and a tense meeting with the harried screeners they hit their stride. All in all it had been a good show. It was getting near the end of the hour, time for the guest to give a final comment and Larry to wrap things up. Jack looked at the camera and said, "I told the jury a story in my closing arguments that I know most of you in America have heard, the story of the Jessup family. Tonight I want to tell you another story, the story of a young boy named Nick. He was a sweet boy, grew up with a very tender disposition, interested in all the normal boy things. He tore home appliances apart and dumped his food in all directions for the dog to eat. When he began school his teachers commented year after year on what a joy he was to have in class.

"But little Nick started to change after switching from a conservative private institution to public school his sophomore year. Out of that comfortable environment of unchallenged propaganda he began to flounder. He became unteachable, belligerent and stubborn. Teachers began to change their opinion and reports came home about a disturbed boy who argued unceasingly with others, always needing to be right. He argued with his Science teacher about evolution. He spoke before the school board trying to stop a presentation on safe sex in health class simply because it was led by a former bisexual prostitute. When he didn't win his protest he led a walkout during the lecture. By high school teachers had to pull Nick out of more than one fistfight. I ask you, what could have happened to such an innocent boy that turned him into a bigoted bully?

"Could it have been his parents, Steve and Ellen Rodman? Could it have been their insistent preaching? Could it have been the Sunday morning and Wednesday night meetings they forced

47

him to attend from early childhood? How about the innocuously titled 'youth group' that subjected Nick to a teaching series on apologetics – a ten dollar word for arguing? Bullying. Badgering others into agreeing with you or giving up.

"My fellow Americans..." and at that Jack paused with his self-conscious grin, as if he found humor in hearing himself say something so lofty. However, as he thought about his next phrasing his face become serious again. He had been in a closed-door meeting all morning with the Attorney General and his staff, the outcome of which was a decision to make the Rodmans the first MPA test case. They also decided that Jack's appearance on Larry King was the perfect time to drop the first hint so they could take a preliminary poll.

"My fellow Americans, Steve and Ellen Rodman have already destroyed the life of one child with their ruinous beliefs. They have another child, a 6-year-old daughter named Gracie. I ask you, should they be allowed to ruin the life of this child as well? Haven't they proven clearly where their beliefs lie? What if they turn Gracie into another Nick, but this time instead of quietly killing herself, the individual Gracie bullies fights back with an AK-47?"

Jack stopped again, overcome by emotion. For a few seconds he worked the knot out of his throat and, had a poll been taken just then, Jack would have had his pick of 32% of the single women in America.

"I fear for Gracie. I fear that this innocent child will have no chance at a normal life growing up in such a hostile environment. I fear that her parents will poison her as they poisoned her older brother. If we don't stand up as Americans and make some tough decisions, if we don't put a stop to this cancer right now, I fear Gracie and Nick will end up in adjoining prison cells."

Larry closed the program off with a poll. Later that night Jack got a call in his hotel room - 56% of Americans believed the President should follow through with his intention to present the Minor Protection Act to Congress after his show Monday.

CHAPTER 5

MOORPARK, CALIFORNIA
OCTOBER 1
6:55PM, MONDAY

The television showed President Farmer's image as he spoke confidently into the silence of the room. A couple just past middle age sat together on the couch barely moving, barely breathing, as they watched Farmer cement the plan he'd been stumping for weeks. "Now that we have reached the necessary popular majority I plan to send the Minor Protection Act to Congress first thing in the morning. Our expectation is that it will pass both the House and Senate within the week and I will sign it into law as soon as possible thereafter. The FBI is prepared to act and will rescue the first child within a few days of the signing ceremony. I hope to be able to report on the success of that operation during next month's show, as well as introduce you to the MPA Advisory Council. Until then, good ni..."

Farmer's self-satisfied image abruptly faded to black as the man savagely stabbed the remote, cutting off the President's final word. The couple stared straight ahead in silence for a full 30 seconds before turning to look at one another. The woman had tears in her eyes and the man looked ready to do to the President in person what he'd done to him with the remote.

"George." The name was all she could get out before she leaned her head on his shoulder and began to cry. He absently patted her back as his mind raced through all the implications of what he'd just heard. He'd known it was coming. He'd felt in his very soul that Farmer had been building up to something like this for years. When the MPA had been introduced the previous month he'd sat in a daze on this same couch for three hours. Tonight when he and Amanda sat down he thought he was somewhat prepared for the worst. But it turned out that nothing could prepare him for

49

hearing those words spoken from the lips of the one man who had the authority to make them a reality. George felt himself burning with an anger he'd rarely experienced during 25 years spent in the Los Angeles Police Department dealing with the unimaginable variety of evil mankind can dream up.

He was glowering at the blackened screen a minute later when he abruptly turned his head as though he'd heard someone in the next room. His face began to relax from its murderous expression just as Amanda lifted her head to look him in the eye. He knew plans needed to be made, but there was something that took precedence. "Amanda, we need to get over to Steve and Ellen's."

THOUSAND OAKS, CALIFORNIA
RODMAN RESIDENCE

Fifteen miles away Steve and Ellen Rodman were still-life replicas of George and Amanda's posture, frozen in stunned silence on the couch. They sat side by side; their only contact the extremely tight grip between them cutting off circulation in both their hands. Neither noticed Gracie, quietly humming to herself as she colored on the floor in front of them. Steve's mind was stuck in slow motion, replaying Farmer's final words over and over while Ellen's was going a hundred miles a minute as the last five years of her life went whizzing before her eyes.

As a family they'd spent the summer before Nick entered 10th grade discussing whether Nick would switch from private to public school. Steve and Ellen lobbied for Nick to continue where he was, but Nick was adamant to move into what he called the "real world." They'd finally agreed two days before the registration deadline and watched with trepidation as he drove his beater off to school that first day. It had been a bit of a shock to Nick's sensibilities to go from praying before every class to the rather liberal education philosophy preached by the California school system, but overall he'd enjoyed the transition.

Steve and Ellen had worked out a system where he went into the office a little later so he could take Gracie to school and she left before dawn so she could pick up their "Little Surprise," run an errand or two and be home by the time Nick arrived. It worked well for them since she was the early bird of the family and Steve mightily enjoyed his extra hour of sleep.

One afternoon halfway through Nick's sophomore year Ellen was standing at the kitchen sink feeling quite virtuous. For once she was peeling real potatoes instead of popping the ever present box of potato flakes into the microwave when Nick came bursting through the door in a huff. He slammed his backpack on the table and plopped into a chair with a big sigh. Ellen had gotten used to such theatrics where her son was concerned and took a deep breath before asking what was wrong.

Nick had lined up 40 students who wanted to get together once a week at lunch to pray, secured a room and found three teachers willing to be advisors. The school's requirements for forming a new club were 10 willing students and one advisor so Nick had expected his petition to be easily approved. That afternoon he'd received his answer. The Student Council denied his request to form a Prayer Club on the advice of their faculty advisor, saying that such a religious club on school property violated the establishment clause. What was most bitter for Nick to swallow was that Carla, the President of the Gay Pride Club, was the one to rather gleefully deliver the news. Her club had only eight members but their six advisors had gotten the 10-student rule waived. Though only eight strong, they were one of the most active clubs in school and had banners hanging throughout the halls.

Steve and Ellen spent the better part of the evening talking over the subject with Nick and trying to calm him down. He wouldn't be calmed and that denial turned out to be the beginning of what Ellen referred to as Nick's militant phase. In less than a month he'd found someone from their church who lived across the street from the school and agreed to have students over at lunch. By the end of the year there were 60 students meeting on Tuesdays for prayer and Thursdays for a Bible lesson taught by Nick's youth pastor.

Since the school didn't officially recognize the club they couldn't hang banners or have announcements broadcast over the PA system, but word of mouth publicity turned out to be just as effective. The group's kickoff barbecue at the beginning of Nick's junior year attracted more than 200 students. Steve and Ellen watched their son's transformation with wonder. Nick met weekly with his youth pastor and began co-leading a Bible Study in the Rodman's living room with him on Monday nights. Sometimes Steve and Ellen would sit out of sight on the stairs and listen to their son talking. They were both strong Christians actively involved in their church and had tried to pass the faith onto their children, but they were still a little stunned to hear their little boy discussing relativism versus universal truth as easily as he discussed football and girls.

What wasn't easy for them was watching the doctor put nine stitches in Nick's forehead when he was attacked in the hall between classes right before Thanksgiving his junior year. Teachers who pulled the fight apart marched Nick and the three boys who'd been pounding him right down to the office. The principal didn't care to hear from the ten witnesses who said Nick hadn't done anything but defend himself and Nick received the same week's suspension as the other boys. As much as it had infuriated his parents, the whole episode had done nothing for Nick but cement his resolve. When the week was up he went right back to school sporting a small white scar.

When Nick first brought Jayla Jessup home for dinner at the beginning of his senior year Ellen was a bit taken aback. The rainbow button was the first thing she noticed, followed closely by the hard look in the girl's eyes. A look Ellen had never seen in one so young, bitterness and anger barely veiling a deep hurt. She wasn't sure what had caused that look, but decided within five minutes of meeting Jayla that she would add the girl to her daily prayer list.

That first dinner was followed by many more until Jayla became an accepted part of the family. Ellen never really talked to her about anything serious, just showered her with as much love as possible. She and Steve had a long talk and decided she'd take the "love the sinner" approach and leave the "hate the sin" part to her son. In reality, Ellen couldn't quite figure out the friendship between Jayla and Nick. They treated each other with affection and joked often, studied together and talked on the phone for hours. But Ellen also heard them arguing loudly on several occasions about homosexuality. An argument about someone named Carla sent Jayla storming out of the house in tears, but a week later she was back like nothing had happened.

Three months passed and Ellen watched Jayla slowly transform. She still wore the rainbow button every day, but the look in her eyes had changed. No longer the hard bitterness and raging anger, now all Ellen saw was an awful torment betrayed in unguarded moments. Time after time that Jayla came over Ellen watched her eyes and her posture and was driven to more and more prayer. In December she began fasting once a week because she felt such a burden for the girl's soul.

New Year's Eve was a difficult day for the Rodmans. Only Gracie skated through unperturbed. They were supposed to go to a church party but after an hour of stilted mingling they caught each other's eyes and headed home. For some reason each of them had felt a concern for Jayla they couldn't shake. Ellen put Gracie down and joined Steve and Nick in the living room. They prayed for three hours before any of them felt peace, then stumbled off to bed. Nick rang Jayla first thing in the morning and that's when they heard the news that she'd killed herself.

The next two years blurred by in her mind's eye. The aching grief she'd felt over Jayla was superseded that horrible day only two weeks later when the police called to say they'd arrested Nick at school. She sat through his trial day after day, clenching her teeth until her jaw ached as the state prosecutor calmly twisted the truth about her son. The final blow of the verdict shattered her. She felt numb watching Nick led away and clung to Steve's hand as he bent over weeping. She didn't even notice the camera crews surrounding them as they stumbled down the stairs to their car.

In the weeks that followed every fiber in her being vibrated with anger toward God. She could barely function when the violence of her feelings threatened to spew out toward anyone in the vicinity. She'd actually packed Gracie off to stay with friends for a week as she paced the rooms of her house like a caged animal randomly yelling at God about the injustice of it all. Hadn't she been a good enough Christian? Hadn't she taught her son the right way? What kind of God would send a 17-year-old boy to jail for simply doing what the Bible said?

Steve didn't handle it well either. His coping mechanism was to work longer and longer hours and shove his feelings into a small corner at the back of his mind. He only allowed them out for an hour each evening when he would pound on a punching bag in the garage until his hands were bloody and he could barely breathe.

Nick's optimism during their weekly visits nearly killed them at first. Both of them had to bite their tongues as they listened to him prattle on about God's goodness and how He had a plan for everything. Neither believed his cliché assertions. They were too overwhelmed by the sight of their firstborn clothed in an orange jumpsuit.

As the first month passed into the second they began to listen to what Nick had to say. Ellen stopped screaming and started talking to God in a normal tone. Steve let the punching bag get dusty again and spent the garage hour reading his Bible. By the time Nick's optimism began failing him they'd both found peace and could honestly repeat his words back to him about God's goodness and how He had a plan for everything.

Ellen was surprised but not destroyed when the subpoena came shortly after and she found herself named in a lawsuit defaming her parenting skills. Again she sat through day after day of testimony, the lies about her not hurting nearly as much as the lies about her son and the many references to his incarceration.

Although she struggled constantly not to fall into despair, most of the time she'd been able to face both the Jessups and their crusading lawyer with calmness and grace, the bitterness in their eyes finding no mirror in hers. She wasn't shocked at all when the jury came back with their judgment, as that was what she and Steve had come to expect after long nights of discussion and prayer. They were appealing the verdict, of course, but weren't getting their hopes up. Meanwhile they did what was necessary to get through each day and Ellen felt a very comforting sense of peace beyond description.

However, when President Farmer announced the MPA and she heard herself mentioned on Larry King Live she felt a dread in the pit of her stomach unlike anything she'd ever felt before. Each day her fears mounted as she sat glued to the television watching Jack's campaign with one eye and her daughter with the other. Tonight those fears had been realized.

Steve's face was pure white when he opened the door to find George and Amanda standing on his front step. George grabbed him in a bear hug while Amanda patted his shoulder before going in search of Ellen. She found her in the living room, crumpled on the couch with Gracie coloring quietly on the floor in front of her.

George led Steve back inside, then knelt in front of Gracie and looked at her drawings while Amanda held Ellen, the younger woman crying silently on her shoulder. After a few minutes George picked Gracie up and took her to the kitchen where he popped in one of the many Veggie Tales tapes stacked nearby.

Once Gracie was out of the room Ellen started talking. "I know it's us. He was talking about us! They're going to take Gracie." She was on the verge of hysteria and Amanda hugged her close while looking in George's direction. Steve stood where George had left him, like a tree that had received its deathblow and was just waiting for the merest wind to topple to the ground. When George returned from setting up Gracie's 37-minute distraction he guided Steve to a seat on the couch.

He cleared his throat and began, "Steve…Ellen…I have no words to say right now that seem appropriate. Nothing I could think of on the drive over would even begin to express what we're all feeling, nor is there anything introductory that seems right, so I'm just going to start."

He looked at Amanda and, receiving her encouraging nod, went ahead. "Amanda and I have known you since you started coming to the church 10 years ago. We've been in Bible studies and served on committees together. We've been to every major event your children have had. We've watched you grow over the years and have been encouraged by your faith. Amanda and I both feel like you're part of our family." He saw his words were starting to bring Steve out of his trance-like state and Ellen had stopped crying and was staring at him. Unnerving as it was, at least she was giving him her full attention.

"Two years ago we watched your lives begin to unravel. Amanda sat with you every day in the courtroom and I got there as often as I could to watch in silence the travesty of justice that sent Nick off to the state penitentiary. We barely had time to absorb the news that he'd be gone for 15 years when you were served with the civil lawsuit papers. Again, we watched in silence as your character was shredded, hoping and praying that the Lord would step in, that justice would not be short-circuited. We waited for a fair and honest judgment and were again disappointed.

"Every day for the past two years we have waited and we have prayed. We waited for the government and our laws to do the right thing and we prayed for God to intervene on your behalf. They didn't, and in wisdom we can't comprehend, neither did He.

"What He did do was impress on both Amanda's and my heart the same words. Amanda heard them a few days ago but didn't tell me, then I heard them right after the President announced tonight that he already had a test case in mind. I knew Farmer was talking about you and I was just sitting there with anger rolling over me in waves. I saw Gracie being taken from you and I swore I would never let that happen. Then I heard the Lord. It was hard at first, hearing Him through all my anger, but eventually I heard Him clear as day: 'the time for waiting is over. You have given to Caesar what is Caesar's and now it's time to give to God what is God's.'

"Now we have a lot to talk about, but Steve, Ellen," and at this he paused and looked them each in the eye. "Amanda and I both believe God has told us that in this case His law is to be obeyed above our government's. With your permission we want to help get you and the children out of the country."

SUPERIOR COURT OF CALIFORNIA COUNTY OF VENTURA
HALL OF JUSTICE
OCTOBER 14
4:30PM, MONDAY

Georgia Hammond stood in front of the microphones with an HPAC spokesperson while Stacy stood to her right holding Gracie. The reporters were getting themselves worked up as flashbulbs went off in the roar peculiar to that singular event.

The HPAC celebrity spokeswoman came forward and introduced herself, unnecessarily, owing to her celebrity status. Once the applause trickled off she began, "As you all know, several years ago I was involved in the fight to repeal the Florida law banning homosexuals from adoption. I was very proud the day I stood next to the Governor when he signed that legislation. I was also proud when, as a result of my efforts, Homosexual Parents of Adopted Children asked me to become their spokeswoman. I believe in their mission and am gratified that I can represent them. Nothing could give me greater pleasure though, than to introduce to you my friends Georgia and Stacy Hammond. I've known them for years and am thrilled at the opportunity they've been given today. But I know you don't really care to hear from me right now," she said, laughing delicately, "so why don't we start with your questions."

Standing in the front row Beth thought the laugh sounded a little forced, like the celebrity was irritated at not being the center of attention this time. As Georgia walked forward Beth pulled her mind back to the story at hand. The CNN reporter on her right managed to drown everyone else out and ask the first question.

Georgia responded with a facial expression that clearly showed what a dolt she thought the reporter must be, "How do you think I feel?"

Beth barely contained a snort and noticed that several of her colleagues had coughing fits simultaneously. Nobody was that fond of CNN.

After waiting a moment for quiet Georgia continued. "Amazed, filled with joy. Stacy and I are so happy right now we don't know what to do with ourselves. We've sat on our living room floor these last three nights just watching Gracie play, filled with awe that we've been given the privilege of raising this precious treasure. It is an honor and a responsibility we feel greatly, the sacred duty of parenthood, teaching your child to relate to the world around her with love and respect for others. What can I say, we've only had her three days but it seems like so much longer already."

Beth watched CBS knock the microphone out of the hand of Fox News and ask quickly, "Why did you never have children before?"

"We have tried numerous times during the past 10 years, but we were unable to get pregnant with artificial insemination."

By this time Fox News had recovered her microphone and was able to drown out the others with, "Will you try to adopt Gracie?"

"Based on her interpretation of the Minor Protection Act, Judge Renton granted us temporary guardianship this afternoon and our friends at HPAC tell us that we will most likely be able to start adoption proceedings after six months. We certainly plan on doing that."

Beth tuned out CNN's next inane question as she pondered the thought that this conference seemed entirely too scripted for her taste. She knew that excuse wouldn't cut it with her producer though, so at the next opportunity she decided to see what the main plot point of the script was. "Do you have anything else you'd like to say?"

Georgia stepped up again and looked straight into the cameras. "I'd like to say thank you. I'm so proud to be an American today. Only ten years ago it was impossible for Stacy and I to be legally married in our home state or adopt a child. I'm proud of how far we've come as a country. Four years ago Stacy and I were married by a minister at our local church after the Supreme Court ruling in Stanton v. State of California upheld President Farmers' Protection of Marriage Act. Three years ago we were told we could begin foster parent classes in preparation for adoption after their ruling in Paul v. State of Florida set a nationwide precedent in favor of homosexual adoption."

At this point she reached back and drew Stacy forward to stand beside her. "It's because of those rulings that we are here before you and we promise to do the best job we can raising Gracie. We will teach her the virtue of treating all her fellow men and women with the dignity and respect we all deserve and that freedom and tolerance will always conquer ignorance and fear. I am thrilled to be living in a free country as I stand here today, next to my wife holding our child. Thank you."

Beth could tell her colleagues were completely won over but she was not quite as taken in. Not that she disagreed with anything they were saying per se. She realized it could just be her distrust of Georgia's chosen profession as she tended to take anything lawyers said with a grain of salt. And after that answer Beth knew for a fact Georgia was reading from a teleprompter in her mind. However, all of that was speculation on her part, so she set aside her misgivings and delivered a stirring introduction for the Nightly News, before showing a montage of the best quotes.

People were so moved that they completely forgot where exactly little Gracie had come from and didn't notice her bewildered and slightly terrified look when glancing between the reporters and her new mothers.

MOORPARK, CALIFORNIA

George flipped off the TV as Amanda leapt from the couch and began pacing the room.

"I can't believe the audacity of that...that woman! How could she stand there so self-righteous and smug when she's no more than a no-good, rotten kidnapper! I wish I could have two minutes alone with her to tell her just what I think she can do with her such and such v. so and so rulings!"

Amanda would have continued spewing exclamation points had George not started laughing. With a new focal point for her anger she turned to him, outraged.

"And just what are you laughing at George Stanley Rochester?"

Normally the use of his full name would cause him to gulp, but today he just continued chuckling. "My wife. What do you think?"

He ducked just in time to avoid the pillow hurled in his direction.

"Honey, can't you see what's happening? They're just throwing out the same politically correct garbage they've been using for years. That woman was so smug because she thinks she's won. But she has no idea that her child," at that he jabbed his fingers up in quotation marks, "is going to be out the door sooner than the paint can dry in their new pc nursery. They're going to have the shortest foster parenting job in history. That's the reality of the situation Amanda they will not win."

She'd stopped pacing at this point and, since she didn't appear to have any other projectiles in hand he continued, "But what I'm laughing at, my dear, is you. I enjoy seeing you all riled up and ready to do battle. After 30 years you are even better than the woman I married and I was laughing at the joy of it."

Amanda pretended to storm out in a huff, but George knew he was forgiven when he heard her humming in the kitchen. While she prepared dinner he went back to studying his plans.

In his garage fifteen miles away Steve Rodman was not laughing. He'd wanted to see the press conference without upsetting Ellen so he watched hunched in front of the mini black and white he mainly used for listening to ballgames. He was infuriated to watch the arrogance of the woman who now had his child.

Steve deliberately turned off the TV and turned back to the desk where he'd been studying Romans. If there were one good thing about the past two years it would have to be his desperate dependence on God. He had always been a churchgoer, faithfully attending his men's group as well as Sunday mornings. He made sure his children knew God and knew what was right and wrong. But Steve had rarely spent more than a perfunctory 10 minutes a day reading his Bible and praying. Since his son's trial, except for the brief period he thought of as the bloody knuckles era, he had spent countless hours at his garage desk studying the Word. He and Ellen established a weekly hour of prayer together in addition to his own half hour a day. It was the only way he was coping - he knew that for sure. Only God could save someone in his position from driving his car over a cliff.

So Steve didn't laugh just then. Instead he prayed.

BALTIMORE, MARYLAND

Sam's reaction to the press conference was a little different. She was riding her stationary bike and merely trying to find a little mindless entertainment after a difficult day, usually not a problem. She'd tried all the other channels, but everyone was covering the press conference complete with gushing LIVE reports.

Surely Entertainment Tonight would have something else on, but sadly, no. Sam switched over just in time to see a celebrity nearly everyone in America would recognize introducing herself almost humbly, then introducing her new best friends. Maybe it was her FBI training that made her so cynical, but Sam found it just a little fishy that the celebrity was such good friends with this random gay couple who happened to be able to take a child on short notice and speak so eloquently on an impromptu basis, all the while looking like supermodels on the catwalk.

Sam decided to flip off the TV and ride in silence, alone with her thoughts about the new assignment she'd been given that afternoon. As if she wasn't busy enough, her boss had put her into the rotation for babysitting America's newest Boy Wonder, Jack Stone.

CHAPTER 6

WHITE HOUSE STUDIOS
NOVEMBER 4
6:30PM, MONDAY

Jack watched from his hard won position in the front row of the gallery as Talk began. He looked a little more haggard than the last time he was in studio; the new lines creeping across his face a visual representation of too many sleepless nights. The President had waited less than a day after getting the Minor Protection Act passed and signed into law before forming the MPA Advisory Council. He appointed 20 members, Jack one of the lesser known among them, and assigned them the purpose of hammering out strict guidelines for enforcement of the Act.

The President wanted them to start right away so Jack hadn't even had a weekend off to fly home. Charlie stayed with a friend and his mom assured him she'd been sending his youngest brother by to pick up the mail every so often. He hadn't really packed for a two month stay, but not being much of a clothes horse, he didn't think too much about it until someone pulled him aside and suggested he upgrade his wardrobe to fit his new position as a Presidential appointee. Thus he sat feeling uncomfortably snobbish in one of the same Brooks Brothers suits he'd mocked most of his life.

Jack was certainly no stranger to long hours having worked his way through college and law school, but the hours he'd been forced to keep the past month had worn him down. He was looking forward to going home and taking some time off. He was also proud of what they'd accomplished in a mere month. Sitting on the President's desk was a 400-page-report outlining everything on which the committee had been able to agree. Thousands more copies were being printed tonight and would be sent out tomorrow morning to federal offices across the country.

It was a difficult process to begin with, time constraints aside, bringing together 20 such different minds and asking them just how much freedom they were willing to give up. The ideas ranged from throwing all people who believe in God into prison and putting their children in institutions to putting all Americans through mandatory tolerance training before they could take their baby home from the hospital.

Jack often found himself dragging back to his hotel after midnight with a vague hope of five hours sleep before heading back. His one pleasure had been telling a new taxi driver every morning to take him to "the White House." Granted, he hadn't actually been in the White House since his first meeting with the President, but most taxi drivers didn't know the difference between the Executive Offices and the Residence and were suitably impressed by their earnest young fare.

Now Jack , he thought, let's be honest with ourself, shall we? Yes, the taxi thing had been his one pleasure for most of the month, but during the last week of meetings a new pleasure walked into the tiny office he'd been temporarily assigned wearing a standard issue blue suit.

"Too bad she doesn't know we exist." The questioning look Jack's neighbor gave him reminded him where he was and he tried to concentrate on the President's wrap-up of last month's new legislative efforts. But all too soon he was drifting back to the morning he'd met Sam Hawthorne, FBI.

"Good morning, Mr. Stone. I'm Special Agent Sam Hawthorne and I'll be your Bureau liaison this week." All spoken in such a no-nonsense, I don't take any crap tone of voice as she jutted her hand toward him for a firm shake. He was charmed in spite of himself.

Jack remembered that, even at the time, he couldn't recall the names of the three Bureau liaisons before Sam, but he knew without a doubt he'd remember hers long after her babysitting job was done. At least, that's what the three previous guys had called the assignment. He hoped she didn't think of it that way.

She'd leaned against his bookcase then, calmly waiting for him to reply. When it became obvious that he was just going to keep staring dumbly at her she rolled her eyes and straightened back up, "Well, I've got quite a bit of work to do so I'll be just outside. Please call me if there's anything you need."

Luckily he'd stayed late again the night before preparing for the morning's meeting, because he didn't do a lick of work in the 20 minutes he had left. And frankly, he was man enough to admit, he had trouble concentrating whenever he was in his office for the rest of the week. He was very thankful that most of the week was spent in conference rooms far away from her little desk.

She'd been assigned to him until he sprinted, with the rest of the Council, to make their "Talk" appointment just over an hour ago. He could still see the little half wave she'd given him as she was packing up her laptop while he threw stacks of papers into his briefcase.

Overall, working on the Council had been well worth it, the long hours, the time away from family and friends, even the preppy suit. He finally was involved in something that would change the course of history and he was proud of the role he had played. Sure, he'd had to concede on several major points he didn't really agree with, but it was his strong belief that no one in their right mind would sacrifice a child for something as trite as religious faith.

Jack's idea of modern faith, apart from the zealotry he so vigorously fought against, was rather hazy. He had basically come to believe it was something you tacked onto an otherwise normal life. Something you would choose based on which type would best enhance your life. He knew several of his lawyer buddies went to church just so they could pass out business cards. That had been his childhood experience and he hadn't seen much later in life to change his mind. Jack just didn't see religion as an integral part of life that might have an affect on every other part so he didn't see how anyone would have a problem agreeing to the requirements they'd set forth and still maintain their beliefs. He didn't like some of the repercussions for non-compliance that had made it into the report, but since he didn't think they would be necessary he decided not to worry about it.

Jack was just about to start daydreaming again about the lovely Ms. Hawthorne when he was startled to hear the President turning to the MPA.

"I'm excited to be bringing this topic before you tonight. We've had overwhelming support for the Minor Protection Act. Since Jack Stone and I introduced it to you we've received hundreds of thousands of phone calls and e-mails from people all over America saying they agreed with the Act. As promised, I took it to Congress that next morning and it passed both House and Senate within the week. Less than a week later we affected our first rescue. Little Gracie Rodman was introduced to her new parents, Georgia and Stacy Hammond three weeks ago and I'm gratified to report that she is doing very well with them.

"I think the best news I have to present is that a poll taken last night showed an additional 6% of Americans now agree with the MPA, bringing us up to 62%. It is with a sense of the strong imperative from the American people exhibited by this massive majority that I make the announcement tonight that we are going to conduct a larger operation.

"After the bill was passed I formed the MPA Advisory Council and, as promised last month, I'd like to introduce them to you now and tell you what they've been up to. The Council is made up of the leading ethicists, moralists, theologians, educators and tolerance experts of our time, as well as a few politicians." Several people in the gallery chuckled but Jack was too focused to notice.

"I know you've heard of most of these men and women and I feel they are representative of the America we all want to achieve." As the President was speaking the camera panned through the crowd and each person's title was superimposed on the lower half of the screen. Jack was sitting between the head of the Christian Faith in Action Association and the Director of the Modern Theology Department at Harvard.

"I charged them with the creation of some governing guidelines for us to follow and they've produced marvelously. Their report sets out strict parameters restricting the MPA to be invoked only in the most critical situations, where it is obvious that if the government does not intervene the family will be producing a new generation of terrorists. They also set up a just and equitable process for rehabilitating children raised in these types of homes so that they can rejoin society in a healthier and more tolerant way. In just under a month they've come up with this massive report which only serves to highlight government efficiency." Another chuckle from those surrounding Jack, but he barely noticed. The next part of the speech held the most interest for him. He'd argued strongly against immediate enforcement but was voted down.

"I asked the Justice Department to compose a list of offenders who met the criteria set forth by the Advisory Council and they had no trouble coming up with 50 individuals, some of whom have been or are currently in prison and have spouses who supported their activities caring for their children. These individuals match all 10 early warning indicators and are therefore certified according to the law as terrorist breeding families.

"In the morning representatives from the Justice Department will begin the process of entering 50 homes in 32 states to remove 127 children. In accordance with Council guidelines, children 16 and over will be sent to a group facility until their 18th birthday where they will finish high school while being instructed in the most current tolerance education curriculum. We have turned a facility in Southern California over to this project entirely and 58 children will be traveling there with federal escorts over the next few days. Those 15 and younger will be placed in foster homes. For now we have also localized these in Southern California because there are enough couples in that area that have already undergone foster parenting classes in preparation for adoption.

"It is our hope that this operation will go smoothly and will serve to rescue these children from the hostile and hateful environments where they are currently being raised. Once again, I believe that recent circumstances require us to take more drastic action. I believe this very strongly, and I know you also believe it because I've seen the VNs. If we allowed these 127 children to grow to adulthood in their current environments we could have another crop of religiously motivated terrorists on our hands. With swift and decisive action, I believe we can educate and love these children into being productive citizens."

Jack tuned out the rest. He remained in his seat long after the on air light had blinked out and the studio had gone dark, trying to account for the pit in his stomach.

CALIFORNIA STATE PRISON LOS ANGELES COUNTY
LANCASTER, CALIFORNIA
NOVEMBER 5
3:01PM, TUESDAY

The cell door clanged and Nate's voice jolted Nick out of the light catnap he'd fallen into. "Time to go to the head shrinker, Nick. He has to see you before class this week."

Nate was the guard who came to take him to his weekly tolerance class, usually followed by an hour with the special psychiatrist who came in to check on his progress. Since Nate was the only guard who treated Nick with any kind of respect he got right up. Most of the other guards taunted him about what kind of God would let a 17-year-old kid take the rap. Nick had yet to come up with the perfect retort but it didn't stop him from trying.

The whole ordeal had been a lark at first. Nick was an outgoing kid and he'd harbored the feelings of invincibility common in his age bracket. He strode down the corridors of his high school convinced that he knew the truth and it was his job to tell everyone else. His t-shirts were a blaring testimony for anyone to read, "WWJD," "Real Men Pray," and "The Cross is a Radical Thing." He had no problem debating classmates and teachers alike and he was proud of the small white scar over his left eyebrow earned after talking the quarterback into turning himself in for cheating; earned at the hands of the D-Line Monday morning after Friday night's loss with the backup quarterback.

When he'd been taken out of math class and handcuffed in front of his locker, Nick had still been sure of himself. He was terribly upset by Jayla's suicide but he couldn't fathom why anyone would find him responsible for it. Throughout his trial he read Jesus Freaks, a book about martyrs for the faith, and felt himself standing tall in the Christian pantheon. He memorized the Christian Hall of Fame in Hebrews 11 and recited it to himself every night in his cell. Even when he was convicted his optimism had not failed him – he was proud he'd been deemed worthy to suffer for Christ. He even comforted his parents and found their lack of faith a little disturbing.

All that changed after the first month in minimum security. The novelty of martyrdom quickly gave way to the reality of 20 hours a day in a 9x9 cell with a string of roommates who were no more than common criminals. The other inmates mocked him whenever he walked past. He read of Paul's escape from prison again and again and asked God why he was stuck there. Four months passed and he spent every minute of the time wishing he were elsewhere and angrily petitioning God for relief.

It was their family friend, George, whom he'd always looked up to as a favorite uncle, who came to visit one day and helped him turn things around. George told him, "Nicky, sometimes you get a raw deal, and I've seen a lot of them over the years, but you have to believe that God has allowed this to happen to you for a reason." George went on to share with Nick how desperately he and Amanda had wanted children over the years and yet for some reason God had not allowed that to happen. Nick was shocked to hear George tell of his years of anger and hostility toward God before he got it straight in his mind that God had other plans. "Nick, if we could comprehend God's ways, you have to admit He'd be a pretty small God. His thoughts are as high above ours as ours are above the ants that burrow in the dirt. Can you imagine an ant looking up at you and asking why he had to march around looking for food all day? God has a plan for you in this place and it's time for you to shape up and get to it."

George talked to him brother to brother that day and Nick felt the truth of the words in his very bones. He went back to his cell, picked up his Bible and began reading again. The man standing before Nate was significantly different than the naïve boy who'd entered the cell almost two years before. He was grounded, solid, mature. No one could say he was enjoying prison, but he knew he was there for a purpose and God would get him out in His perfect timing. In the meantime Nick enjoyed debating the other prisoners, leading a Bible Study full of felons, reformed or otherwise, and eating the chocolate chip cookies his mom baked him by the cell-full.

Another favorite pastime was his weekly brainwashing session, as he liked to think of the tolerance classes, and the shrink hour that went along with it. The class and the shrink were part of Farmer's program to educate and reform hate crime offenders. Unfortunately for their statistics, they could not count Nick among their converts. He enjoyed watching the psychiatrist become completely frustrated when the "kid" didn't sit meekly by and accept the standard pc party line. It was one of the few forms of entertainment Nick had left and he looked forward to it.

Nate led him through the circuitous route necessary to get from the bowels of the prison to the friendlier visiting rooms. He wasn't sure why Dr. Frink was early, but he sent up a prayer that he would think clearly and represent himself well before stepping through the door that Nate opened for him.

He was just about to turn around and tell Nate there was no one in the room when he heard a voice from the corner, "Hello Nicky." No one called him Nicky anymore except...

Nick turned around and flashed a big grin.

OAKS MALL
THOUSAND OAKS, CALIFORNIA

70

3:11PM, TUESDAY

A middle-aged woman sat in a gray car that looked like it may have been borrowed from a police pool of nondescript stakeout vehicles. The engine idled as she watched Gracie swinging along between her foster mothers. Each held a hand as they crossed the parking lot and entered the mall. Switching the key off, the woman quickly exited and began to follow them, a slight grin on her face as the Mission Impossible theme played in her head.

Inside the Gap Stacy held up a piece of overpriced cotton on a plastic hanger. "Look at this darling jumper! What do you think Gracie? Would you like to try this on?" Stacy looked down to see Gracie nodding enthusiastically - pink was her favorite color.

"Stace, come look at this one," Georgia called from the next rack. As Stacy started to walk over, her cell phone jingled. She let go of Gracie's hand and juggled the jumper while trying to unzip her purse and walk toward Georgia at the same time.

"No, I can't come in tomorrow. I told you I was taking the day off - you're going to have to ask Liz or Linda to come in, I've already made plans...well I don't know...the itinerary is in my top drawer...right, it's all set, I already told Linda to call and confirm with the travel agent tomorrow...right...ok, ok, I'm hanging up now."

Exasperation was evident in her tone. "I swear, Georgia, if they call one more time I'm getting a new cell phone and this time I'm not giving them the number."

"Yeah, yeah, where have I heard that before?" Georgia rolled her eyes, and said, "Now look at this." They began to discuss the merits of pink versus blue in the formation of the feminine ego.

It was only a few minutes, understandable in that they'd only been "parents" for just over a month and weren't used to always keeping one eye on the escape artist. Besides which, up until last week they'd had a federal escort with them whenever they left their house because of worries that the Rodmans would attempt to take Gracie back. It was also one of the first times they'd been out

71

in public without photographers hounding them for a family photo op. As much as Georgia believed in the cause she and Stacy were representing, she was a little relieved to have America's attention turn elsewhere so they could get back to their new life.

When the conversation ended with the pink jumper placed back on the rack they began to look around for Gracie. She was nowhere to be seen.

BALTIMORE, MARYLAND

Sam was riding her bike again when she heard about the kidnapping. She switched her thousand channel satellite so that she could watch the local California broadcast. Local was always more entertaining than national. The serious faced, serious haired anchorman Jim Sarton looked serious as he introduced Laura Liu standing in front of the mall with a LIVE report:

"Jim, I'm standing outside the Oaks Mall in Thousand Oaks, where earlier this afternoon Gracie Rodman was kidnapped while clothes shopping with Georgia and Stacy Hammond. At first they believed she had just wandered off and alerted store Security, but after a thorough search the police were called in. It was then discovered in a related search that Gracie's brother Nick was missing from the minimum security prison where he's currently serving a 15-year sentence for the murder of Jayla Jessup. Prison officials have been unwilling to explain the details of his escape, but nevertheless they announced it a little over an hour ago."

The camera switched back to Jim so he could ask his carefully prepared question, "Laura, what is the response at the mall to all of this? Do they feel the need to install extra security cameras?"

"Well, Jim, that is a very interesting question and I placed it to the mall's spokeswoman. I will be giving a full account of that interview later in the broadcast."

"Thank you, Laura. And now as we continue with our LIVE team coverage of this shocking turn of events we go to Jenifer Hernandez, who is standing outside the Rodman residence. Jenifer, what is the situation there?"

Jenifer stood bravely against the Santa Anna wind whipping her long brown locks out of position. "Well, Jim, as you can imagine, the police came right over to the Rodman residence and found that Mr. and Mrs. Rodman were not at home, apparently having plenty of time to pack for a trip since the home was not in disarray. None of the neighbors we asked can remember seeing them in the last week. The police have issued an all points bulletin for the Rodman's car, a blue 1987 Chrysler LeBaron. They also activated the nationwide Amber alert system, but so far no sightings."

Back to Jim for another intense question, signified as such by his posture leaning slightly toward the camera. "Jenifer, can I assume the FBI will be called in on this kidnapping?"

Sam chuckled to herself at the sheer predictability and wondered, not for the first time, if they learned in broadcasting school exactly what degree of tilt to go for based on the severity of the crisis. Jim looked like he had about a 10-degree angle going on so Sam knew this was semi-serious.

"Yes, Jim, the FBI have already been called and have assigned a special kidnapping unit from their LA office. They should be arriving at the Hammond home any minute. We'll stay here to give you continuing coverage throughout the evening."

"Thanks, Jenifer. You know that we'll stay with this story..." Jim continued, but Sam was no longer listening. She flipped the TV off on her way to the kitchen, the better to think about the Boy Wonder in silence.

Jack Stone had not been exactly what she'd imagined. He came across as so passionate and articulate in all the TV footage she'd seen of him. Who knew he'd be a blushing introvert in person. Ok. Really she hadn't seen him blush…really it'd been her blushing when he wouldn't say anything and just kept staring at her that first morning. She'd gone in there with her usual take-charge attitude, unhappy about the assignment but determined to be professional.

It had been one interesting week, that's for sure. Jack was rarely in his office, but when he was she was very aware of him. For reasons she couldn't quite pin down, even though their only conversation had been the stilted introductions, she was drawn to him. He always politely offered to bring her coffee when he was walking out to get some for himself. He didn't order her around, didn't ask her to get him lunch or pick up his dry cleaning like she'd heard some of her colleagues had been forced to do for other Council members. A whole week...and that was about it for interaction. She'd given him a little half wave as he ran out the door for his big appearance, then sighed and finished packing her bag.

Definitely not enough to be mooning over, she sternly told herself.

CHAPTER 7

WHITE HOUSE STUDIOS
NOVEMBER 5
6:45PM, TUESDAY

"We interrupt this program to bring you a special broadcast from the President of the United States." The bulletin broke into the middle of NBC's top rated comedy and a highly anticipated game between the Washington Redskins and Philadelphia Eagles. Ed Gonzalez had been against it on the grounds that it was a little beneath the office of the President to announce a kidnapping, but Farmer was so ticked off that he shook off the advice from his more level-headed Press Secretary. "This was a personal attack against me and my administration. If I don't make a big deal of it and get these criminals caught quickly I'm going to be a laughingstock! Besides, I've worked toward this for too long to let it unravel."

He looked grim to the legions of twenty somethings accompanying the sitcom's laugh track and the largely male contingent caught mid-cheer for a Redskins touchdown.

"My fellow Americans, we all remember little Gracie Rodman. Only yesterday she was playing in the front lawn with her new parents." As he spoke a video rolled in the background showing Gracie laughing as she chased a cat while the Hammonds looked on from the porch.

"This afternoon while the Hammonds were shopping at a local mall, Gracie was kidnapped as their backs were turned for just an instant. Less than a hundred miles away, Nick Rodman simultaneously escaped from his prison cell. Neither has been found.

"According to information the FBI has been able to gather, they believe Steve and Ellen Rodman are responsible for this. It's easy to see how they managed to get Gracie and I can assure you the prison is being carefully looked at to determine how they got their son out. I urge you in the strongest terms, do not let this kidnapping go unnoticed. If you have any leads, call local authorities. I've put the full resources of the FBI and Homeland Security behind this effort. We will not allow anyone to terrorize innocent families and flout the American justice system in this fashion. The Rodmans will be caught, Nick returned to prison and Gracie returned to her family.

"Finally, I believe the Rodman's actions today solidify our case for rescuing Gracie in the first place. They resorted to terrorism and broke the law less than a month after Gracie was lawfully removed from their home."

It took 33 hours to get from Union Station in Los Angeles to downtown Seattle on Amtrak's Coast Starlight. Nick and Gracie stayed in their private compartment the whole time watching the scenery go by. They kept track of their trip by the water they saw, first an hour or so after departure, then again in the Oakland area, and finally an hour or two before their scheduled arrival in Seattle. Amanda told the steward that her grandchildren had strep throat. She didn't even flinch at the lie and he certainly didn't believe the kind woman who looked too young to be a grandmother could be harboring a convicted felon and hiding a kidnap victim the entire country was looking for. Amanda cut off Gracie's long blonde hair and dyed it black while Nick chose to hide in the uniform of his gender and generation, baseball cap pulled low and baggy clothes.

George's older brother Phillip met them at the train station in the shadow of Safeco Field with his ancient station wagon. Not too beat up, it had made the three hour drive from Vancouver, B.C. in fine shape. Amanda had an hour layover before catching her train back, long enough to transfer the children, give Phillip a hug and a letter for Steve and Ellen and wave good-bye as they headed north to be reunited with their parents. As the train pulled out she decided that on this leg she would have strep throat. She spent the time fasting and praying.

Amanda went to work the moment they walked in the door after George picked her up. She turned her computer on and called up the database from last year's leadership conference. As chairwoman, she had organized the four-day event that brought together women's ministry leaders from all over the country. The conference was by invitation only and the invited leader could bring along one woman who helped her with day-to-day planning. 456 women showed up and spent a long weekend sharing tips and learning new methods. At the time she'd thought it a smashing success, but thinking about it now Amanda knew the best was yet to come. She quickly began scanning locations and noting which names might be helpful to her.

George was also busy mapping out strategies for the largest mission of his career. How in the world could he organize so many different kidnappings, all within the space of an hour? As the task loomed to overwhelming in his mind, he went to Amanda's office, grabbed her hand and pulled them to their knees to pray for guidance.

LAS VEGAS, NEVADA

A large shape hunched in front of a blinking 42-inch flat screen monitor in the dark room. The young man looked more like a football player than a computer geek. Junked computer parts were piled around the room in seeming disarray and the only clean item in sight was the computer monitor.

To the untrained eye the code scrolling across the screen looked more like Matrix-inspired gibberish than anything else. To the young man, however, it made perfect sense as he snipped statements here and added commands there. Finally, leaning back for a monstrous stretch, he hit the execute command. The code evaporated as the screen went blank, and then a swirling blue hive faded in. After it bounced around for a few seconds a bee appeared out of the eye and the entire image dissolved, a logo taking its place - Blue Honey.

The perfect intro for the perfect website. Joshua Naylor was a web designer, but not just any average high school punk - he was a visionary. Though it wouldn't be obvious from the clutter surrounding him, the only thing of value besides the computers was the comfortable leather chair he sat in, he was one of the most sought after website designers in the nation.

However, he didn't have much time for personal designing anymore. Straight out of college he'd started a small website called believe.net. What began as a hobby on the side of his web design business soon grew into a million+ member online community. Now he spent most his days dealing with administrative headaches at his 50 person office down the street. It was only in the wee hours that he could sit quietly at home and fiddle with his first love.

He was also the nephew of one Amanda Rochester, who rang his phone at that very moment.

"Hello," said a gravelly voice that hadn't been used in six hours. "Hello, Josh, it's Aunt Amanda."

He smiled at the familiar voice and glanced at the clock as he flipped his feet up on the desk. Amanda was always good for some family news. "Hey, Amanda, you're up late."

"Well, George and I have gotten ourselves into something and we need a little computer help."

"Did you open another anonymous e-mail?" Josh sighed and closed out the program he'd been working in, preparing to spend an hour helping his aunt debug her computer from a seemingly endless supply of e-mail viruses.

"No, Josh, this time it's a little more serious. Have you heard the latest on the Rodmans? How Gracie was just kidnapped..."

"Yeah, I read something about it online." He pawed around the clutter, looking for his latest anti-virus disk.

"Well, the villain who masterminded it all was none other than your Uncle George," Amanda said, with a little giggle.

Josh sat bolt upright, disk forgotten. "Amanda, we can't talk about this over the phone. Have you ever been in a chat room?"

"Umm, no." There was a pause on the line. "Well, wait a minute. I went into one I found on America Online that was supposed to be about quilting, but there was some guy who kept typing swear words so I left."

Josh was busily pecking at his keyboard while he half-listened to the story. "Ok, here's what you need to do. Get online and type keyword chat. I've just created a private chat room named josh1201. The password is Amanda."

"Josh, are you sure that's necessary. I'm not using the cell phone because I saw that story on Dateline about cell phones and scanners."

"Amanda, trust a paranoiac, will ya?"

"If you think we need to, ok. It'll take me a few minutes to get there."

"I'll be waiting for you." He hung up and took a breath, then sat staring vaguely in the direction of his monitor.

aroch: hello?

jdog: amanda?

aroch: yeah

jdog: what nickname did you call me by that i hated as a kid?

aroch: joshposh :)

jdog: now start over and tell me what you're talking about. just don't use their name

aroch: ok. well, you know they are some of our dearest friends. your uncle george and i couldn't stand it anymore, and when the president announced the mpa we knew just who they were talking about. so, we've been planning for a month and i actually just got back from dumping the kids on george's brother phillip in seattle.

the, uh, parents are staying at his house in canada and when the kids join them they're going to fly to indonesia on a plane that's being donated to mission work down there. The pilot will take them to some missionary friends of ours where we think they'll be safe

jdog: Amanda

aroch: yeah?

jdog: when did you and george become james bond and bond girl #1?

aroch: very funny

jdog: i'm serious - how did you plan all this? aroch: well, we prayed and God led

jdog: holy cow!

aroch: that's just the background, here's what we need you for...

jdog: i can't wait to hear this

aroch: george and i are arranging to "kidnap" the children announced monday, but since there are so many more we're going to need to get connected with a lot of people across the country. getting steve and ellen out was actually pretty easy, only a few people knew about it - but this is going to be a huge undertaking

jdog: understatement of the year

aroch: josh, george and i both feel God leading us to do this - will you help us?

jdog: of course i will! we'll need to get more secure connections, that's for sure. first thing, i'm going to send a courier tomorrow morning to bring you a disk i want you to load on your computer - it's chat software that will dial directly from your modem instead of using aol - it's easier to avoid being traced. i'll put complete instructions inside about what to do and where to meet me tomorrow night. if you could have preliminary plans and numbers for me i'll try to have some logistics mapped out

aroch: you're a gem josh! i knew we could count on you!

jdog: count on God, not me, this isn't an easy thing you're asking

--

One of the unforeseen side effects of VN controlled broadcasting had been a resurgence of talk radio programs. Those who were not satisfied with the direction the media was taking began to find other avenues of entertainment and news-gathering. This became particularly true about those the media labeled right-wing Christian fundamentalists. There were few labels that would shut the door faster because it was a codeword with so many negative connotations. Through endless repetition fundamental Christian had come to embody someone who was right wing, racist, bigoted, sexist and homophobic. The mere attachment of the label sent a person into violent protestations of innocence. Any candidate who ran on a platform of faith in God or, worst of all, anti-abortion was labeled accordingly with bragging rights going to any reporter who could dig up some dirt on the self-righteous candidate.

In the 90s and early 2000s conservative talk radio had certainly been flourishing, but the industry boomed with the introduction of the VN system and the continuation of the media's trend of

81

reporting on anything related to Christianity as an oddity, a joke or outright antiquated barbarism. Out of sheer desperation fundamental Christians soon had hundreds of choices. They joined the Internet in record numbers to listen to programs when they couldn't get local stations to carry them and Christian websites and chat rooms flourished. One program in particular had the most meteoric rise, owing to its coincidental launch the first year of Farmer's presidency. It was from a diminutive young man in a small room that the most violent protest of recent events was being broadcast.

Rick Stanley had a face made for radio. Not that he was grossly deformed, but he would have never made it in the image-conscious world of television broadcasting. However, what he lacked in good looks he more than compensated for with a mesmerizing voice and powerful intellect.

Rick moved to Los Angeles right after graduating from college and, after bouncing around at various temp jobs for a year, managed to land a gig on a radio station run by a mega church. Given free rein he quickly became too outspoken for their image and was asked to leave after his one-year contract expired. Luckily, a year had been sufficient to gain several wealthy sponsors who agreed to underwrite his own program. He relocated to Colorado Springs because two years in Sodom and Gomorrah, as he jokingly called Los Angeles, had been enough for him.

The first few years of "As4Me" had been heady. There was nothing quite like the feeling of having one of the most powerful voices on earth aiming to bring you down. Or at least that's how Rick described it to a daily audience that averaged 500,000 by his third anniversary.

Rick joked that Tobias Snelt, owner of the largest media conglomerate in the world, had put a price on his head. He sent out a "hit" to two networks, four cable stations, six weekly news magazines and 36 newspapers. Anyone who could come up with some solid dirt on Rick Stanley would have their choice of posts, up to and including anchoring the evening news.

Despite the best efforts of thousands, no one was able to come up with credible dirt, although they often ran material that was less than credible. Rick slept like a log every night after thanking God for his Christian upbringing and the strange sense of destiny he'd always felt, which had helped him avoid several big mistakes.

A funny thing happened after Rick's third anniversary. He went from an almost weekly topic of conversation in the news to a non-entity. Mr. Snelt decided his wisest course would be to ignore the boy he couldn't take down and other media outlets followed suit. The show's fifth year coincided with Rick's 30th birthday, a daily audience of one million and 10 million hits a week on his website. Although that didn't touch the numbers of the most popular talk radio hosts, Rick's sphere of influence put him on equal footing with some of the lower rated network news programs. However, as far as the mainstream media was concerned he was blacklisted.

Rick did manage to appear every year in an anonymous e-mail that circulated through the media, Top 10 Most Hated Conservatives. That "status" and his subject matter notwithstanding, Rick had a pretty good reputation and counted several good friends among the liberal establishment. They would never have admitted the friendship to their bosses of course, rather saying they were keeping tabs on the enemy, but nonetheless tabs were kept several times a month.

Part theologian, part political pundit, Rick spoke about anything and everything related to Christianity in the modern world. His opening monologue generally related to current events but the rest of the two-hour show was up for grabs. He brought to light news stories that the networks wouldn't touch and gave air time to politicians who couldn't get more than a five second out-of-context quote onto the evening news. Rick felt it was fair game as long as it related to the title of his program, which came from his favorite verse "As for me, it is good to be near God."

Josh met Rick when they were thrown together as freshman roommates, Josh studying new media and Rick, radio broadcasting. Many were the times Josh laughed at what he considered the Dark Age major Rick had chosen. But many times since the jokes had been good-naturedly returned to him as Rick rose higher and higher in the public eye.

Josh and Rick remained close through the eight years since graduation and Josh was one of the handful of people who received a monthly update of Rick's new cell phone number. Rick had to change it so frequently because of forms of harassment far more ugly than his face in the National Enquirer, digitally altered to look like he'd gained 300 pounds.

Most of their conversations these days centered around their disbelief at being the center of such massive businesses and trying to best each other's stories of administrative chaos. After a few hours cogitating on his aunt's phone call it was Rick's number Josh dialed.

Phillip Rochester tipped his hat at the Canadian border guard, an elder from his church who hadn't looked too closely at the big pile of blankets in the rear of the wagon as he carefully examined Phillip's passport and Canadian Certificate of Residency. Pulling back onto Provincial Route 99N he accelerated to his usual 120 kilometers and called back, "Come out, come out, wherever you are!"

Two pairs of eyes peeked out from under the blankets, followed closely by two identical grins.

CHAPTER 8

The children to be rescued were supposedly on a secret list, but the secret was spilled to several key members of the press just as the President was making his announcement. Farmer sent a personal note to the media requesting they exercise prudence by not releasing the names or pictures of the families. He wrote in gentle terms that the children had been through enough being raised in such hostile environments and would need a stress-free period to readjust with their new families. The note was widely reported for the twin benefit of making both Farmer and the media look compassionate. Consequently there was always at least one camera crew available to film the scene and one editor along to black out the faces involved. Although the rescues were all completed within the first week the most incendiary footage was endlessly recycled accompanied by equally endless debate and commentary. Each network came up with dramatic promos including some variation of the word rescue that ran between segments, combined with a kickin' soundtrack and the scariest snapshots.

Without releasing names or faces the media had a tough time. They couldn't do their standard reporting package of interviewing anyone who'd ever met the subject, up to and including their former kindergarten teacher. They had to improvise and ended up running anything they could find that was somewhat related, always accompanied by a panel of experts.

Beth had jumped at the assignment in the beginning, but soon grew bored with the formulaic reporting that seemed to her like reading the sports page. "So and so was involved in such and such locally and fit the terrorist profile sections A, C & D." She passed the assignment on as quickly as her producer would let her.

The next few weeks were a little discouraging for 43% of Americans. Although 62% agreed in theory with the MPA and the President's decision to more widely implement it, some were finding it more uncomfortable than they had thought to watch hysterical parents as children were ripped from their arms. Even with facial expressions obscured, the body language and audio of children screaming was enough to portray extreme anguish.

There was only one variation to the news and that was the daily Rodman report. The FBI spokesman who got stuck giving the briefings was wholly sick of seeing himself say, "We have no new information" on the five major channels every evening and was beginning to daydream about early retirement.

VN-S dropped across the board so precipitously that, after two weeks watching the numbers plummet, Farmer made a personal call to an old college pal over at HPAC and a special news conference was staged. Fifty attractive couples lined up behind the celebrity spokeswoman as she gave her speech. During the key 15 second sound bite she quoted CPS statistics of overcrowded group homes and the overwhelmed foster care system, then held up a large binder full of names of couples who had gone through foster parenting classes and were willing to take one or more children on short notice. She also made a point of saying that, except for those 16 years and older, all families would remain intact with siblings staying together, glossing over the possible hole in her logic that families were no longer technically intact.

The public began feeling better after that comforting conference and VN-S slowly returned to a more normal level when rescue stories began to be interspersed with "happy news" showing how well the children were adjusting to their new environments. Great care was taken in subject selection for these "happy news" stories and mostly showed younger children as the older ones could not accurately be described as happy. Each network retained a parade of experts who explained in careful detail how crucial these rescues were to the healthy development of the children. 20/20 dedicated an episode to some of the more infamous cases of children raised in cults.

Not to be outdone 60 Minutes did interviews with 25 adults raised as fundamental Christians who had seen the light and could now talk freely about the trauma of growing up in such hateful homes. The program's most fiery words came from a woman raised in Africa by missionary parents. At the age of 15, after spending all her life helping her parents run a small medical clinic, she watched in horror as warring tribes went on the rampage and her parents were killed in the crossfire. She now lived in Washington and ran a small lobby intent on getting citizenship revoked for Americans arrogant enough to interfere with other cultures for religious purposes. After the program ended her website received almost a million hits before it crashed, 400,000 of them asking for membership information.

The Today Show did a week-long series on their own version of the roots of terrorism, each day recounting the childhood experiences of four of the 9/11 terrorists. Finally, on Friday they arranged an interview with Fasoud Mohammed, a Palestinian man convicted of attempting to bomb a synagogue in France and sentenced to five years in prison. Katie Couric flew to Paris and sympathetically listened as Fasoud recounted his childhood among the radical Hamas. She passed him a tissue when he broke down over the fact that he had not been allowed to martyr himself for the cause when his pack didn't detonate as expected. His family was now unprotected and had not received the money he'd been promised since he was seven years old and begging on the streets.

The highest rated program that made the biggest impact on VN-S was a Barbara Walters hour long special with HPAC's celebrity spokeswoman. The celebrity spoke at length about her fundamental Christian upbringing and the traumatizing effect it had on her psyche. Ms. Walters got a little choked up when she heard that the celebrity had experienced a lot of the same feelings Jayla Jessup had written about in her journal. The interview was interspersed at that point with scenes from the Court TV coverage of Nick Rodman's sensational trial when Roselyn Jessup spent an emotional two days on the stand reading selections from Jayla's journal.

The celebrity continued with her story about how her parents' bigotry had sent her through a self-destructive path of sex, drug addiction and several suicide attempts. She confessed she'd even fantasized about buying a gun and shooting her youth pastor after he told her he was going to tell her parents about her drug problem. Barbara was her most empathetic self when she asked what had turned her life around. The celebrity teared up again talking about a teacher in college who had helped her see her parents in a new light, that they were just living in an antiquated moral system and couldn't help the hate they tried to pass on to her. The unknown college student shed a conservative background and reached the heights of her current fame once she realized that the most important thing she could do was find her own universal truths and treat everyone around her with respect and tolerance.

Some commentators thought Barbara's closing remarks were a bit more over the top than usual, making it sound like the celebrity had overcome parents who locked her in a closet and beat her senseless every evening, rather than parents who forced her to get out of bed as a teen and go to church once a week. Regardless, those were the commentators whose VNs were bad enough that they only spoke on talk radio.

Jack agreed to stick around DC for a month after the President's announcement of further enforcement. He spent his days ironing out minor details that the Council hadn't had time to finish and his nights glued to the television in his hotel room. The pit in his stomach had turned into a big ball of unease that gave him trouble when he tried to sleep. Or eat. Or work.

He was glad when the rescues were accomplished within the first week, but as he watched the media try to make sense of it all with their endless expert panels he realized he wasn't experiencing the relief he'd been expecting. Jack really thought that, overall, the MPA was the right thing to do. He didn't agree with the additional rescues, true, but he saw the ends justifying the means. After that bit of unpleasantness was over he really expected to feel better and move on. The fact that he didn't was a great cause of concern.

In his last week he decided it was all just anxiety about being a displaced person for so long. Knowing he'd be heading back to California at the end of the week he decided to take a leap he normally wouldn't have.

7:15PM, MONDAY

Sam was working late again. She sometimes wondered if she'd ever really get a life, or if 70 hour work weeks were all she was destined for. Her office phone rang at that moment and broke her train of thought.

"Sam Hawthorne." There was just enough silence that she wondered if anyone was on the other end. "Hello?"

"Yes, Ms. Hawthorne. This is Jack Stone. From the Advisory Council..."

She was still processing when she noticed a few moments had passed and he was obviously waiting for some kind of response. "Um, yes. Mr. Stone, hello. What can I do for you?"

"Well. Uh. This may be totally inappropriate Ms. Hawthorne and please feel free to tell me if it is, but I don't really know anyone in DC and I'm getting ready to head back to California at the end of the week and I was just wondering if maybe you might like to get some dinner tomorrow night?"

Sam was so taken aback that she didn't say anything.

"I know you don't really know me and all, but I think you know enough about me to know you'd be safe. Not that you would really have to worry or anything since you're an agent and carry a gun and everything, but I thought it might be nice to have some company before I left because I've been eating room service for so long and I wanted to thank you for being such a good liaison and everything you did for me..."

He trailed off into silence. During his ramble she'd moved rather quickly from disbelief at what he was asking into stifling a laugh at how absolutely non-eloquent he sounded.

"Mr. Stone, I don't see that dinner would be inappropriate given that our working relationship has terminated. I think that would be nice."

She could hear the relief in his tone. "Great! Then can I ask you to call me Jack?"

"Alright…Jack." Was that sigh from him or me? She couldn't tell. How embarrassing.

"I really have been eating room service all this time. Do you know any good spots?"

"If you're still at the Four Seasons there's a nice Italian restaurant just down the street. Do you like pasta?"

"Love it! Is 7 to early?"

"Nope, I'll just come from work."

"Well, great. I guess I'll see you then."

"Yep. And Jack?"

"Yes?"

"I'll leave my gun in the car."

5:31PM, TUESDAY

Jack was glad he didn't have much left to do because he was experiencing a sore lack of concentration. He'd been incredibly relieved when the reporters interviewing him during the Jessup case had been more interested in his cause than his personal life.

How embarrassing to have to admit to the world at large that he hadn't been on a date in over two years – even more embarrassing if they'd gone further back and found out just how infrequent dates had been most of his life.

Not exactly for lack of trying, although that was definitely some of it. "Just listen to how that call went," he mumbled.

JOE'S ITALIAN GARDENS
6:59PM, TUESDAY

Sam made it through her day with not much more success, work wise. Her concentration was all over the place. Only after she'd given herself a firm lecture while eating a quick sandwich at her desk during lunch was she able to finish some important paperwork.

As she sat in a back corner waiting for Jack she had finally calmed herself into thinking he was just looking for a dinner companion and she'd been the only person available. Not a date, she told herself firmly. Again.

Just then Jack entered the restaurant and immediately started scanning the room. Even though he knew this wasn't necessarily a date date, he had the feeling in his gut that he'd gotten the two times his mother had set him up on blind dates. And it was not a good feeling.

As he was about to ask the maitre de if his "date" had arrived he caught a motion out of the corner of his eye. He turned to see Sam waving at him from a small table in the back corner. He noticed she was wearing another blue suit, though like the ones she'd worn during her babysitting assignment it was more stylish than his idea of the average g-woman dress code. He nodded in her direction and set off, sliding carefully between the crowded tables.

As was her habit, Sam hadn't waved right away and watched his eyes pass over her. She was used to watching people, checking them out and gathering as much information as possible from a distance before identifying herself. Only as she saw him move to ask did she raise her arm.

As he approached the table she'd asked for, where she could sit with her back to the wall, another habit, she stood to say hello. "Hi Jack. I hope you found the place ok."

"No problem at all, I asked the concierge and he knew right where it was." Jack signaled for her to sit down and he sat a moment after she did. They stared at each other for just a second too long and then both laughed.

"So I see from the news that your little project is going quite well." She was surprised to see a cloud pass over Jack's face.

"Could we, I mean, I know that's what we have in common and that's obviously why I've been in DC and all, but could we just not talk about the MPA tonight?"

He asked with such earnestness that she readily agreed, but that took away all of the conversation starters she'd come up with while waiting for him.

"Of course." She looked around the restaurant for a moment, then turned back and said, "so what do you think of DC?"

After a bit of awkwardness they fell into conversation about his first trip to DC, which led to his upbringing and how he'd chosen law school. To avoid talking about the Jessup case he asked her why she'd chosen the FBI. Before they knew it they were on their second cup of coffee and their waiter was shooting them a dirty look.

Jack signaled for the check and in the space of the 30 seconds it took the waiter to run over with it Sam had quite an argument with herself. She heard her best friend's voice in her head, if it looks like a date and acts like a date…maybe you should let him get the check. It was always tough for her, especially in a somewhat ambiguous situation like this. Finally she decided to follow her friend's advice and looked around the restaurant while Jack paid.

As they walked out into the cool night air Jack was congratulating himself on the fact that Sam let him pay. In his albeit limited experience, if she let you pay it was definitely a date. In that case, "Sam, would you like to try another hot spot tomorrow night?"

She just smiled.

--

Meanwhile the Rodmans were winging toward freedom, getting a little closer every day. They left Canada about an hour after the President's announcement and spent the week hopping from strip to strip and continent to continent in a small Cessna Turbo 210. Even with its long-range tanks the six seater could only fly about five hours at a time. At an average speed of 160 knots per hour and only 8-10 hours a pilot could safely fly each day it was an incredibly long trip.

The interior of the plane was too loud for normal conversation but their pilot had the foresight to bring along headsets for everyone, including a miniature pair for Gracie. Tim had spent 20 years as a jungle pilot in Indonesia working for Mission Airmens' Fellowship and passed the first leg of their journey by telling them about the history of MAF and how he and his family had become involved. Nick was enthralled with the story that unfolded in his headset as he watched the Alaskan tundra passing beneath.

The history lesson had a pregnant pause when it came time to make their first landing in Sitka, Alaska. Nick was sitting in the front passenger seat amazed by watching everything that went into a smooth landing. When the plane taxied up to the hangar there was stillness in the cockpit as the Rodmans held their breath.

Tim had explained to them what would be involved in their journey. He'd filed an international flight plan and faxed the paperwork necessary to make fuel-only stops in some places, and to stay the night in others. He told them he'd needed to give nationality and passport information on his passengers, as well as a description of cargo, but since they were under the 10 seat minimum they didn't get looked at as closely. Obviously he'd lied about the number and identity of passengers he was carrying, but they were only stopping at strips where he had close friends to fuel them up. It also helped, he said, that he'd never done anything remotely illegal in his flying life and there was no reason to give his flight plans further scrutiny.

He'd been very clear that, because they were still in America and landing at larger strips, during their fuel stops in Alaska they all needed to lie down. He gave Nick a hat and told him to pretend to be a sleeping copilot. They would spend the night at a small strip in Adak run by a friend, then cross into Russian airspace the next day. After that they could get out at any time they wanted to.

So in Sitka there was silence as a truck rolled up to refill their tanks with jet fuel. The plane was back in the air thirty minutes later without a hitch and Tim continued his story.

Tim spent hours in the following days regaling the Rodmans with tales of some of the wilder things he'd done during his time with MAF. Even Gracie was in stitches when he told them about the first time he and his wife spent a night in one of the more remote villages. The Indonesians had prepared a feast for their honored guests, unfortunately comprised mostly of the "delicacy" sago, a starchy staple made from a tree that tasted, as Tim delicately put it, like snot. The great honor of the chicken eyes was bestowed on Laura by the head of the tribe. An honor which she gratefully transferred to Tim while she nibbled her blackened sweet potato.

They were all understandably jumpy that first day, but after crossing into Russia the edge of fear wore off and was replaced by both glee and boredom. Nick lost track of how many times they had landed, the days passing in a numbing wave of sameness. They never went farther than the hangar where they were sleeping so that they wouldn't have to go through customs and the only variation was the quality of the picture passing beneath him and the stories Tim spun into his headset.

After escaping North America they hopped from Russia to Japan and spent a night with a very kind Japanese man who spoke no English beyond "Ok." After Japan they flew through Taiwan to the Philippines and another cot in a hangar in Bagabag. This time the man spoke English and gave them all hugs as he blessed them as brothers and sisters. The last day brought them to Sentani, Indonesia and they spent the night in the home of an MAF family that knew Tim and had been expecting to receive the new plane for their work. The extra "cargo" was overlooked.

They had taken off again for the last time only an hour ago and Nick felt his excitement level rise exponentially as they got closer and closer to Mulia. Watching the endless jungle slip by beneath them Nick was reminded of something their host had said the night before, "If you go down in that jungle you'll be swallowed up. There have been hundreds of planes lost because you just sink right into the swamp."

Nick shivered a moment at the thought but it went right out of his head when Tim tapped him on the shoulder and pointed out a small sliver he'd come to recognize as an airstrip. Tim did a quick flyby and then lined himself up for landing. It was only when they were within 100 feet of the ground that Nick was able to get his perspective right and see the angle and the cliff. He held his breath as the wheels touched down within a few feet of the abrupt edge.

While the Rodmans were stuck in the air George Rochester was making plans with his feet firmly planted on the ground. In the first flush of research he'd realized rather quickly that the President hadn't been exactly truthful in his address to the nation. Farmer made it sound like the 50 cases were all hardened fanatics riding on the edge of the law and, more frequently than not, slipping into illegal activities and taking their children with them.

In fact, other than two ladies who had finished the three-year Reproductive Freedom Act prison term, none of the other parents had any kind of criminal record. They did, however, have a history of speaking out against Farmer's policies. One man in Chicago organized a rally when Farmer came to visit, a move that was particularly embarrassing to Farmer when it was highlighted on the national news and overshadowed the message he'd been bringing. Another man was in charge of nationwide letter writing campaign that had squashed one of Farmer's pet projects by convincing enough people to use their VN options against him.

The rest were involved in local politics or school boards. One woman in Farmer's home state of Nevada had been speaking up in front of her school board for the past 10 years trying to get them to include intelligent design in the biology curriculum. All of them were at home with their families and quite shocked when federal representatives showed up at their door with official papers telling them they had no further right to their children.

George and Amanda talked and prayed late into the night one evening and decided that their primary planning responsibility had to be for the children. They would try to nab all 127 of them simultaneously and send them out of the country together. The parents would all be notified one week prior to get permission. Amanda felt very strongly that if they didn't ask permission before taking the children they were as bad as Farmer. George didn't totally agree, thinking logistically about the multiplied risk of exposure, but he bowed to her wishes.

The parents would also be notified so they could make their way, separately, to an address outside Fort Worth, Texas. Amanda had a contact willing to meet parents and lead them to a ranch where they'd all be staying until it was time to leave the country. Josh was setting up a closed circuit video conference so that George could talk to the parents an hour before the kidnapping and tell them what the plans were.

Luckily the Justice Department had picked families who were spread all over the country, no two in the same city, so it was hoped that the parents could get away without raising suspicions. They were counting heavily on the idea that couples who had just had their children taken away would not raise too many eyebrows by leaving town for a week.

George felt pretty secure in the kidnap and travel plans they had prepared for the children. He even felt pretty secure about their plans to get the parents together in Texas. But at that point they were stumped. Phillip had been able to get his friend, Tim on short notice, but even if Tim shuttled back and forth constantly it would take months to get everyone out of the country. That was just too much time to try and hide over a hundred people, even in Texas cattle country.

While George struggled with that problem Amanda was having far less trouble with her assignment. She had determined that she wanted 10 women praying for each of the 50 families and spent days working through her database of contacts. She asked each woman she contacted to recruit one absolutely solid Christian woman to the prayer team. In less time than it took George to assemble his team she had 512 women who had agreed to pray for an hour a day. As she watched George struggle with this last hurdle she did what she could, sending the request out through channels that he needed wisdom.

A few days later the problem was solved when George logged on and found two e-mails waiting for him. Josh had tried to explain his e-mail security strategy to George and Amanda when they first started using it. He didn't get much beyond the general concept before he gave up and just told them what they needed to do. Josh had set up a funnel that all messages from a hundred different anonymous e-mail accounts went through, and then got scrubbed of actual address data and forwarded through several different international servers before arriving with nonsense addresses. His system meant it would be difficult for the average data mining program to track them and George and Amanda checked only their personal e-mail account. A message was sent to that account whenever a new e-mail was waiting. All they had to do was dial into a secure dedicated server sitting about two feet from Josh's left foot, enter their 6-digit passkey and they had the decrypted message, ready and waiting. After spending a minute completing the process he hollered for Amanda. When she came running he began to read exultingly from the first one.

George and Amanda,

Phillip gave me your e-mail address - thought you'd like to know I just got back from dropping the R's safe and sound. They seemed pretty excited to get out of the plane after all this time. G. was running wildly up and down the runway when I took off. Anyway, don't have a lot of time before my flight leaves. If I survive Garuda, which is always a matter of speculation, I will contact you in a few days.

Oh, almost forgot, my son Jason asked me to tell you he's checked out on 757's from some time spent in the Air Force. He's unmarried, much to his mother's consternation, and furious about the MPA. He was pretty jealous when he found out I got to do something about it and told me to tell you he'll do anything he can to help out.

Tim

He quickly called up the second message. It read:

G&A,

Rick and I have solved the Texas connection! The only hiccup is that we need a 757 pilot willing to stick his/her neck out. Can you work your contacts and see if you can rustle one up? I'll tell you more when we chat tomorrow!

Josh

CHAPTER 9

WHITE HOUSE STUDIOS DECEMBER 2
6:30PM, MONDAY

Beth was back in the audience again, hoping against hope for a story to work on besides the MPA. She'd just returned from her first two-week vacation in years. Her producer had been only halfway surprised when she asked for the time. She'd been increasingly vocal about her unwillingness to interview more experts, or really to have anything to do with the MPA. Two weeks of not much more than sleeping on the beach had relaxed her and she was ready to dig in.

She leaned forward a bit when she saw the 100-watt smile on Farmer's face that he had to work at toning down to a more appropriate Presidential expression before the on-air light blinked on.

"I have the opportunity tonight to make the most exciting announcement of my Presidency. I could build up to it and drag it out, but the topic is too momentous for that. As you may know, my administration has invested almost a billion dollars over the last five years funding stem cell research. Unlike my predecessor, whose executive order banned the research, I felt the possibilities were too valuable to restrain. One of the first acts of my administration was to lift the ban on federal funding for embryonic stem cell research and sign the Stem Consortium creation bill, better known as StemCon. Tonight I am pleased to announce the biggest breakthrough in medical history since...well, I don't know what would match this."

Here the President paused for effect, the drama he was building belying his former promise of expediency. Beth was not the only audience member on the edge of their seat at this point.

"This afternoon the Director of StemCon, Dr. Fred Conklin, met with me and filled me in on their discovery. The cure for

Alzheimer's has been found." Another dramatic pause, this one necessary as Farmer delicately cleared his throat.

"I apologize. My grandfather suffered for 10 years before succumbing to an Alzheimer's related death. This news has taken me by surprise. Dr. Conklin told me this afternoon that StemCon has unlocked the mystery and found the cure to a disease that has debilitated millions of our parents and grandparents."

A graphic appeared to the left of the President as he began to explain the mechanics. "As most of us know, Alzheimer's is more than just a loss of memory. It affects every part of the brain and causes deterioration on all levels. Six months ago StemCon doctors saw a breakthrough by injecting genetically altered embryonic stem cells into the spinal cord at the base of the neck. Now I don't pretend to understand anything about the science involved, but when Dr. Conklin informed me of his preliminary results I directed the FDA to expedite approval of human testing. Because of the nature of this discovery we kept it from the public until we had solid evidence. Today Dr. Conklin brought me conclusive proof that shows the procedure is 90% effective.

"I don't have to tell you how many possibilities are open before us. If we can cure Alzheimer's, we're only a few steps away from curing AIDS, cancer and all the other diseases that are wreaking havoc on humanity.

"I have before me a two-part executive order I signed just before coming on the air tonight. First, I am ordering that 10 billion dollars in additional funding be appropriated to StemCon during the final three years of my administration. I can only hope my successor will continue funding.

"StemCon has assured me they will step up research on all fronts while perfecting the delivery mechanism for the new Alzheimer's medication. In order to accommodate this expanded research StemCon will open four new facilities by the end of the month, with more to follow next year.

"Dr. Conklin has informed me that culturing and cloning is too time consuming and more gains would be made faster with a ready supply of embryonic stem cells. Therefore the second part of my executive order lifts the ban regarding certain methods of harvesting those cells for research purposes. I believe there is simply no excuse for continuing this ban when the need for embryonic stem cells is so great. Adult stem cell research has stalled and, though I know this decision is controversial, I believe it is the right thing to do. Our scientists simply need more cells to continue these exciting research possibilities and I will do whatever needs to be done to provide them. A society without disease is within our grasp."

AS4ME STUDIOS
COLORADO SPRINGS, COLORADO
DECEMBER 3
1:50PM, TUESDAY

The President's announcement the previous night really fired Rick up and he was still going strong as he neared the end of his second hour.

"Why is it that people change their mind on moral issues when a friend or family member is affected? Either something is morally wrong or it isn't. How can you just flip flop? It shouldn't matter the circumstances. Either there are universal truths that apply to everyone in every situation in the same way, or there aren't. Either it's wrong for the government to perform abortions to harvest the cells of babies for research purposes or it isn't. Frankly, it shouldn't matter that they've found the cure for Alzheimer's. If it wasn't wrong Farmer should have taken care of that ban when he took care of the one regarding research with baby cells. But he only does it now when there's a good enough reason - now the end justifies the means.

"I want to ask you something. How would you feel if you got a heart transplant from the cells of your aborted grandchild? Would that end justify the means? Because let me tell you, the President is telling young girls everywhere that if they have an abortion they'll be providing the research material that could cure grandma's cancer. The small black moral mark that is abortion is now completely wiped out by the good of saving humanity.

"And I'd like the President to explain what he means by harvesting methods and what exactly the new StemCon facilities are for. Because I'm taking it to mean the government is going to get even further into the abortion business. I think StemCon is going to become the center for baby harvesting.

"Oh brother. A story just popped up on Fox News. Ten Hollywood celebrities have joined together this morning and are donating a million each to StemCon. Their spokeswoman said they each have family members with life threatening diseases and they want to follow the President's example of doing whatever is necessary to further this research. The spokeswoman also said the ten are planning to fly out to Washington next week to lobby for quicker action.

"This brings up another topic. Why are celebrities given the right to speak before Congress with their pet diseases? Who are they? Are they intellectuals who have earned the right to speak with any kind of expertise? No. All they are is people who look good and can memorize lines…in most cases. I appreciate that they have people close to them suffering from some agonizing diseases, but why are they given the right to lobby Congress and I am not?

"Plain and simple, it's because they're famous. With all due respect to their Oscars, who are they? What right do they have to lecture Congress about what should and should not be done?

"Like the HPAC celebrity spokeswoman. Did anyone see her interview with Barbara Walters a few months ago? She is trotted out every once in awhile to justify a position. But the woman doesn't even think logically. And I quote 'the most important thing I can do in life is to find my own universal truths.' Does the woman understand what universal means? Applying to everything, i.e., universally. So when she says she finds her own universal truths what she's really saying is I don't understand the dribble

I've been asked to parrot so I don't see the inconsistency. How is this woman a representation of America? Why is she given such a large pedestal to preach from? I guess this is America, and in America celebrity is god. With celebrity you can do anything. Sometimes I think it's time to move.

"Before I close the show I want to switch to a positive note for a minute. I can't stand the taste in my mouth after this last topic. There is a group of volunteers heading out to Zimbabwe to start a clinic for AIDS victims and an orphanage for children whose parents have died of AIDS. This is a worthy cause and I ask you to think about contributing. They're pretty much set to go and have been almost fully funded by the government's Aid to Africa program, they just need to collect enough for plane tickets. For more information go to aidtozim.org and check them out. If you send checks here write Zim in the memo line and we'll forward them on."

LOS ANGELES, CALIFORNIA

George had attended a Promise Keepers event at the Anaheim Pond five years before with 50 other men from his church. At the time one of the speakers challenged the 20,000 men present to get into small accountability groups. George took up the challenge and went home that evening to draw up a list of men he worked with who lived close enough to be able to meet weekly. What came of that list was a group of six men who met together every Tuesday morning from 6-7:30. They shared their lives and struggles and held one another accountable for being men of integrity in their homes, families and careers.

It was not an easy task. One of the men dropped out for a year as he went through a divorce and didn't want to be reminded of his failings as a husband by looking across the table at the five other men. But six months after his divorce was finalized he called George up and asked if he could return. He had been welcomed with the male equivalent of open arms, a pat on the back and a stiff one-armed hug.

It was to this group that George went when Amanda came home after dropping the children with his brother in Seattle. Her fired-up response echoed what he'd been feeling and the men of his group were the first he called. They met that Tuesday morning at George's house, Amanda's pancakes and coffee filling in for their usual restaurant fare, and George watched their faces as he explained exactly why Steve Rodman would no longer be attending their church. When he described what they wanted to do for the next step there was stillness around the table for a full minute. Then, one by one, the men committed to help. Each agreed to bring two men they could trust to the next week's meeting, along with ideas for how this colossal idea might be achieved.

The group had grown each week as members brought one or two other like-minded men along with them. The ideas had been both simple and preposterous and there was much argument before a decision was made. In the end they had 61 men who would be involved in the kidnappings, almost all members or former members of the LAPD and other police departments. They even counted a current US Marshal among their ranks.

George intended for the group to be composed only of men with adult children or no children, like himself. He was optimistic about their success, but didn't discount the danger and hadn't wanted to have other children put at risk. However, he was soundly vetoed within the first few meetings when one young father announced that he wanted to earn the respect in the eyes of his wife and children, something he would not see if he remained out of harms way. In a group of hardened law enforcement officers there weren't many dry eyes when the young man finished by asking that his wife and children be included in the exodus.

Not everyone made the same decision, but as final plans were drawn up there were an additional eight wives and 14 children added to the roster.

After one meeting the US Marshal came up to George, introduced himself as Bill Brubaker and asked if George might have time for lunch that week. When George showed up at The Grinder he saw Bill was already seated in a booth with another man. George sat down and Bill introduced his friend Tom. Over hash browns and eggs George's eyes got bigger and bigger as Tom told his tale of working for the Mafia as a counterfeiter for 15 years before finding God and turning himself in to the FBI. He gained immunity by testifying against his former bosses and was now in the witness protection program with Bill as his handler. For the past five years he'd been living in a seedy part of Los Angeles and working with Inner City Missions.

At this point in the story Bill took over and told how he'd thought of Tom when they were discussing different scenarios for getting the parents out of the country. Tom's specialty had been identity theft for the purpose of getting hit men in and out of different countries and Bill was certain he could forge the necessary papers. George's eggs over easy grew cold as Tom earnestly told him, "God has already redeemed my life from the path I was on, now I think He's going to redeem the skill I learned in the service of evil. Will you let me help?"

George nodded as a slow smile spread across his face.

ALEXANDRIA, VIRGINIA KLEIN RESIDENCE

The knock on the door shook Jackie Klein out of her numb reverie. She'd been sitting all morning on her living room floor looking at picture albums. Actually, she'd been sitting in that position or a similar one for the last three weeks, ever since people in blue suits came to her door with the police and took her daughters away.

The blue suits said she and Frank were unfit to be parents because of her involvement in the campaign that took down the Governor of Virginia when it was leaked that he'd smoked pot with his teenage son in the Governor's mansion. He'd almost escaped unscathed with some slick spin by his PR arm, but Jackie had been so infuriated at yet another morally reprehensible politician that she'd overcome her introverted nature and spearheaded Mothers for the Recall. Six months later the man who had been slated to be Farmer's running mate was cooling his heels on a month long vacation overseas.

George was right when he suspected some of the 50 families on the list had no idea the President was talking about them. Both Jackie and Frank were concerned with the MPA and appalled by the direction they felt the President was heading, but they were totally shocked when the knock came at their door one Wednesday morning as they were getting the girls ready for school.

That had been three weeks ago and this was the first morning Frank felt able to go into work, mainly because his boss was hinting about having to let him go and they certainly didn't need that adding to their problems. They'd spent the time on the aforementioned floor, interspersed with discouraging visits to their lawyer and new and inventive ways of avoiding the press camped outside. The networks only stayed for a day since there were so many other places to get to, but the local news and papers stayed for a full week and still popped by now and then to film an MPA report with the Klein household as a backdrop.

Shaking herself she got up and went to peek through the window to see if the knock was friend or foe. When she saw it was her friend Lucy she went quickly to open the door. Lucy gave her a big hug and headed into the living room. Jackie looked around self-consciously and bent to clean up her album mess. "I'm sorry, I've just been looking at pictures this morning."

"Don't apologize," Lucy said with barely contained excitement. "I think I have some good news for you."

Jackie's head shot around at both the words and tone and she forgot the albums in her hand.

Lucy moved forward and took the albums from her, guiding her to a seat on the couch. "Why don't you sit down and I'll tell you about the phone call I got last night."

Lucy sat beside Jackie and held her hand. "Do you remember that conference I went to with Jean last year in Los Angeles?" At Jackie's nod she continued, "Well, the woman who planned it gave me a call last night and had me meet her in a chat room on the Internet. It was all very secret agent with passwords and such, but basically she told me that she and her husband helped the Rodmans escape."

Jackie opened her mouth to interrupt so Lucy spurted out the rest in one breath, "They're planning to kidnap Sarah and Jessie and they want to know if you and Frank will meet them. If you're willing, they've got a new place for you all to live outside the country."

Jackie opened her mouth again, but this time no words came out. Lucy was thrilled to watch as her friend's face shed the tragic veil it had been wearing for nearly a month.

Jackie called Frank as soon as Lucy left, telling him to make whatever excuse necessary but get home fast. Thirty minutes later Frank walked in to find a tornado had hit his house. Jackie was tearing around trying to get together the two suitcases she'd been told she could bring to their new life.

Two hours later Frank pulled out of the gas station with a full tank. He called work and pitifully begged his boss to hold onto the position for two more weeks. He actually had a grin on his face after hanging up thinking about the surprise the jerk was in for. They stopped by the bank and cleaned out their accounts, telling the manager they'd decided to switch to free checking at another bank.

DEAR RENA & SUZANNE JENKINS,

Foster Parents United would like to invite you and your new foster daughters, Sarah and Jessie, to a luncheon held in your honor Tuesday, January 7 at 12:00 at the Grand Vista Hotel in Simi Valley. The guest speaker will be Francis Paulson, Director of Homosexual Parents of Adopted Children.

As press will be attending, please rsvp your acceptance as soon as possible to RSVP@FPU.com.

Planning Committee
FPU Foster Parent of the Year Luncheon

CHAPTER 10

WHITE HOUSE STUDIOS
JANUARY 6
6:30PM, MONDAY

The New York Times ran a 50 point headline above the fold Monday morning screaming "Farmer Schedules Another 10,000 for MPA." A mid-morning poll showed MPA VN approval slipping to 30%, its lowest level since Farmer signed the bill into law. He was planning to feign anger about the leak, though in actuality Ben had ordered one of his staffers to do it so they could have some sample numbers to work with. 30% wasn't as bad as some of their projections.

Adding to the pleasant surprise of the approval rating were two unpleasant events whose outcome was positive for Farmer's agenda. First, one of the worst Hamas bombings in a decade occurred that morning in Israel. Four suicide bombers, ages 15 and 16, had blown themselves up at the same time, taking 150 Israelis with them and injuring another 600. Second, a senior in Northern California was caught in time to make the 6 o'clock news with several guns in his locker and a list of students belonging to the school's chapter of Fellowship of Christian Athletes. The boy's sound bite saying the students had bullied him off of the basketball team because he wouldn't go to church with them was the last story on the news before Talk.

As the red light flickered Ben stared intently, not at the President, but at a small monitor full of numbers. Tonight was the first time they were testing the new VN reporting system where, so they had been told, the numbers on their monitor would be updated in real time with every vote that was cast. Despite all assurances to the contrary Ben wasn't so sure it wouldn't just crash the whole system. Nonetheless he was paying close attention.

"It seems our press corps has been diligently digging once again. I had hoped to present this new information to the American people myself." Here he paused and directed a stern look at the camera, as if trying to shame the Times editor who ran the story.

"However, I hope you will all listen with an open mind. I have here in my hand a list of 10,000 names. These names have been pulled from FBI files and belong to people who have been arrested for various hate crimes and violations of the Reproductive Freedom Act, as well as individuals the FBI has been monitoring for years. They belong to people who are known for preaching hatred and intolerance and clearly fall within the MPA Advisory Council's guidelines for fostering terrorism. It is my intention to hand this list over to the FBI tomorrow morning for action beginning a month from now. But first, I wanted to talk to you about a few things."

Ben watched VN approval dive down ten points, just as his analysts had predicted.

"First of all, I want you to know that I believe this is the right thing to do. I have always said that we must take strong measures if we are to turn the tide of hatred in our country. The events of the last few months, not to mention the tragic events in Israel and California today, have only served to further convince me of this path. If we continue to allow children to be raised in these violent, hateful homes we will see more and more cases of children plotting to kill one another, both in hate crimes and in retaliation for harassment.

"This step was suggested by the MPA Advisory Council and when my staff and I decided to move forward we took it to 10 different town hall meetings across the country. All of them were supportive of the idea, but with reservations. Those concerns came back to us here and we have worked on them during the last weeks. Mostly the concerns centered around second chances. All our focus members believed that people deserve second chances, especially where their children are concerned. They felt people would mend their ways, attend parenting and tolerance classes; in short, do whatever was necessary to keep their children. We agree."

Ben glanced away from the monitor for a minute to watch Farmer deliver this important introduction and when he turned back to it the numbers had updated again. Farmer had gained a few points back. "Now comes the big jump," he murmured to himself.

"I'm now holding in my hand a document worked up by the MPA Advisory Council. It's called the Tolerance Oath and consists of four simple points. I want to read it to you."

Each point appeared in thick black letters along the bottom of the screen as Farmer came to it.

1. I believe in freedom for every individual, regardless of race, gender, sexual orientation, physical ability or religious belief.

2. I believe in the right of every individual to practice their personal beliefs to the extent that those beliefs don't infringe on the rights of others.

3. I pledge to uphold the American ideals of diversity, tolerance and respect for my fellow man.

4. I further pledge that I will raise my child(ren) in a loving environment, teaching them that others have the right to believe what they wish and that those beliefs are as true and valid as my own.

"As you can see, it is a very simple document, merely affirming each person's right to believe what they want and act upon those beliefs as long as they don't infringe upon the rights of others. Signing this is a mere act of 'good faith' that we will ask of each of the people on this list. Justice Department officials will join with local law enforcement and members of Children's Protective Services to begin making these visits next month. All we require is that the parent or parents living in the home sign the Oath and a form contractually obligating them and their children to attend tolerance training and adhere to certain tolerance standards set forth by the MPA Advisory Council as part of their rehabilitation program. As the terms are very reasonable, we don't believe we'll be removing more than 100 children from these homes."

Farmer set the sheet down and bent his head for a moment to arrange the parental face Ben had convinced him to wear for the closing remarks. "Once again I want to say to you, I think drastic measures are called for in this age of violence and hatred. However, I also believe the threat of legal action is, in most cases, enough to force a change in behavior. You've all experienced it, when you're on the freeway going 80 and pass a police car you slow down. You change your actions to follow the law because of the threat of a ticket. I believe this law is such a measure. The threat of a child being removed is enough to change parental actions and reduce the level of hostility and intolerance in a home.

"I can tell you that, in the event we need to place more than 100 children in foster homes, HPAC has provided us with a list of 10,000 couples who have completed extensive foster parent training and are ready to take the younger children. This is a critical component since our current foster parent roster is completely swamped. We are also converting five juvenile detention facilities to take care of the older children.

"Make no mistake, bigotry that leads to hate crimes will not be tolerated. Let me be clear. If you choose to raise your children in a hostile home that preaches hatred of others and religious superiority, you will be held accountable. You will no longer be allowed the privilege of raising children in an environment that damages them for life and insures acts of hatred and terrorism outside the home. These latest incidents in Israel and California have only strengthened my resolve, as they should yours.

"I called the Israeli Prime Minister this afternoon to offer my condolences. He overwhelmed me with his statement of support for what we're doing here with the MPA. He said, and I quote, 'Tony my friend, if you can stop this from happening in your own country you must. You must turn the tide before the ember becomes a flame. I only wish we had been able to take the same course 20 years ago, perhaps we would not be engulfed ourselves.'"

Farmer paused for a moment and took a deep breath. "We simply cannot allow another generation to be poisoned by hatred. We must do whatever it takes to rescue them and our country from the devastating effects of bigotry and intolerance that lead to terrorism."

On perfect cue the camera lights went off. Farmer sat calmly for a few moments while the TV crew swarmed around him.

When they finished he left the studio closely paced by a manic Ed Gonzalez clutching a single printout in his hands.

"Sir, you started the night at 30% approval. When you announced the new list it dropped to 20% - four points less than we projected. But when you began talking about the focus groups it started edging back up and when you finished explaining the Oath there was an instantaneous 16-point jump that kept climbing through your close! We ended at 53%!"

The Press Secretary was not generally known for gushing, but there was no other description suitable to his current mood. "Sir, as you know we were hoping to end at 40-45%. You beat our best projections by eight points! It was remarkable!"

"Thank you, Ed. I couldn't have done it without you." Tony's rolled eyes in Ben's direction sent Ben's eyebrows arching toward a staffer who quietly latched onto Ed's arm and started to ask him a question. Tony and Ben swept alone into the Oval Office. "He'd be a little surprised to hear we knew the results beforehand, don't you think Ben?" The President was grinning at his reflection in the mirror as he patted his perfectly positioned hair.

Ben did a double take in his boss' direction before answering. "Tony, didn't we agree not to talk about that here?"

"Sure, sure. I'm just glad we decided to leave Ed out of it. Now he and the rest of the country think my persuasive skills are out of this world." The President chuckled his way over to his desk and the AG nervously tugged at his tie as he started to sweat, remembering all the times secret tapes made in the White House had come in handy.

BALTIMORE, MARYLAND

There was another person not surprised by President Farmer's announcement, Sam Hawthorne. She'd already been surprised with the news during the morning's briefing. Sam was a member of a relatively small FBI team whose sole purpose was to investigate violations of the Reproductive Freedom Act. This responsibility encompassed boring hours of background checks for newly assigned agents, high adrenaline arrests for the more senior ones, and everything in between.

Sam began her stint with a year solely dedicated to surfing the Internet for anti-abortion websites and passing herself off as a supporter to get more information. Over the next four years she slowly worked her way up the ladder. Part of it was due to a work ethic that had her clocking 60-70 hours a week and part of it was due to her background. Since Sam grew up in a fundamental Christian home she had a unique perspective some of her superiors could never see, but nonetheless appreciated. As one of her bosses put it, she had the ability to "think like the enemy," and equally important she'd "come to her senses." It was this ability, as much as the long hours she put in, that helped Sam climb to her current position.

That ability was acquired without much work on her part through 18 years of weekly church attendance and summer camps. She was involved with the youth group during junior high and high school, mainly because her parents didn't question anything church-related and she had a lot of fun with the activities. Some of her friends got involved in small group Bible studies but Sam seemed doomed to get matched with a series of leaders who couldn't stick out the year long commitment.

Sam began dating Glenn, the extremely popular youth group president, in their junior year and finally gave in to his pressuring to have sex early in their senior year. That concession didn't turn out to be enough to hold onto him and they broke up before Christmas. Sam took her broken heart up to winter camp determined to "get right with God" as the popular youth group saying went. However, before she could make much progress Glenn got up in front of the group and resigned as president, confessing he'd been involved in sexual sin and asking for the group's forgiveness.

Sam was mortified. Though he didn't mention her name everyone knew they'd been dating. It was the longest, most humiliating weekend of her life as everyone carefully avoided the topic around her. She went home and told her parents that, since she'd just turned 18, she would no longer be attending church and they couldn't force her. After hearing what had happened from another parent they decided the best course was to let her be.

Upon graduation Sam went off to college and studied criminal law, followed closely by her application and acceptance to the FBI. Two years at Quantico and five years on the assignment her instructors felt she would be perfect for had mellowed her feelings of humiliation, but she still hadn't returned to church. Anytime she started to think about God she buried herself in work.

In five years Sam had never had a problem with her job. She enjoyed the respect of her peers, as well as the knowledge that she was helping make the world a safer place by helping get fanatical wackos off the street. Whenever a long case was finally solved with a website shut down and the administrator trotted off to jail, or on more rare occasions, some clinic bomber or doctor murderer captured, Sam felt her job was incredibly fulfilling.

She did have problems with her parents but they'd learned not to talk about work after the first few blow-ups when they found out her job was to enforce Farmer's "horrible" new law. Sam drifted from the closeness they'd always had, knowing that silent disapproval lay somewhere under the hugs and protestations of accepting love.

It was true that she sometimes felt a tug at her conscience when she saw the look on some housewife's face getting dragged off to jail because she'd stepped, accidentally or purposefully, inside the 100 foot boundary and was going to be made an example of for her friends. Sam had been feeling those tugs more frequently in the past year and began to wonder if she'd have to change jobs. Sometimes she felt like they were pokes from God but that just made her ignore them all the more.

When the MPA was first introduced Sam had been all for it. She supported the idea because, like most people, she thought Farmer was talking about truly disturbed individuals such as she'd seen in the course of duty. She didn't think too much about the enforcement clause because she couldn't see MPA being broadly applied to the public. In her experience the vast majority of "true believers" were decent, law-abiding citizens. "True believers" were those her department classified smack dab in between "fanatics" and the "culturally religious."

When the President announced the first list of 50 Sam had been surprised because she of all people knew just how few violent religious quacks there actually were. Aside from what the media led people to believe in that they put every weirdo with a sign on TV and made it seem like they represented mainstream Christianity, Sam knew from daily contact that only a handful of the thousands of anti-abortion activists ever got violent. Considering the thousands who opposed abortion and showed up at clinics on a regular basis to protest, Sam was always a little amazed by how few ended up doing something that required her team's intervention. She'd helped out with dozens of rallies in Washington and seen people get out of hand much more frequently who supported causes supposedly more peaceful.

In fact, out of curiosity she'd done a little digging and determined that the President's list wasn't exactly as he'd presented. However, before she could think too much about it a case came up that took her mind off her misgivings for another month.

When she'd sat in the briefing room this morning and heard about the new list, unaccountably all she could think about was her own parents. Using the standards the President was evidently going by, she herself could have been "rescued" from her parents' home. Try as she might to focus and get back to work, her mind kept creating an image of the look her parents would have had if someone had shown up to take her away.

For once she'd gone home early and spent the evening on her couch looking at a family photograph taken when she was a child. She watched the President's speech and when she heard him read the Tolerance Oath something shifted in the region of her stomach. She knew it was not as innocuous as he claimed. Her parents would never have agreed to that sleeper fourth condition. Sam couldn't imagine anyone trying to make them agree to teach her that every single other belief out there was as true and valid as Christianity. And she couldn't for the life of her figure out how that simple belief had a thing to do with fostering terrorism.

Sam suddenly found herself standing firmly against the MPA. If the President was going to expand enforcement to any fundamental Christian parents and force them to make a choice between their integrity and their children she could not have any part of it. Moreover, she could not continue in a position whose sole responsibility, she now thought, was to give the President more names for his list.

Before she could change her mind or think through the consequences she flipped open her personal laptop, called up Yahoo and quickly created a new anonymous e-mail address. The whole process took less than five minutes, after which she clicked the compose button and addressed the one person from her old youth group with whom she still kept in contact. He had been the only friend who stuck by her side during that fateful weekend, publicly lecturing then ignoring his best friend Glenn. Owing to her grueling work schedule she hadn't made too many close

117

friends and still considered him one of the best people she knew. For his support Sam still felt grateful, though she had a poor way of showing it with shoddy communication skills comprised of twice-yearly e-mails. Mostly due to his efforts they'd kept in spotty contact since high school.

Just as she hit send on her brief note the phone rang.

AS4ME STUDIOS
JANUARY 7
1:00PM, TUESDAY

"Don't you see, he's never going to stop. Last month it was 50, yesterday it was 10,000, tomorrow it will be every Christian in America. We have to do something. Pretty soon Farmer is going to say, heck, this is too difficult, why don't we just sterilize the Christians. I'll tell you what, I'd like to get my hands on that simple contract he talked about, I'm absolutely certain there's more to it than he mentioned.

"And I'll tell you something else. I had a hunch about the 10,000 foster parents with such extensive training that HPAC could pull together on such short notice. I called their headquarters this morning posing as a prospective foster parent excited about the President's announcement last night. This is what the receptionist said, and I quote, 'I know, isn't it awesome! We're finally going to stick it to those self-righteous bleeps.' When I expressed regret that I hadn't begun the training program earlier she said it was just one weekend. If my partner and I came in for next week's training we'd be certified in time to get some of the kids. Apparently being gay is qualification enough for being a tolerant parent. She didn't even ask how long my partner and I had been together or if we had any experience with children.

"Let me tell you, the regular foster parenting program is more difficult than this. I checked it out a few years ago. It's different in every state, but in Colorado the whole application process takes up to six months. You have to have background checks, psychological screenings, in home visits and attend all kinds of training classes. They do quite a bit to make sure you're going to be alright taking care of a kid.

"We've got to take a break and it seems ludicrous to be bringing this up now with everything that's going on, but I promised my producer I would mention it before the commercial. One of our sponsors is giving away 50 African safari trips for two. If you're interested, go to our website and register. We'll do a random drawing and contact you if you win."

LAS VEGAS, NEVADA
2:30AM

Josh was running through the plans for maybe the millionth time. Normally he didn't go to bed until 3:00 or 4:00 in the morning even when, like tomorrow, he had to get up early. Tonight he wasn't sure he'd be able to sleep anyway with all the adrenaline pumping through his system. Finally he decided to just give up the plans and spend the rest of the night praying. His mouse was making its way over to the start menu to shut down when his computer chimed softly, signaling new e-mail. He detoured and double-clicked.

To: josh@believe.net
From: shaw@yahoo.com

josh,

I've had a change of heart re: my work situation. Could we talk? Please respond to this e-mail address rather than my work one, for obvious reasons.

sam

MOORPARK, CALIFORNIA

A month after the MPA Advisory Council released its findings
Jack headed back to California and discovered with mixed
emotions that even the wildest celebrity fades quickly, especially
when there's a bigger story to cover.

As the weeks passed he watched the news with a heavy heart as
more and more children were shown screaming from the arms of
FBI men. He became a bit of a news addict, sometimes forgetting
to go to sleep as he watched scene after scene and digested the
endless commentary. Jack couldn't shake the feeling that this chain
of events had started with him, that he'd unwittingly lit the fuse
burning closer and closer to a final explosion that would leave
America in ruins. He'd even begun to have a recurring nightmare
where he played the part of the FBI agent ripping a screaming
child from the arms of its parent.

He spent hours at the beach, wandering aimlessly as he tried to
pin down his uneasiness. Hadn't he done the right thing with the
Jessups? How had he moved so quickly from that case to having
the President announce the Tolerance Oath?

In fact, the Tolerance Oath was one of the issues where Jack
strongly disagreed with the majority of the Council. He'd finally
compromised with the understanding that the Oath phase was years
away and possibly would never be announced. There was supposed
to be a large gap between the first major test case and wider
enforcement to give people a chance to get used to the idea and
voluntarily change their ways.

He saw it a lot like the campaign to make Americans quit
smoking. First you shock them with huge lawsuits, then give them
time to change, then start enacting different laws to move the
intransigent. No Smoking in public buildings. No Smoking within
20 feet of doorways. No Smoking with children in the car. No

Smoking any place where non-smokers might possibly breathe in the slightest wisp of smoke. No Smoking.

Jack had always been a bit of an egghead, dealing in theory and hypothesis, and he was finding it difficult to watch his theories become reality. Like the Tolerance Oath. Although he'd strongly disagreed he'd still allowed the Council to talk him into signing off on it because it was all theory. Hearing the President explain it on national television last night struck Jack differently than tossing the idea around in an intellectual gathering where enforcement was hypothetical. And quite frankly, he didn't even want to think about the contract Farmer had mentioned, as he'd not participated in all the Council's enforcement discussions.

Since he'd left Washington he'd been out of the loop and had been as surprised as anyone by the announcement. He'd been so shaken he'd stared into space for a couple hours before he realized the time and called Sam. Bad idea. The unease he'd been feeling got cranked up a few notches when she called him an idiot and hung up on him.

He'd gone out to the beach one more time today and been blindsided by doubt. Who was he to say how people should raise their children? Who was he to make someone sign an Oath that they would present all sides in every debate? He certainly would want the opportunity to teach his children what he thought was right. And how in the world did teaching your children there was one way to heaven relate to creating a new generation of terrorists? Never in his life had he pondered these questions, ever and only interested in the blind pursuit of his idea of justice. Now he began to wonder if Sam was right in her assessment.

As he sat watching the sun go down he had a brutally honest conversation with himself. He'd been more and more despondent as the weeks went by watching the 24/7 MPA coverage, and he had mountains of doubt about what he'd done. But somehow his blossoming relationship with Sam had been a light at the end of the tunnel. He'd allowed it to temper the horrible depression that should have been a sign that he'd done exactly the wrong thing in Washington.

Jack had analyzed their brief dates so many times he could rattle them off like box scores in his sleep. First date: dinner at an Italian restaurant – wonderful. Second date: dinner at a Mexican restaurant the next night – fabulous. Third date: she'd actually taken the day off to show him the sights, topped off with dinner at a steakhouse and a long walk on the Mall – blissful. Fourth date: breakfast and a ride to the airport – disappointingly short.

They'd talked almost nightly since he returned to California, sometimes for a few minutes and other times for hours. One memorable night they'd talked from the time she got home from work until she had to get ready the next morning. He'd had a triple espresso delivered to her office.

Jack knew without a doubt that he had never met anyone like her. She fascinated him. His times with her, and the time he spent thinking about her, were the only thing keeping him sane in between MPA assaults. He almost felt schizophrenic, bouncing between such highs and lows so many times a day. And when she'd hung up on him last night, that was a low.

CHAPTER 11

BIG JAKE'S TEXAS BBQ
JANUARY 7
11:15AM, TUESDAY

Big Jake was keeping one eye on the grill and one on the couple in the corner booth that had come bolting in a few minutes before. When his wife Jan came up with three more rib orders he winked and nodded in their direction. Jan pulled a slim folder from behind the soda machine and glanced inside. She nodded imperceptibly back at Jake and headed in that direction.

Frank and Jackie Klein had driven nonstop from Virginia to make the noon deadline and were understandably pale as they watched the waitress approach them. The instructions had been clear but Frank felt a little uncomfortable following them in this environment. When Jan reached the table she asked her usual, "What'll it be?" She couldn't hear Frank's mumble so she asked him to repeat himself. Once again he mumbled and irritated, Jan asked one more time, "What'll it be?"

This time Jackie answered loud enough to earn a chuckle from Big Jake behind the grill and dirty looks from every burly trucker within hearing distance who had barbecue sauce prominently painted on their chins. "Do you serve tofu?"

Thirty minutes later they pulled up outside the Double S Ranch. They had followed Jake and Jan's son Jimmy from the restaurant. Jimmy got out of his truck and drawled, "Head on inside the barn there. I'll take yer car round back."

Opening the door caused the low murmur inside to stop completely as nearly 100 eyes looked at them. From the group emerged a dusty looking cowboy complete with wranglers and an enormous belt buckle. "Mr. and Mrs. Klein! Ya'll barely made it, we were starting to wonder."

A woman approached who could only be described as the dusty cowboy's better half and said, "Now Earl, don't give them a hard time. They look like they've been through the ringer sideways. Why don't ya'll follow me and I'll show ya'll where to freshen up. The meetin's gonna start in about ten minutes."

Eight minutes later the Kleins reappeared with shiny faces and clean teeth. A woman who looked about their age beckoned them over to some empty seats beside her. "I heard Millie say you're the Kleins. I'm Sharon Mitter and this is my husband, Gary." She pointed to the man next to her who was engrossed in another conversation. "We're from Pittsburgh." Hands shook all around and Jackie was trying to think of something polite to say when Earl cleared his throat and spoke loudly from the front of the room.

"Well folks, looks like everyone made it just in time. The meetin's about to get started. Millie's just gettin' us connected."

Millie was typing furiously on a shiny laptop that looked just a little out of place positioned as it was on a bale of hay with a saddle blanket separating the two incongruous elements. With a few last clicks she seemed satisfied and adjusted the cord between the laptop and a mini projector aimed at a white sheet hung on the wall. A small video camera hung just above the sheet and appeared to be held in place by duct tape as it panned back and forth over the crowd.

Through the magic of technology George Rochester's face was now four feet wide on the sheet and he began to speak. George's features were darkened just enough to be indistinct but the group could still see his mouth moving in time with the audio.

"Welcome parents. My name is George. I'm the lesser half of the organizer of this shindig, but she made me do the talking." Nervous laughs rippled across the room.

"What I'd like to do is explain our plan and then answer any questions you might have. It won't take me very long but it's imperative that we be finished before 1:00 so I ask you to be brief and concise when it comes to your turn. Don't worry about the camera, it's a closed circuit connection and we only have it running so I can see you when you ask a question. It's not recording."

George appeared to take a deep breath, took a sip of water and continued. "Ok, first things first. If you give us permission we will be taking your children back in approximately two hours. The plan is very non-confrontational and we foresee no problems. Should any occur our people are equipped with rubber bullets so that no one will be seriously injured. We will take your children out of the United States and have them rendezvous with you in another country.

"Those of you who agree to go with us will be moved from here to transportation we have prepared. There will be nothing violent done to get you out, though there will be a few illegal things happening, as well as some general sneakiness and subterfuge. Those of you who got here early in the week know this already, but we've taken several cars and transported them to different locations around the country. We're trying to throw off the authorities for as long as possible so in about an hour we have volunteers who will be driving your cars over the borders into Mexico and Canada and logging your names into the immigration systems. I'm sorry for those of the rest of you who love your cars, Earl will be crushing them and burying them on the ranch.

"Now, as to where you're going. We have taken the liberty of placing you where your skills will be of use. Each of you will need to work, but you will be with your children and your work will be in the service of God's kingdom. We're not sure if this will be permanent or if this current madness will go away, but we've got you set up for at least five years.

"For the safety of everyone involved I cannot be more specific as to plans and locations, but I assure you much prayer has gone into this and the people involved in planning are your brothers and sisters in Christ. I tried to be vague so that anyone who decides against going won't have anything to hide from the authorities who will be investigating this. Those of you who go will have plenty of time to hear the whole story. Now, I'll try to answer any questions you might have."

George looked around the room as the camera panned and saw a few shocked expressions but most faces were nodding in agreement. After a full minute of silence he said, "Ok, anyone who doesn't want to go please stand up. We'll leave your children where they are and ask you to take advantage of Earl and Millie's hospitality for a week, then you'll be free to go."

No one stood.

GRAND VISTA HOTEL
SIMI VALLEY, CALIFORNIA
11:55AM

Rena and Suzanne Jenkins were having quite a bit of trouble with their new foster daughters. Sarah at 12 and Jessie at 8 were proving far less malleable than the Jenkins had imagined and turned out to have quite strong feelings about being taken from the home of their parents, no matter the logical reason. The girls had tried sneaking out the first night, only to set off the alarm and bring the police running. Since then Rena had to change the alarm code every few days so that the girls would have trouble getting hold of it. More irritating than having to call Suzanne three separate times because she couldn't remember the code was that the girls wouldn't just sit quietly and listen to the wisdom Rena had to impart. Instead they argued vehemently. When they weren't arguing they were crying and when they weren't crying they were quoting Bible verses and singing religious songs at the top of their lungs. If Rena heard "Arky, Arky" one more time she thought she might lose her mind. It was too hard to concentrate in a staff meeting with "The animals, the animals, they came in by twosies, twosies" running through her head.

Rena found herself working later and later to avoid the chaos formerly known as her quiet and ordered household. Of course Suzanne didn't anticipate nor appreciate having to foster parent alone so there were arguments no matter how late Rena came home.

Rena almost cancelled this outing as too much trouble but Suzanne had a fit saying she'd looked at FPU's website and this was a serious up-and-coming organization. Rena had also received a call from an HPAC representative the night before who was checking that they were still planning to attend. Put upon and guilted into it, she felt obligated to go. For once, even the prospect of listening to her favorite speaker wasn't enough to lighten Rena's mood.

Nevertheless they were here. Silence reigned in the car as Rena pulled into the parking lot. Suzanne wasn't speaking to her since she'd dropped the bomb that she had to go on a business trip to New York for two weeks of training on a new system. As for the girls, Rena definitely preferred their passive method of the silent treatment to some of their more aggressive options.

Rena winced as three of the four doors on her BMW slammed shut and the family trouped into the hotel looking for Ballroom C. Two smiling hotel employees greeted them at the door and directed Rena and Suzanne inside to table four, then herded the girls into Ballroom D where they were going to be entertained with an educational film.

Two hours later Rena thought she was going to die of boredom. It turned out that all the couples that took MPA children had been invited and they'd all been welcomed and congratulated by the head of Foster Parents United. He spoke inanities for a few minutes, then introduced their speaker Francis Paulson before heading to the back of the room to dim the lights. And then the came worst part, no one had said Ms. Paulson would be speaking via satellite! Rena felt royally jipped.

She didn't know who had given Ms. Paulson instructions but two hours was too long for any speech and yet she showed no signs of slowing down as she carefully catalogued 50 destructive influences of patriarchal society in the last 2000 years. Rena leaned over to tell Suzanne she was going to sneak out to the bathroom, then exited as quietly as she could. It seemed everyone else in the audience was raptly listening to their hero and not worried at all about such pedestrian things as time and bladders.

On her way back Rena peeked in on Ballroom D. The place was pitch dark other than the screen and through that dim light she could see the outline of a number of couches and the backs of heads. She didn't see the woman standing in the corner of the room who slumped with relief when Rena closed the door as the speakers thumped out a very recognizable tune. Rena threaded her way back to her seat wondering who had made the call that Star Wars was an educational film.

FOLSON RE-EDUCATION CENTER
LOS ANGELES, CALIFORNIA
1:15PM

The staff at Folson Re-Education Center was enjoying a live lecture, via satellite, from none other than Francis Paulson, director of HPAC. She was a hero to many of the counselors at Folson and the excitement level had been high for a week in anticipation. The director had even agreed to the rare privilege of a movie in the afternoon to entertain the inmates so all the staff could enjoy the lecture. Of course, they weren't supposed to be called inmates anymore that's just how the staff referred to the Tolerance Education students when no one was looking.

CALIFORNIA/MEXICO BORDER CROSSING
3:30PM

Mike and Sue Snider idled in their borrowed Ford Taurus with Oregon plates as they edged along in line. The heat wave was unseasonable, even for Southern California, and even with their air conditioning cranked on high they were getting concerned their masks would start to melt.

A friend of a friend of one of George's team was a Hollywood prosthetic specialist who had fashioned 32 masks for the volunteer border crossers. Another friend provided unedited media footage that showed the parents from all angles so the masks had turned out quite good.

Mike and Sue dutifully glued them on that morning and then picked up their ride at a Texaco outside of San Diego where it had recently been dropped by a semi from Texas Trucking. Sue's mother was tailing them in her Camry, which was how they planned to get back after ditching the car as quickly as possible…if they could ever get through this line.

Finally it was their turn and Mike handed over the fake driver's licenses supplied by Tom the counterfeiter. A cursory look, two questions and a scan of the license bar code took all of 10 seconds and they were waved through.

GRAND VISTA HOTEL
3:45PM

Rena was ready to bolt and impatiently bounced from one foot to the other as Suzanne chatted with their tablemates. Three and a half hours had crawled by when Ms. Paulson finally started to wrap up. To add insult to injury, the closing was also taped. The hotel sound technician merely switched tapes when the speech was over and the head of FPU thanked them for coming. He said he thought it'd be fun to tape his close after enjoying Ms. Paulson in the same manner, and then invited everyone to get to know their tablemates. They had picked a long educational movie so that the new foster parents would have an additional 30 minutes to compare notes after the talk. Rena snorted at that but couldn't convince Suzanne to leave.

Promptly at 4:15 Rena made a dash for the door, yanking Suzanne behind her. When they reached Ballroom C the door was locked. Rena knocked as loudly as she could but when no one answered she went in search of a hotel employee with a key. By the time she returned with the manager a crowd of grumbling parents was impatiently waiting.

When the door swung open Star Wars appeared to be halfway through which seemed odd to Rena since it was close to the same scene she'd heard two hours before. Everything was explained when the manager flicked on the light switch to reveal a room full of couches and chairs with strategically placed head-shaped pillows.

FOLSON RE-EDUCATION CENTER
4:30PM

Ms. Paulson wrapped her talk up magnificently, but before anyone could get away the Director thought he'd take a few minutes to give some of his thoughts. Fifteen minutes later the first staff members escaped and headed to the main room where the inmates had been watching their movie. When they unlocked the door and flipped on the light they found Star Wars playing to an empty house.

CHAPTER 12

WHITE HOUSE
JANUARY 8
WEDNESDAY

The President was furious. It was evident in every line that his makeup artist was valiantly trying to powder over. He had come straight from a closed door meeting with the Attorney General and the rest of his inner circle of advisors - a meeting that began with fifteen minutes of yelling dutifully ignored by the Secret Service agents posted outside the door. Farmer raved about the personal attack and had to be talked down from declaring martial law and bringing out the National Guard to, as he put it, "capture the terrorists trying to ruin my legacy." He was taking this latest kidnapping exponentially worse than he had the Rodman situation. Only Ben knew the real reason why and it certainly had nothing to do with Farmer's legacy.

It was true that at this point in their lives they were concerned about the "legacy," but that was an ancillary matter. Ben had known the real reason for Farmer's current flip-out for over 20 years, ever since the day he stood by while his best friend sobbed beside a gravestone.

Ben didn't like to think about those days, but watching Tony rage brought back memories of a lifetime of such incidents. It started almost from the first day they met in the Young Democrats club in junior high. Tony had already been elected 7th grade class president when he befriended the nerdy student body secretary. A faculty advisor had appointed Ben when no one wanted to run for the ignoble post that did all the work for none of the glory. He didn't mind. Ben had always been a background guy, content to work overtime on the message as long as he didn't have to be the one standing in the spotlight to deliver it.

It was a well-matched friendship, though Ben often wondered in those early days why the popular and dashing Farmer wanted to hang out with the most introverted guy in their class. He didn't find out for sure until their senior year when Tony showed up on his doorstep just after midnight, suitcase in hand.

Ben snuck some beers from the refrigerator and they sat in the park across the street all night long. Tony talked until dawn and by the time the sun rose Ben understood what was going on beneath his friend's smooth exterior more than anyone ever had, or would.

Tony's dad was a certifiable nutjob. He was the preacher of a 100-member congregation he'd started in town, The Church of God's Sinful Children. That night Tony told him a thousand horrible stories, one after another. How his father had disciplined the tiniest infraction with a large belt buckle. How he'd been forced to recite long portions of the Bible since before he could read and sent to bed without supper if he missed a word. How he'd watched his mother shrivel over the years, his father enforcing submission with words that cut her to shreds.

Around five in the morning, after Tony had downed a six-pack of beer, he finally got around to explaining the suitcase. He'd turned 18 at midnight and walked out of the house. Tony lived in the den at Ben's house for the last month of school, and then they both moved to New Haven where they'd been accepted to Yale.

Those first two years Ben thought Tony was going to overcome his dad's early influence. He was elected to the student government both years and thrived in the environment. More important, in Ben's mind, was that Tony was making fewer and fewer derogatory comments about the "fundies." He was extremely popular with the ladies, although his heart belonged to a girl back home whom he'd dated for four years.

At least one night a week Ben could awaken to find Tony hunched over his desk writing to Mary. He had Ben read many of the letters and they had long discussions on how best to convince her to come to New Haven and get married. Tony took a lot of goodnatured ribbing over pining for his long distance love, but only Ben knew why she stayed away. She'd grown up in The Church of God's Sinful Children and, though she loved Tony with all her heart, the preacher had commanded no one in the congregation could speak with Tony since he'd "gone to the devil."

During their third year Mary stopped returning Tony's letters. Ben watched as he grew increasingly desperate, writing to her almost every night. They were both at Yale on scholarship so neither had the money to fly home until the summer. When Ben could stand it no longer he wrote his parents, asking them to find out what they could. He kept their answer to himself for almost a week before he could work up the nerve to tell Tony.

Mary's parents had found Tony's letters and taken her before the preacher. Threatened, battered and in fear for her very soul, with Tony nowhere in sight, Mary agreed to their punishment. Within the week she married a lawyer in the church whose wife had just died, leaving him to raise four young children.

When Ben gave Tony the letter he had no idea what to expect. He watched in silence as Tony finished it, packed a change of clothes and walked out the door. One week later Tony returned, unpacked his bag and resumed his life. He never told Ben where he'd gone and killed the subject anytime Ben tried to get him to talk about it. Other than a more pronounced dark side that caused his temper to explode more often than in the past, Tony acted like nothing had happened.

Ten years later Ben had returned to their hometown with Tony for his father's funeral. Always thinking of the long-term plan, Ben convinced him to go. They were only lowly assistant DA's at the time, but Ben told him it would be difficult to get elected as governor of a conservative state if the press got wind of the fact that he'd skipped his father's funeral, no matter what kind of whacko he was. Tony dutifully agreed, but didn't shed one tear. He didn't stay more than 10 seconds after the service was over, just gave his mother a hug and strode away.

Tony hadn't wanted to stay over, but they couldn't get a flight out until the next morning. Ben was working on his laptop that night when Tony knocked on the door and silently motioned for him to follow. He had no idea where they were going as Tony drove in silence, but ten minutes later they pulled into the cemetery. Tony strode right by his father's grave, not giving it even one glance. However, when he arrived at Mary's grave he crumpled to the ground and wept.

To this day Ben had no idea how Tony found out about Mary. His parents had called him the day she died from complications in childbirth nine months after her wedding day but he could never tell Tony. Twenty years later and he could still recall the image of his friend sobbing in the mud as if it had happened yesterday. Twenty years later, in the exact spot they'd worked toward all those years, and still his friend mourned.

The MPA was born that night. Tony explained the seed of the idea at breakfast the next morning. Ben listened, as he always did, but didn't think they'd ever get this far with it. He agreed with his friend's opinion of the fundamentally religious, if not with the level of hatred Tony had for them. And this was just one plank in the platform of good they planned to do together. At least, that's what Ben had thought. He was beginning to wonder if this was Tony's sole endgame.

With a sigh Ben tuned back to the present and let Tony rage on. He was less than thrilled with the information the FBI had been able to gather during the day. Almost immediately after the kidnapping story broke the press was able to figure out that the parents had all disappeared. What they didn't have the FBI's clout to find out quickly was that each of the parents had cleaned out their bank accounts and disappeared at various times during the past week. To muddy the picture, immigration registered border crossings into both Canada and Mexico for 16 different couples around the same time the kidnappings took place and before the borders could be notified.

Upon relating this information to Farmer the Secret Service heard another profane outburst along the lines of "how could we not know this" and "what kind of operation are you running?" Ben calmly responded that, with the years of budget cuts, they didn't have the manpower nor the directive to surveil each family. The FBI had already been stretched to the limit when MPA duty was added without additional staffing. "Frankly, Tony, we weren't watching them."

Farmer whipped around from where he'd been pacing and said menacingly, "Well, we should have been."

An hour later the men exited with grim faces and the President stalked to the studio.

"Tonight I'm announcing the formation of a Task Force whose sole responsibility will be investigation and enforcement relating to the Minor Protection Act. I've asked the Attorney General to submit candidates for heading up the MPA Task Force. It will be transferred to Homeland Security as soon as possible, but until someone is chosen he will be directing it out of his office. Members will be pulled from the FBI and Homeland Security and will work in conjunction with local law enforcement."

Farmer's skin tone reddened through the diligent powdering efforts of the makeup artist and the combined effect left him looking like he might have a minor case of hives. "This terrorism of our citizenry will not be tolerated. It was obviously well planned and carefully orchestrated and I will use whatever means necessary to bring these terrorists to justice. Especially if they turn out to be treasonous Americans. Anyone who flouts the laws of the US government will be held accountable.

"If you know the whereabouts of any of these families, contact local law enforcement immediately. Some may feel sympathy toward these terrorists, but they are breaking the law nonetheless. Let me assure you, they will be brought to justice, as will anyone aiding and abetting them. To quote my predecessor, you are either for us or against us. If you harbor terrorists, you will be brought to justice alongside them."

He took a few seconds to quiet his breathing and then, with a forced smile said, "I was going to save this until the next Talk but I feel the need to end on a positive note. The four new StemCon centers are ready on schedule and will be open for business next Monday morning. I have no doubt in my mind that I will be announcing another medical breakthrough in no time."

Ben blinked at the announcement. It was true, but he hadn't expected Farmer to include it. They'd had a heck of a time getting the centers up and running. He'd sent two of his staffers over to help Dr. Conklin find the medical staff to perform therapeutic abortions in-house since they'd been told that was the easiest and quickest way to get embryonic stem cells in mass quantities. They were genuinely surprised to find that not every doctor in America wanted to be involved in that particular medical procedure. It turned out that pretty much every doctor who was willing was already performing abortion on demand in a wide variety of public and private clinics.

Ben learned that, though abortion training was an ob-gyn requirement for the Accreditation Council for Graduate Medical Education, doctors and institutions were still allowed to opt out due to moral or religious objections. Throughout the country older doctors were twice as likely to perform abortions as younger ones, and the older doctors were too close to retirement to consider a career move with StemCon. It had proved more difficult than anyone had imagined to find staffing for the research centers. To meet the President's deadline they'd had to beg, borrow and in the end, steal from the larger reproductive health centers with promises of higher salaries and beefier security. Ben was still hoping to smooth things over with the heads of several major clinics before the centers went online. With the President's early announcement that bit of diplomacy was out the window.

BALTIMORE, MARYLAND
7:45PM

Sam looked over her shoulder. Even though she was home alone on her personal laptop accessing an anonymous e-mail

136

account, she of all people knew the spying capabilities of the FBI had greatly increased since the Patriot Act. What she was doing had her spooked. However, she also knew that in the worst case scenario her e-mail would get flagged, but it could be two years before anyone saw it. Thank goodness for budget cuts.

The room was dark, the only light coming from the laptop she was hunched over. The somewhat innocent message she'd sent the night before seemed ominous after today's events. Five minutes before she'd left for the day her boss took her aside and said he had just received a call from the Director regarding the new MPA Task Force and he had recommended her for a critical position. She nodded somewhat stiffly and thanked him while continuing to pack her briefcase.

When Sam got home to an e-mail message directing her to a chat room she was understandably a little nervous.

A few minutes later she'd maneuvered to the site.

shaw: Josh?

jdog: I'm here

shaw: You got my message. I was hoping you were still using that address.

jdog: Forgive me, but what was my favorite drink in high school?

shaw: Oh, right. I could never forget that - it was the most tart concoction I've ever tasted. Dr. Pepper with lime Kool-aid ice cubes.

jdog: Hi Sam, it's been a long time

shaw: I know Josh. I'm sorry about that.

jdog: What can I help you with?

shaw: I'm still working with the Reproductive Freedom Task Force so I have access to information the general public doesn't. I was initially supportive of the MPA but when the President announced his first list of 50 "religious fanatics" I was curious where he'd found 50 – we certainly don't have that many we can locate at the drop of a hat. Anyway, I got sidetracked by another case...and then the President announced the other night his new list of 10,000. Josh, I sat on my couch for 6 hours imagining my parents' facial expression if I had been taken from them, because by the standards the President is now using my parents could have easily made it onto his list.

jdog: That's true, your parents raised you in a fundamental Christian home – defined by MPA as a home where parents take their children to church every week and teach them there are moral absolutes.

shaw: Exactly! And you know my parents, they weren't hateful or bigoted, they were just as loving as I could have hoped.

jdog: That's how I remember them

shaw: Anyway, that's why I initially e-mailed you – but my boss told me as I was leaving today that I was being recommended to the MPA Task Force

jdog: The new task force supposedly formed this evening? they're certainly moving fast

shaw: Well according to my boss it's the Bureau's new #1 priority and quite a coup to be assigned. He said he thought they could really use my ability to "think like the enemy" jdog: I can see why they'd think that

shaw: Josh, I haven't spent significant time with Christians besides you and my parents since I left school. I know I'm a horrible correspondent and you haven't approved of my job, but you're still my oldest friend and I didn't know who else I could talk to about this. I don't know exactly what my job will be, but I might be able to get access to the list and maybe I'll be able to let you know sometimes when we're planning on taking children from a particular house. I thought maybe you would know someone who could help through your believe.net contacts, or maybe your friend Rick...

jdog: I may know someone, but Sam - I need to know - why are you doing this?

shaw: I know the truth Josh. I've been living as if I didn't for over 10 years now, but I've always known. I thought I could forget, could turn my back on God. I've been feeling Him tug at me for the past year but I kept ignoring Him and working longer and harder hours. Two days ago I watched President Farmer announce the new lists and when he read the Tolerance Oath...it was like a bolt of lightning. Josh, I've been on the wrong side for too long. I need to help make things right.

jdog: Wow! Well, you know I've been praying for you since we graduated so I guess I shouldn't be surprised that God finally got your attention. :) I don't think I have to tell you that we need to be extremely careful. I'll do some research and get back to you. Can you meet me in this chat room tomorrow night at 10?

shaw: Yes.

jdog: Ok, I'll see you then. I'm so glad you got in touch with me Sam.

shaw: Me too

JANUARY 8
8:47PM, WEDNESDAY

Amanda was working at her desk when the phone rang.
"Hello?" "Our prayers are answered. Meet me in 10 minutes on
B3." Click. Great. Now how do I get to B3? She fumbled through
her papers trying to find the instructions Josh had sent her. Amanda
was not the greatest computer expert living by any stretch of the
imagination. She had just learned how to use e-mail in the last few
years, but Josh's instructions were clear and it took her just under
nine minutes to log into the chat room and type the password.

aroch: JOSH?

jdog: I'm here.

aroch: WELL, WHAT'S GOING ON...

jdog: First of all, turn your caps off - you don't need to shout :)

aroch: Oh, right, sorry

jdog: A friend from high school I've been in touch with on and
off contacted me last night. She works at the FBI and I bet you
can't guess the new assignment she's been recommended for

aroch: the MPA Task Force?

jdog: How did you know?

aroch: You're kidding! I was just kidding...

jdog: Well, anyway, yes. She's just been recommended and - even better - she said she "might" have access to the list and "will maybe" know ahead of time what days they will be executing each order

aroch: Josh, do you trust her?

jdog: She's been fighting God for ten years, but when I asked her why she was doing it I believed her answer. Yes, I trust her.

aroch: Then praise God. He'll take care of the mights and maybes

jdog: I told her I might know someone to pass along the information to...so "someone," whaddya think? ;)

aroch: I think our prayers HAVE been answered! I'll start working on call lists right away. Let me know as soon as she can get any information to us.

jdog: I will. Right now I'm working up a chat room schedule for us and writing instructions like yours so she'll be able to get in and out without being tracked.

aroch: Hopefully she's a little more computer literate than me, at least your instructions won't need to start with 1) make sure the computer is plugged in and 2) telling me what in the world the colon and parenthesis is all about :)

jdog: I think she can handle that part. I'm meeting her in a chat tomorrow night - how about we meet Friday morning at 10 in C7?

aroch: I can do that. I'll see if George can get off and meet with us jdog: Be careful Amanda, we'll be in even more trouble now if we get caught. Remember to follow the instructions when leaving the chat room and logging off

aroch: Aye aye Captain. You be careful too! I'll pray for you.

jdog: Ditto

SEATTLE, WASHINGTON
JANUARY 9
1:05 AM, THURSDAY

The two white semis pulling up to the docks didn't look out of place, but if the dockworker routinely checking the manifest had taken a closer look he would have seen their cargo certainly was. But the paperwork was all there, including the requisite permission from customs, so he just waved them through. Inside there was a collective sigh of relief from the 142 passengers passing a big hurdle.

Despite the cramped quarters and going on 23 hours of rolling movement the passengers were in good spirits. A lot of it simply had to do with the recent circumstances the children had experienced. In one semi the 16 and 17-year-olds sprung from the re-education center talked quietly or slept most of the way on some of the many cushions the semi was fitted with. They had only one adult volunteer riding with them who had their complete attention when he told them what was happening.

The rest of the adults were in the other, better-equipped semi. Amidst the cushions, books and Gameboys there was a steady flow of children to the makeshift restroom and much hubbub, but the discussion was not as frank as that which the teens received. However, most of the children figured it out fairly easily and were calmly accepting. They knew why they'd been taken from their parents and gathered that they would be rejoining them at the end of this journey. The six eight-year-olds, including Jessie Klein, were fairly well entertained by the big stack of video tapes as they bounced along I-5 while the older children played cards and listened to music from the boombox. Twice during the trip silence had reigned for the half hour it took to make it through a gas station.

When Josh initially called Rick they'd decided one of the first things they needed was money. Rick immediately called one of his major benefactors, a financial guru who'd made a killing in the stock market against all conventional wisdom by only investing in small companies he felt he could support morally.

Rick's friend agreed to set up an account in Switzerland that Josh could access and seeded it with two million dollars. Josh jokingly referred to it as Rick's superfund, but it became less of a joke as word went round, discreetly, and the money came pouring in. Rick's friend also had his lawyers set up several shell companies to operate under. It was in the name of one of those companies, Burke Industries, that Josh had rented the Seattle warehouse the previous week.

Trucks had been coming all week at odd hours to drop off supplies so the two semis caused no untoward stir. As the drivers maneuvered the trucks carefully into the warehouse the children were all giving each other silent high fives. When the door slid closed behind the trucks the drivers hopped out and came around back to unlock the doors. A quiet group assembled and waited for instructions.

The young father from George's meetings climbed onto one of the trucks and introduced himself as Paul. He told them they were all going on a cruise and quickly explained the procedure they would need to follow in the next few hours. Each would spend a wretched half hour packed in boxes, which would be loaded as supplies onto the cargo ship. Once aboard they would need to stay below deck for a few hours until the ship was out of sight of land. On the open sea they would have a big party on deck. At this some of the younger children cheered. Closing up Paul introduced his wife and the 13 other adults who had volunteered to pull up stakes and move with the children. Among them were six cops, four teachers, two nurses, a doctor, a housewife and an out of work actor.

CHAPTER 13

True to his word, George explained everything a few minutes after the plane was off the ground, this time in a pre-recorded video Jimmy started.

"I'd like to congratulate you all on winning the As4Me Great Safari Getaway! You and a guest will fly first class to Harare, Zimbabwe where you will be wined and dined, inasmuch as that is possible in the bush, for two weeks, before returning to your normal lives."

At this point George's game show voice went back to normal, "Of course, you won't be enjoying that return flight. You all met Tom when you boarded, he'll be taking new passport shots during the flight." Tom nodded self-consciously at the group from his position up front with Jimmy.

"I don't know if any of you heard Rick Stanley on his radio program a few week's back, but there is a group of volunteers working to start a clinic, school and orphanage at what has, up to now, been a fairly successful children's camp in Kadoma, Zimbabwe. They received most of the necessary funding out of the government's Aid to Africa budget and have been in country getting things going for the last week. When you meet them you will see that some of their names are familiar. Actually, all of their names will be familiar once you get your passports. They came into the country and registered your new names, you will come in registering their names and they'll leave on their own passports next week after experiencing the safari of a lifetime." George paused for a moment and smiled. "We sort of made the assumption you'd all take us up on our offer.

"This will be your new life. The country of Zimbabwe has been hit as hard as the rest of the African continent with AIDS. Fifty percent of the population is infected and there are thousands of children wandering the countryside. With the successful coup that threw out President Mugabe last year, aid groups have been swarming in and are finally beginning to make a difference. Your work will be helping to build a new and stronger foundation for this devastated country. I hope that excites you as much as it does me – the chance to have such an amazing eternal impact.

"You'll need to organize yourselves into work details. Jimmy will pass out the plans and explain a few things. The work that needs to be done is outlined and we've chosen team leaders based on what we knew of your former jobs, but it's ultimately up to you to figure out who wants to do what. Jimmy is going to give you a history lesson, then you can spend the rest of the trip getting to know each other and figuring out how to run your new commune.

"Finally, the rescue went off without a hitch, thank God, and your children are on the proverbial slow boat to China and will be arriving in a month's time. We thought this was the safest way to get them out, but we also wanted to give you time to get set up. If you have any questions you can ask Jimmy, he has all the details that will help you get familiar with your new life. Good luck and God bless!"

The screen went blank as Jimmy stopped the tape and turned to face the cabin and 100 beaming faces. They were quiet for about three seconds before a cacophony of questions burst forth.

Jimmy, it turned out, was experienced in more than cattle farming and had a degree in developing Third World cultures from the University of Texas. He gave a very cogent history lesson on Zimbabwe, its leaders, culture and people. He then spent about an hour describing the project and explaining the ten team responsibilities. He talked about the camp and what its focus had been and would now be, then closed by naming the team leaders and handing out information packets.

Their plane landed in London and all stayed onboard while it was quickly refueled. Ten hours later they woke to green fields speeding by outside the windows as the plane descended into Harare.

J EDGAR HOOVER BUILDING

WASHINGTON DC
JANUARY 13
8:00AM, MONDAY

Even though the President had announced the MPA Task Force as a high priority, Sam knew the slow pace at which her government usually moved and was therefore quite surprised at how quickly her transfer orders came through. Sunday afternoon her boss called to tell her to report to the new Task Force office at Hoover.

The Assistant Special Agent in Charge met her at the elevator and took her around to meet everyone. She had to stop herself from cringing every time she was introduced as their secret weapon. Apparently her boss had included her Christian upbringing in his recommendation.

Sam hadn't left her apartment all day Saturday. She wandered from room to room analyzing the last 10 years and at the time she should have been heading for bed, found herself instead sitting on the floor of her living room staring sightlessly into the darkened fireplace. Sam had an epiphany. She had been starkly, completely wrong for as long as she could remember. That fact she knew and had felt ever since the announcement of the Tolerance Oath. She had been sick to her stomach from the moment the words came out of Farmers' mouth, further compounded by the knowledge that she would probably be assigned to enforce the Act. The small step she'd taken in contacting Josh and offering him information did nothing to ease her conscience but as she sat dismally contemplating her choices in life she felt a peace steal over her that she couldn't account for.

Sam snapped abruptly back to the present as the fifth group of agents broke into laughter at the ASAC's joke. Luckily this appeared to be the last group and the ASAC led her to her new desk.

"Because of your unique position and background we've decided to place you in charge of the List Management and

Logistics team. You'll have 10 agents here in the office reporting to you who will help make all the travel arrangements for the field recovery teams. Over the next few weeks we'll have other agents helping you do background checks on each of the names.

"What we want you to do is sort the data and give us a ranking. Your first priority is to compile a list of the 100 subjects most likely to roll over and sign the Oath. This is a directive from the President himself. The first 100 cases will be filmed and he wants there to be no problems until the media loses interest. Also, you need to find us two of the biggest quacks you can identify. He wants those interspersed with the first 100 to emphasize why this is a good idea.

"The President has given us a month deadline to get started. Your deadline will be February 5th so we can get the logistics together. After that you'll have two more months to rank the rest of the list. We also want an assessment of what you feel the reaction of each subject will be so we can plan accordingly." The ASAC stood upright from where he'd been leaning on her desk and wrapped up with, "That's about it. Any questions?"

Sam shook her head no and watched the ASAC walk briskly away. Looking around, she nodded at the agents seated near her, then turned to her computer and booted it up. She knew what her first order of business should be, but she was still working up the nerve.

Jack had called more than 20 times over the weekend. He didn't leave messages after the first several weren't returned, but caller id spoke loud and clear. She couldn't face him then, but she knew she'd need to get in touch soon with a plausible excuse for her behavior. Now that she'd thrown herself into actively breaking the law she couldn't exactly tell him the truth.

Well Jack, I called you an idiot and ignored you all weekend because you sold this pile of crap law to the country and this debacle may or may not end with me thrown in jail for treason. Nope, that wouldn't do.

Sam was having a hard time reconciling her budding feelings for Jack with her new perspective on the MPA. Much as she had begun to care for him, it was difficult not to focus her MPA-fueled anger on him.

With a sigh, she decided the best course was to blame her outburst on the same thing women had been blaming outbursts on since the beginning of time. She picked up the phone and dialed from memory.

BORAH HIGH SCHOOL BOISE, IDAHO
JANUARY 14
3:45PM, TUESDAY

Dee Tell was zoning off in her white Camry while edging slowly forward in the endless parent pick-up line when Sue surprised her by opening the passenger door and jumping in.

"Hey Mom."

"Sue! You about gave me a heart attack - I was in lala land." Dee pulled out into the exit lane, narrowly missing a Volvo mom trying to drive and yell at her daughter at the same time. She looked up just in time to screech her brakes for the orange vested, pimple-faced crossing guard defiantly holding up a stop sign.

"How was your day?"

"It was fine, I guess."

"You guess."

"Yeah."

Pulling answers from her 16-year-old daughter could be like pulling teeth without Novocain. She'd tried many times to convince her husband that punishing Sue by taking away her car was more a punishment for herself but he was unmoved. Dee tried again. "So could you expand on that for me – it might make the traffic seem less irritating."

Sue sighed and picked imaginary lint off her cheerleading uniform, then began. "Well, I know you don't really want to talk

149

about this, but I need to. I don't understand why you didn't protest the opening of the new StemCon center." She rushed to complete her thought when it looked like Dee would break in, "I know, I know, you say it's because you love me and don't want to lose me - but Mom! You've always taught me to stand up for what I believe in and you aren't! You've let this new law bully you. How is this any different from having the mayor publicly tell you to shut up and get back to your housework? You said someone has to take a stand, even if it doesn't necessarily accomplish anything, just to bring attention to something that is wrong. You said we each have to speak up and do our part. You told us God's laws were higher than Man's. I know you're worried that it'll call more attention if you get arrested, but this is just what you lobbied against last year. Fetal research in our own city. You came so close to getting your bill on the ballot, if it wasn't for the mayor spiking it you know it would have passed."

She finally had to take a breath and Dee saw her chance to cut in. "You know very well why I didn't go. I will not risk you being taken away. I won't do it. Not for anything. You know I have one strike on my record from when you were little. The law says I'll spend a night in jail if I'm arrested protesting within 100-yards. Not that a night in jail matters that much in light of eternity, but it will certainly bring attention to me. If I get close enough to see the building you'll be introducing yourself to your new parents."

"But Mom, you said yourself that you weren't ashamed of that citation. You stopped Lisa from having an abortion, even though you had to chase her onto the clinic property – and she named her daughter after you!"

Sue paused for a minute to see if her argument was working. Dee wasn't saying anything so she went in for the kill, "Remember how you told us the story of Jim and Elisabeth Elliot when we were kids? I was always mad because Jim spent his whole life preparing to be a missionary and he was only there a couple years before the Aucas killed him. I used to ask you all the time what good it did when Elisabeth and all those other wives and children were left without their fathers. Wouldn't it have been better for everyone if they had just left those Indians alone and stayed in the good old U.S. of A.? You told me God had a higher calling for them and they wouldn't have been happy here. You said God told them to go to Ecuador and it doesn't do any good to go against God, even if it means danger for your family. You always said we're supposed to make a practice of following Man's law, but God's law is higher."

Dee looked at Sue's face flushed with the excitement and righteousness of her cause. What could she say? It was only a story...you don't have to listen to your calling when you're a parent...God wouldn't ask a mother to risk losing her children. None of the responses that came quickly to mind would satisfy her daughter who always saw things in stark black and white. After all, Sue was practicing one of her most irritating habits, quoting her mother verbatim.

When Dee remained silent for a telling amount of time Sue continued in a lower, but just as passionate voice. "Mom, you're wrong. Ever since you took that debating class five years ago you've said you felt God called you to speak out against fetal research. You testified in front of the state legislature for Pete's sake! Remember how petrified you were? You had to take along a towel just for your sweaty hands. You always tell people about how ill-prepared and over your head you were, but God was big enough to handle it. Look at you now! When the situation is even worse, when the stakes are so much higher, you're doing nothing."

Their car was just now clearing the school grounds and Sue pointed to a white van parked near the curb. "You see that van? It goes around to each of the schools, picks up girls who need abortions and takes them to StemCon. They took two yesterday and three today. They even picked up a freshman from East Junior High. The girls came back with $250."

Dee's white knuckled grip on the steering wheel was the only visible sign she was listening. "Mom, the school isn't going to give out free birth control anymore since the girls can pay for their own

151

after they have one abortion. But I already heard some girls joking with their boyfriends about not taking it anymore. They were laughing about how this was a great new way to get spending money and they were even helping mankind. Another girl, a sophomore, was really serious about how her aunt had breast cancer and she was going to give as many embryonic stem cells as she could for research to help her aunt live. How can you stand by and watch that happen? I just don't understand!"

Spent, Sue stuck her feet on the dash and pressed her forehead to the side window. The rest of the drive home was made in tense silence.

CHAPTER 14

STEMCON - TRAVERS CENTER FOR FETAL STUDIES
BOISE, IDAHO
JANUARY 16
8:01AM, THURSDAY

The Chief of Police had been enjoying a leisurely breakfast with his wife when Director Travers called and balled him out, telling him to get his bleep down to StemCon and get this bleepin' woman out of here! As soon as he hung up, his phone rang again and the mayor started balling him out about how hard he had worked to get StemCon to build in Boise and how many jobs it was bringing to the beleaguered economy. The Chief listened to the mayor repeat almost verbatim his press conference speech about the wonders of StemCon while he drove to the site, whereupon he abruptly cut the mayor off by hanging up.

The scene was chaotic. Word had spread quickly and people shouted from the sidelines. Policemen used hastily constructed barricades to hold back the gathering crowd and cameramen filmed from every auspicious angle. All of the attention was centered on one small blonde woman holding a sign that said, "All Life is Precious" and standing directly in front of the entrance to the building. As he got out of his cruiser and began walking toward the woman the crowd quickly settled down, straining to hear what was said. Chief Eggert tipped his hat as he came to a stop, "Dee."

"Joe."

"Dee, I'm going to have to ask you to step back to a 100-yard radius from this building."

"I can't do that Joe," she said calmly.

"Now Dee, we've had this discussion before. You know what they're doing at StemCon is perfectly legal. If you have a problem you can take it up with your congressman, I know you have his number on speed dial." Joe's attempt at levity fell flat, only garnering a sad smile from her so he continued. "I don't have any problem with you being out here as long as you stay 100 yards from the entrance."

Dee's voice was firm and loud enough for the cameras, "I can't, Joe. You know I can't. They're taking girls out of school and paying them to have abortions here."

Chief Eggert moved a little closer and spoke fervently in a near whisper, "Dee, I know you believe in what you're doing. Heck, I even think you might be right, but I have to fill out MPA paperwork now on any of these types of arrests. I don't have to tell you that they'll notice someone who gets arrested less than three months after the Act was passed. Dee, didn't you see the news last week? The President has formed a Task Force to follow up on this stuff. You're not gonna slip through the cracks like you might have before. Think of your girls. Think of Alan!"

Dee spoke again, this time her voice directed at two girls standing quietly behind the barricade. "I am thinking of my girls. You see them over there, Joe? They're the reason I'm here. All their lives I've told them one thing – God's way is the right way. But two days ago I couldn't look my daughter in the eye when she asked me why I didn't do anything to try and stop the government from paying 13-year-old girls to have abortions."

The cameras immediately swiveled to zoom in on Sue, calmly standing in the front of the crowd holding Anna's hand. Alan stood behind them with his hands on their shoulders. "Alan and I have taught our daughters to believe in the God of the Bible since the day they were born when it didn't cost us anything. If we don't stand up for what's right now, when it costs more than we can bear, all our beliefs will be just a bunch of words."

Though her face bore signs of the last two sleepless nights she and Alan had spent talking, Dee spoke with such dignity and poise that the crowd forgot to heckle and watched in stillness. Joe stood quietly, staring into the distance for a full minute, then sighed and said, "Alright Dee, you're bringing this on yourself. I wash my hands of it." Joe stepped back and retrieved a pair of handcuffs from one of his officers. He quickly cuffed her and walked her to his car. The cameras rolled until the car was out of sight before their owners scrambled to make the noon news.

AS4ME STUDIOS
11:30AM

Rick was energized, finally someone had taken a stand! "This is amazing! Someone should give Dee Tell an award! You have got to watch this footage folks. She's got some extraordinary courage, this woman. I've got to check with the Legal Department on the particulars, but I'd like to set up a legal defense fund for her because I'm sure Farmer will be on her in no time. Look at what this woman has done! She has effectively turned her children over to God's protection when Farmer swoops in and takes them away. I'm telling you, I can't believe what I'm seeing. You who aren't married or don't have children yet – you need to get out there and do something to act. What she's done should spur you on, if it doesn't make you downright ashamed. Don't make another mother protest these abortion centers, strap on your courage and do it yourself."

MOORPARK, CALIFORNIA
THURSDAY EVENING

Jack was not energized. Seeing the footage of Dee Tell driven off in handcuffs while her daughters watched was the final straw that tumbled a lifetime of beliefs. If Dee Tell was a terrorist, he was the Queen of Sheba and he knew with absolute, blinding clarity that he was responsible for this tragedy. The weight of it knocked him off the couch and face first onto the carpet. Charlie nuzzled up next to him but he never noticed. Though his eyes were closed he saw image after image flash by like his own personal news channel, all the lives ruined because of his arrogant belief that he alone was infallibly in the right. The crawler along the bottom shouted his guilt in 100 different ways while he heard his own voice, anchor like, listing his various crimes.

He was already weak from the endless days of guilt gnawing away at his gut, now he felt he might never rise from the floor. He knew one thing for certain, he didn't deserve to.

shaw: Josh?

jdog: I'm here

shaw: Josh, if at all possible, you have to get Dee Tell and her family out of the country in a hurry!

jdog: We're actually just discussing that in another "room." Is there a rush we should be aware of?

shaw: I just got paged, Farmer called the Director tonight – personally. He was really ripped when he heard about it. We're moving on the family Monday at noon, early enough that any problems can be contained in time to make the evening news. Ms. Paulson, HPAC Director herself is so peeved she called the President and asked to be the foster parent for the younger girl

jdog: We'll get right on it Sam, thanks for the info

shaw: Talk to you tomorrow

BOISE, IDAHO
JANUARY 17
9:00AM, FRIDAY

Alan Tell sat at his kitchen table with Sue and Anna, staring at the empty chair across from him and half waiting for the Feds to

156

knock at the door. Considering the circumstances he'd decided it was best if they stayed home from school again today. He had been told he could pick up Dee at the stroke of 5:00pm. Just as they joined hands to pray over their cold cereal the knock came.

Alan wasn't sure whom he would rather see, the blue suits or the media who had camped in the open field across the street all night. He carefully poked his head around the stairs to see out the window and heaved a huge sigh of relief. He quickly opened the door to a hail of flashbulbs and let in his pastor, Carl and Carl's wife, Debbie.

Carl grabbed him in a bear hug while the girls launched themselves at Debbie. Once they'd moved into the living room Carl began, "We've got some good news for you Alan. Debbie got a phone call this morning. Do you remember the leadership conference in California that she and Sandra Feely attended last year?"

"The one in Los Angeles?" Alan had trouble seeing the relevance of the question to his current nightmare, but he was too polite not to answer.

"Well, the call was from the woman who organized it. She saw the news about Dee last night, then tracked Deb down through the conference database. Apparently she has connections with the people who helped the first MPA parents kidnap their children and disappear. She says she can help you guys."

Alan felt his heart begin to beat steadily again as it hadn't since seeing Chief Eggert lead his wife away yesterday. He could hardly get the words out fast enough. "How? When? What can they do?"

Carl laughed, feeling his own heart lightened for his friend. "Hold on, hold on! She called us because there would be less suspicion, but she said she'd need to contact you for specific instructions and that it'd be best if we didn't know. We're supposed to be able to say we just came over for a pastoral visit to comfort you."

"Oh, you'll be able to say that alright!"

"You have to meet her in one of those chat rooms on the Internet." He pulled a piece of paper from his pocket and passed it to Alan. "Here's how to find it and the password. Someone will meet you at 9:30 tonight."

As the couple headed toward the door Deb turned back and said, "Oh, I almost forgot, your favorite fruit is broccoli."

"What?"

"That's what she said to tell you, your favorite fruit is broccoli."

atell: Hello

jdog: Hey. Is this Alan?

atell: Yes

jdog: Alan, what's your favorite fruit?

atell: broccoli?

jdog: Authentication is the key to spywork Alan

atell: ok, but I'm not really the spy type. I'm an accountant.

jdog: Well that's alright, that's what I'm here for. Now let's get down to business

atell: alright

jdog: We have a source on the MPA Task Force who's let us know that because of the media attention Dee's arrest is getting, her case is a high priority. They plan to execute an MPA warrant on Monday. Up to that point it's top secret, but once they announce they're coming there'll be plenty of media with them. They'll transfer Sue to one of the re-education centers in Los Angeles and the HPAC Director has personally asked the President to place Anna in her home. We expect the media to stay at the courthouse for the DA's press conference where the local FBI Director will announce the MPA warrant. I don't know if you and Dee ever did any acting in the past, but this next part is crucial in case any crews decide to stick with you – we're not expecting it but there still might be witnesses. A little after 11:30am four men will show up knocking on your door. Make a fuss, cry, carry on, but let them get the girls out of the house. Remember, you didn't know they were coming so the girls shouldn't have a suitcase or anything. When they knock let them shove you back in the house because one of them will squirt some fake blood on your face before hauling you all out in cuffs. We have to make it look authentic. Dee will also be cuffed and put in the second car. All of this needs to happen in five minutes or less, that's imperative because we'll only be about 30 minutes ahead of the real FBI team and the media. Do you have any questions?

atell: um, wow! I don't think so, it seems pretty simple

jdog: Simplicity is the key to a good spy plan Alan

atell: where will you be taking us?

jdog: It's best if you don't know, in case something goes wrong. But if all goes well you will be together, I promise you that

atell: why are you doing this?

jdog: Alan, what you and your wife did was incredibly courageous. She was the first person to protest StemCon since the MPA passed. We can't protect everyone, but the people I work with feel it's important to protect your family - as a symbol

atell: i don't know how to thank you.

jdog: it's not a problem. Now one more thing, you need to trash your computer. I mean completely trash it. The FBI can get data out of the smallest chip left intact so you need to burn everything to cover up this conversation we're having. Can you do that?

atell: sure, I'll do it right now

jdog: alright, well that about covers it. Good luck!

atell: God bless you

CHAPTER 15

When they landed in Harare the parents, joined by Jimmy, Tom, Jason and Tim walked through the customs line with some trepidation. However, the customs men didn't even look at them as they quickly stamped their passports and hurried them along. All 104 crammed into a bus that would hold 50 in America. Three hours and much dust later they arrived at their new home. Standing outside to greet them was Art and Sheila, the couple who ran the children's camp, surrounded by the 50 volunteer couples who had been living in tents while slaving for a week making bricks by hand from vast mud pits. It was a warm reception.

The next week went by in a blur as Art and Sheila and the volunteers helped the parents get acclimated to the culture as best they could. The first hour of every day was spent in prayer, and then the group broke up into their respective duties. Art and Sheila held half hour meetings every night after dinner explaining the history of the camp, culture and anything they could think of which would help the parents. Then they had committee meetings for as long as they could keep their eyes open before everyone trudged off to bed.

Other than the 10 women on the food prep team and the four men assigned to drive from town to town garnering supplies, every able bodied man and woman among them worked 12 hour days putting up buildings. The untold thousands of bricks the volunteers had made lay scattered about in various enormous piles. They fell into a routine very quickly and were soon masters of the building process, from hand mixing cement and mortar to stacking bricks together into recognizable structures.

Each small housing unit held two families and new couples moved from the tents into their new homes every evening. With 200 dedicated and highly motivated people on the crew the work went quickly. All 50 houses were up within the first three days and the next three saw the majority of the other planned buildings nearing completion. They weren't the best looking buildings, surely none compared to the homes they'd left, but all looked with pride on what they had accomplished.

It's amazing what formerly pencil-pushing men and women can achieve if they are adequately motivated. The days went by in a blur and before anyone realized it, the week had passed. The clinic and general meeting room were done and the orphanage, school and main kitchen were almost there. The whole group had a bry, as they were told barbecues were called, and it turned into quite a party. The next day the volunteers piled into the 50-person bus and made the three hour trek back to Harare. Again the customs officials didn't pay any attention so they didn't notice the changed faces on the passports. Each couple was given several souvenirs and a disk with 1,000 digital pictures to account for their two-week safari.

Jason and Tim took turns flying back to Texas and trying to convince Jimmy and Tom about who had bigger blisters from the week of hard labor.

FEDERICA, SEATTLE
SOUTH ATLANTIC

While their parents were feverishly working at setting up their new lives in Africa, the children were enjoying a cruise unlike anything they'd ever experienced. Long sun-drenched days were spent on the deck and everyone aboard soon turned a toasty brown – after a week of toasty pink because Paul's wife forgot to pick up enough sunscreen for everyone.

The friend of Rick's who owned the cargo ship Federica hadn't wanted to draw undo attention to the fact that he had almost 150 extra passengers going on this cruise so there were many mislabeled crates of farming machinery to sort through. There were also four large crates brought aboard that caused the captain to balk. A well-known actress was planning on taking a two week safari in Zimbabwe and was shipping three Land Rovers and a veritable boatload of supplies to keep her in the comfort to which she was accustomed.

What was not as well known was that, owing to similar religious and political beliefs, she had been friends with Rick for much longer than she'd been famous and was now a large donor to his superfund, as well as not being averse to being called a flaky actress if it would help the cause. The captain strategically complained all over the docks about the special stop his owner was forcing him to make to drop off her cargo and the actress made the cover of the National Enquirer within two days.

The first day at sea everyone pitched in to uncrate the army cots and room dividers and set up the smaller hull to look very much like a dorm room. Cots lined the walls, each with its own trunk at the foot filled with outfits garnered from three huge crates of clothing.

The ship was well traveled and entirely mechanized so that the crew of twelve could handle the main sailing duties. However, with the additional passengers everyone needed to pitch in. The older teens were thrilled to get on the steering rotation, even though it meant getting up for a middle of the night watch every now and then. Everyone rotated through kitchen and cleaning duties and there were surprisingly few complaints.

Besides rotating through different jobs, everyone went to school. The teachers taught the more routine fundamentals while the cops taught self-defense. The doctor and nurses held basic first aid seminars on deck and the younger children always fought over who got to play the patient. While the youngest children were learning the three R's, the older ones received more comprehensive medical education, as the doctor taught them whatever he thought they could handle that would help in the jungle.

CORNERSTONE COMMUNITY CHURCH
MOORPARK, CALIFORNIA
JANUARY 19

10:25AM, SUNDAY

Amanda was standing at the back of the gym chatting with a few friends when she noticed a very familiar face come through the door. After doing a double take she made a beeline for George who was standing with another usher discussing the previous night's Lakers loss.

Jack had spent all day Friday and Saturday lying in his bed, unable to move. He was contemplating suicide for the thousandth time this morning when he felt an intense pressure to get up and go to church. He almost laughed at first, so random was the thought. He fought it, but the feeling grew more intense until he finally got up and into the shower. Now that he was here he felt as out of place as the proverbial bull in a china shop. He hadn't set foot in a church since childhood and, with his current status as destroyer of the faith, he halfway expected the burly looking ushers to come tell him he wasn't welcome. It was only that intense pressure on his shoulders that kept him moving forward.

His stomach flip-flopped when he saw a middle-aged couple bearing down on him, the man a physical epitome of the usher/bouncer he had imagined. They looked vaguely familiar but he couldn't place them before, much to his surprise, they both broke out in smiles and greeted him.

"Welcome to Cornerstone. I'm George, this is my wife Amanda." George shook Jack's hand rather firmly before letting go so Amanda could have a chance.

Jack's voice came out as a squeak, "I'm Jack."

"Welcome, Jack. Are you meeting someone?" Jack shook his head and she continued, "Well, you'll just have to come sit with us then, won't you?" She didn't really wait for a response before latching onto his arm and pulling him along toward the seats.

Two hours later Jack parked on the street after following George home from church. He was feeling approximately ten million different misgivings about what he was doing and almost sped away before he got himself into even more trouble. However, before he could floor it Amanda was standing in front of his car smiling and waving him in. With a forced smile back at her he shut off the engine and pulled the keys out of the ignition.

Lunch was rather forced in the beginning, but Jack loosened up a little when George started telling old police stories. Jack found himself laughing more in the hour that followed than he had in the past year. Amanda forced second and third helpings on him and he felt like his stomach would explode by the time she shooed them out to the living room and brought them coffee. When she slipped back into the kitchen to do the dishes Jack felt his uneasiness quickly returning and looked everywhere to avoid George's direct gaze.

He was startled into eye contact at George's words, "I know who you are, Jack."

"What," Jack choked, "do you mean?"

"I know who you are and I know what you've done. I can see in your eyes that you recognize us from somewhere but you haven't been able to place us. Am I right?"

Jack nodded uneasily.

"We sat in the courtroom every day and watched you lie about our best friends, the Rodmans. We watched you destroy their lives with a few well turned phrases before skating off to get your picture taken."

Jack suddenly had trouble breathing; his face flushed bright red as George's image started blurring before his eyes. Shaking himself he started to rise in his haste to get away.

George's firm, "Sit down, young man" stopped him in his tracks and he weakly sank back into the couch.

"Now I have a feeling I know why you risked showing your face in church this morning but I want to hear it from you." George's gaze never flickered and Jack shifted uncomfortably under it. Silence reigned in the room for a full minute and Amanda, intently listening with her ear pressed against the door, had to talk herself out of bursting in to see if George had Jack in a chokehold.

For some reason Jack felt he had no choice but to answer this man with the laser beam eyes. After a few false starts and throat clearing he softly began. The first words came out slowly, but suddenly he felt if he didn't bare his soul now he would die. "I was wrong, what I did. I was all wrong."

The bald admission broke the dam and words, long pent up, came tumbling out. Feelings he'd had for months but couldn't express poured out as quickly as he could gather breath to speak them. "All my life I've been fighting for justice. Fighting for freedom. Fighting for the ideals of tolerance. And all my life I've been on the wrong side. I've looked down on you Christians; I know that's probably patently obvious. I don't know what to tell you George. I was wrong. I've been watching things unfold since MPA passed and sinking lower and lower into my skin. I can't believe what's happening. I feel sick and ashamed and just plain wrong. I can barely get out of bed in the morning. I haven't been to work in months. My boss has stopped calling, not wanting to hear another lame excuse but unwilling to fire his celebrity. I watch the news for hours on end. I can't seem to turn it off. Over and over they show the result of what I've done. Screaming children. Screaming parents. Women standing up for what they believe getting their children stolen. When I do get out of bed I just wander from room to room not recognizing anything. I used to go to the beach to clear my head but all I could think of the last time I went was walking into it until the waves took me away so I haven't gone back. I don't know how to fix what I've done. I don't even know if it can be fixed. All I know is that most days I can barely breathe. I know that I should have enough courage to do myself in. I should make up for what I've done by eating a bullet or something equally noble. But I'm such a lily I can't even work up the courage to go buy a gun. But I have to make up for it somehow. There is a weight on me, a weight so heavy I can barely move. In my head I'm always screaming, 'What have I done? What have I done?' I know it was wrong of me to come to your church today. I thought I happened to be lucky enough to stumble across the two Christians

166

in the world who didn't recognize my infamous face. I just felt like I had to come. Last year someone at my office mentioned his church was starting a plant near my house. I made some joke about being sure they had enough fertilizer to make it grow. He didn't mention it again. I'm sorry. I'm so sorry. I just didn't know where else to go."

Amanda was on her knees in the kitchen, brought to the floor by the anguish in Jack's voice. With her forehead pressed to the linoleum she prayed that George would have the words to say to comfort this broken young man.

Jack fell silent and stared at the floor. Having bared all to this relative stranger he found he had no more words to say and could only wonder about the look on George's face. He suspected it would be displaying hate and rancor, but didn't have the nerve to check his suspicions. He knew he should leave and was just working up the energy when George spoke in an even tone.

"Amanda read your article in People magazine to me. It said you went to church as a child. Do you remember the story of the apostle Paul?" George seemed to be waiting for a response so Jack made a slight negative motion with his head, eyes still focused on the brown carpet.

"Well, I think it's very apt right now so I want to tell it to you if that's alright." Jack made no indication either way so George continued. "Paul used to be called Saul and he was a Pharisee in Jesus' time. The Pharisees were the Jewish religious leaders of the day and for the most part they hated Jesus and what He stood for. Saul was present when the first apostle, Stephen was stoned to death, but that wasn't enough for him. He procured letters from the chief priests in Jerusalem saying that he could imprison, persecute and kill anyone he found who was following Christ. He was zealous in his pursuit of Christians and he did terrible things. Persecuting and killing innocent men, women and children for simply professing their faith that Jesus Christ was Lord."

Jack heard the similarity of the story and wondered if George was going to tell him he was worse than Paul. Maybe George wished they'd bring back the Old Testament practice of stoning just for him. If they did, Jack wasn't sure he would put up a fight.

"Now Saul was on his way to Damascus where he'd heard about a large contingent of Christians, and lo and behold, who should meet him on the road but Christ himself. In a flash of light Christ spoke to him, 'Saul, Saul, why are you persecuting me?' Saul was struck blind and for three days didn't eat or drink anything. Finally the Lord sent along a Christian in the same city to go heal Saul. He repented of his ways and became a follower of Christ. You see Jack, Saul of all people knew what it was like to sin against God and feel His wrath for persecuting His children. But Christ spoke to Saul and gave him a new life. God changed his name to Paul, and Paul went on to become arguably the greatest missionary apostle and write a good portion of the New Testament.

"I have to tell you, Jack, I think God has been following hard after you and you better do something about it. You don't need me to tell you that you've sinned – every person on earth, in the quietness of their heart, knows they're sinful. God has impressed the weight of your sins on you; I can see it in your face. You think that religion is just something that enhances the life you have. I'm here to tell you that the life you have is a breath, a mist that's here one minute and vanishes from all memory the next. You need to be worried about what happens after the vapor of your life floats away. And if you think that taking your life is the noble way out then you have no idea what awaits you on the other side. I can tell you with absolute certainty that the hell you're experiencing now is a fairyland compared to the hell that will greet you if you continue on this same path. Jack, you've made some tremendously poor choices and you've been an instrument of the devil for some pretty serious events."

Jack's shoulders caved even further during George's verbal barrage.

"I'll tell you something else, Jack. I was once a cocky young man just like you and I thought I had it all together. I thought I knew everything there was to know. I had just graduated from the

Academy and was in my first year as a beat cop. My partner was this stark, raving loony tune of a Jesus Freak. I tell you, I made fun of him like you wouldn't believe. I called him all kinds of names, thought he was going to fold at the first sign of trouble. But he took it all good-naturedly. He never spoke an angry word at me. We'd been partners for about a year when we got a domestic disturbance call in the middle of the night. John wanted to wait for backup but I just charged right in there, arrogant as always. And John backed me up, as always. Except this time the husband was a drug dealer who had a gun loaded with cop killers. When he shot at me John stepped in front and took the bullet. I watched in slow motion as John slid to the ground and couldn't even follow the dealer when he ran out the back door."

For the first time in as long as he could remember, Jack was caught up in a misery not his own and his head slowly came up to watch George as he told his story. George was staring, eyes unfocused, in another direction.

"He died in my arms, Jack, and it was my fault. I had to be the one to wake up his wife Joan at 4:00 in the morning and tell her that her husband had died for me. And I'll tell you, Jack, I could barely get it out. I was crying like a baby and she was the one comforting me. It was my fault her husband wasn't coming home ever again. It was my fault he wouldn't see the first steps his new daughter Sheryl took a month after the funeral. He wouldn't see her go off to kindergarten or graduate from high school and join the policy academy. It was my fault Jack and I think about it every day though it was over 20 years ago. And you know, I would have eaten a bullet that night if Joan hadn't seen it in my eyes and not let me go home by myself. She didn't blame me, not once. She never blamed me and after his funeral she took me aside and said she knew where John was and that she'd see him again. She said he'd loved me like a brother and she knew why he took that bullet. He'd told her ahead of time that he would step in front of me every chance he got until he knew he'd see me in heaven. And she said I didn't have to live with any guilt about that because he was in a

169

better place. She said I could see him again too if I got myself squared away with God. Then she led me in a sinner's prayer as I wept on my knees in the mud beside John's grave."

George was quiet for a long moment before clearing his throat to continue. "You see, Jack, we're not talking about life enhancement. It isn't about making yourself feel better or being a good and charitable person. Christianity is about recognizing the fact that you are a sinner, that you've done unforgivable things that deserve the wrath of a holy God. Recognizing that you can't make it up to Him, the gap between one little white lie of sin and His holiness is just too great. That, by all rights, God could strike you dead here and now and be justified. And the fact that He didn't, that instead of justly killing us all He sent His Son to pay for our sins instead, that is the most amazing thing I have ever heard.

"You think I'd be a Christian if I didn't have to? Let me tell you, I've taken enough ribbing in the last 20 years to put my teasing of John to shame. But I know the score. God created us all with free will. The upside is we can freely choose to love Him. The downside is we can tell Him to buzz off and live our own lives. But telling the Creator of the universe to buzz off has its own set of consequences. I know that if I didn't admit my sin and accept Christ's sacrifice for me I would be headed to a place so horrible I don't even like to think about it. Forever. That's the bottom line. Christ saved me. In every sense of the word. He saved my life here and now and He saved me from an eternity in hell. He even saved me from what my life would have turned into without him. I'd probably be a divorced, cynical alcoholic fighting to stay on the force. Now He's giving you the opportunity to grab onto the life vest Jack. And if you want my advice I'd say you better take that opportunity and hold on for all you're worth. You never know when your time is going to be up and this is not the kind of thing you can leave hanging."

Jack fell off the couch like a rag-doll and landed on his hands and knees, forehead smashed into the carpet. George knelt down and put his hand on Jack's shoulder and led him in prayer, Jack chokingly repeating what George told him to say. A few minutes later Jack raised his head from the floor, lifted high from the simple absence of the weight that had pushed him down so long.

Amanda came bolting out of the kitchen, tissue in hand, and wrapped Jack in a huge, motherly hug. "Jack! Welcome to the family!"

An hour later Jack was still on an adrenaline high about 10,000 times better than any endorphin rush he'd ever experienced as a runner. He sat comfortably in the living room and listened in awed wonder as George and Amanda told him a bit about their little project over the last months. He couldn't stop grinning and laughed out loud when Amanda told him about Big Jake's Texas Tofu.

When their laughter finally died down George looked seriously across the room at Jack and said, "Now I have to tell you, Jack, the apostle Paul got two years to recover from being a persecutor before he went back into the battle. I'm not sure you're going to get that kind of time."

CHAPTER 16

TROLLEY HOUSE
BOISE, IDAHO
JANUARY 20
7:45AM, MONDAY

Joe Eggert was sorely in need of his coffee this morning. He'd barely gotten a chance to change into a fresh uniform since spending the weekend doing phone interviews with different news organizations around the country. The questions were always the same, as were his answers.

Have you arrested her in the past? Yes, once almost 10 years ago. Did you advise her of the fact that this arrest would qualify her for MPA action? Yes. And she still wouldn't move? No. Has she ever shown signs of mental illness? No, she's actually quite sane. Where was her husband? He was standing with their children watching her.

Between interviews he'd taken several calls from the irate mayor who continued to browbeat him. After all the hard work he'd done getting one of the StemCon centers to locate in Boise he was not at all thrilled with the negative publicity. When Joe made his appearance at the mayor's office he had to just sit and nod while listening for the umpteenth time to how bad the economy was and how this center was bringing so many jobs and how he had better get on the ball before he found himself writing parking tickets in Garden City.

Frankly, Joe was glad to be sitting at his favorite breakfast spot for a few minutes of peace and quiet when the radio at his hip squawked "Chief Eggert, this is Officer Jefferson, come in."

"Yeah, this is Eggert. Go ahead."

"Sir, you'd better get down to Travers."

"What now?" he asked, a bit ungraciously. "Do I have to do another interview?"

"No sir, you won't believe it." Eggert recognized the panic in Jefferson's tone and started moving to deal with some huge disaster. "Spit it out, Jefferson." He was in no mood for guessing games as he spilled the last sip of coffee on his fresh uniform in his haste to get out the door.

"Sir, there's 10 women down here. They say they won't move." Eggert got into his car and felt the familiar burn of his ulcer begin to light up for the day as he peeled out onto Warm Springs.

--

Courtney Daniels was walking her dog down Sunrise Rim when she saw two black sedans race by before turning into the driveway of the Tell home. Four men in blue suits piled out. The leader pounded on the door while signaling two men to go around back. Courtney had a front row seat to the action and later took great relish in describing it to a parade of reporters including the current Molly Jackson of KTVB, Idaho's News Channel 7.

"I've gone to school with Sue since like the sixth grade and been to her birthday parties and stuff every year. Her parents are like, the nicest people I've ever met."

Molly, wanting to get to the juicy stuff, urged her on, "And what did you see today, Courtney?" Courtney flipped her hair and tugged on the leash. With all the interviews she hadn't yet had a chance to take her dog home. "Well, I was walking Molly here - don't you think that's funny, like my dog has the same name as you?"

The cameraman found that quite a bit funnier than Ms. Jackson as he panned down to show the shaggy mutt lounging on the sidewalk. Ms. Jackson merely gritted her teeth and icily nodded for Courtney to continue.

"Mom said I didn't like, have to go to school today cause of all the like, excitement so I was walking Molly before lunch, probably about like 11:30 when I saw these two cars go flying by - nearly ran me over – then like, they screeched into the driveway and four guys in like, nice suits piled out. The guy in charge walked right through the flowers on his way to the front door while two other guys went around back. Mr. Tell answered the door, but he barely like, got it open before the leader kicked it in. I think it musta hit Mr. Tell in the nose or something because like, they brought him out in handcuffs and he had blood all over his face. And like, the guy that brought Mrs. Tell out had her handcuffed too, except it looked like she mighta nailed him, prob'ly for trampling her flowers. Cuz you know like, she always had lovely flowers…"

Courtney was threatening to veer off track again but a stern look from Ms. Jackson brought her back on target. "Well anyway, the guy was holding his gut and stuff. Then there was one guy with each of the girls. They loaded them all up in the cars and totally peeled out. I don't think the whole thing took like more than five minutes. I ran up to the Johnson's house because it was closer than mine and called the cops and that's like, the whole story."

The camera panned back to Ms. Jackson for a moment so she could finish her LIVE report, then she sent it back to the studio where the anchor spent another few minutes recapping the dramatic exclusive interview for anyone who hadn't been watching the last five minutes before moving to the next story.

RED CARPET ROOM
BOISE INTERNATIONAL AIRPORT
3:42PM, MONDAY

Beth was getting the chewing out of her life as she held her tiny cell phone six inches from her ear to avoid permanent damage from the high decibel diatribe issuing forth. She had been under strict orders to fly to Boise and not return until she had secured an on camera interview with Alan Tell. Mike didn't want to hear any lame excuses like the Tells had split town just as she was collecting her baggage at the airport. In a three hour blitz she spoke with the mayor, the chief of police and the truly intriguing high school witness who like, totally filled her in.

Now she was heading back to New York and having to endure the aforementioned yelling session. Her mind began to wander as she threw in an occasional "Uh huh" to signify she was hanging on his every word.

Beth really had wanted to interview Alan. Even more she wanted five minutes with Dee. She was completely flummoxed as to what would make a calm, rational, everywoman housewife take such a stand. From what she'd been able to gather, Dee was as normal as they come. Friendly, kind, responsible. She substituted two or three days a week and volunteered in her daughter's classrooms. Besides the arrest years ago the most outrageous thing Dee had ever done was campaign last year for a bill outlawing fetal research, and that had failed due to the mayor calling in every favor he'd ever earned in 20 years of public life. Beth could not for the life of her figure Dee out. All she knew was that she had to find what made that woman tick and why she would voluntarily end her parenting career.

Beth had friends who called themselves Christians, but she couldn't imagine any of them making such a drastic decision. Well, she knew one man who would, but he was a lunatic anyway so he didn't count. Beth smiled at the thought of him and was just starting to daydream when she realized the lecture had come to a close.

"Yes sir. I'll be there first thing tomorrow morning." Looking at her watch she realized her plane was boarding, threw a tip on the table and made a dash for her gate.

NEVADA AIRSPACE
LEAR JET CHARTER 0930

There was a great debate raging as the Lear rocketed along at 500 miles an hour 20,000 feet in the air. The eight passengers and two pilots pushed the weight limit, but since there was little baggage and two of the passengers were small teenagers they weren't having too much trouble. Sue told her parents with firm conviction that she was not escaping with the rest of them. In his blue suit George tried to be as unobtrusive as possible while Sue countered every argument her parents laid forth. He tried to hide his grin at the girl's spunk, but realizing it was impossible, headed up to the cockpit. Not that it would drown out the conversation, but at least he could smile all he wanted at Tim and Jason who had returned from Africa just in time to make this trip and were guiding the plane southward.

"As a 16-year-old I'll be sent to one of the re-education centers. I think it's really important that they have strong Christians there to combat the junk they're preaching. I realize you need to get away with Anna so that horrible woman won't get her, but I don't feel I have that luxury. Besides, they can only hold me for two years and then I can join you if this hasn't been sorted out." She tossed her ponytail and smirked while delivering her finale, "And quite frankly, if you even think you can talk me out of this you've lost your minds. You're the ones who raised me this way so it's your own fault!"

Silence reigned for a few moments, then George looked up to see Alan standing in the doorway with an exasperated expression on his face. Not a word came from the cockpit as Alan informed them there would only be three for the trip. After that decision was made things calmed down in the cabin and Dee proceeded to stomp her family in a board game.

George stayed in the cockpit where Tim entertained him with a recitation of how things had gone in Boise. While the fake fibbies went on their mission Tim and Jason entered the Executive Terminal and loudly solidified their alibi. The Lear had been chartered for an economical $1,500 an hour to fly Rick's actress to her vacation home in Sun Valley. When Rick called she'd been quite willing to go on a quick retreat to provide an alibi even though she was "indisposed" due to needing to memorize her lines before filming started the next week. This was in spite of the fact that she'd just done time as tabloid fodder over her African safari. She told Rick all this flaky behavior would keep her agent on his toes and probably increase her earning power.

Tim and Jason took turns complaining in an aggrieved tone to the enthralled secretary about their high maintenance charge while they filed a change in flight plan. Jason did a fair imitation of her voice, explaining how she had forgotten the particular brand of water she loved and knew for a fact the Sun Valley grocery store didn't carry it so could we pretty please stop for a few minutes in Boise. Her bodyguards were forced to tromp off to the closest Albertson's while she stayed onboard receiving a facial and pedicure.

Of course none of that was true. The actress was actually sipping an Arrowhead as she studied in the back of the plane. The secretary saw the four "bodyguards" quickly exit but Jason was doing such a good job entertaining her that she didn't notice when they returned with four extra passengers in lieu of bottled water.

The actress had casually chatted with the somewhat star struck Tells for the 20 minute flight to Sun Valley, then wished them luck and deplaned. It was once they were back in the air headed south that Sue got in the argument with her parents. She ended up getting off the plane with George and the other three fake fibbies a little over an hour later at the small airport in Oxnard. Tom got on with his usual bag of tricks and the plane took off within five minutes of being refueled.

Sue got to know George and Amanda while she stayed in their basement for a week before Amanda drove her down to San Diego. She took the shuttle to the Mexican border and wandered around for about a half an hour before someone recognized her and called the Feds.

During a few hours of intense questioning Sue did a fair job of appearing distressed and not wanting to give up her family, but she finally "broke" under the pressure and said they got separated at the bus station in San Diego. Her finest acting moment came when she told the Feds her family was trying to get to Mexico City where they planned to make a new life for themselves.

After that revelation a short straw lotto was held to see who had to drive her up to Folson Re-Education Center. The surly fed who lost didn't speak the entire trip as he envisioned the glory his buddies would receive when they captured the Tells. When they arrived he unceremoniously dumped her at the door, signed the transfer paperwork and peeled out for the freeway in the hopes of getting in on at least some of the action.

The recent kidnapping and the lull before the next rescues meant that Folson had 35 staff and no inmates, or Tolerance Education Students, so when they took possession of Sue they watched her like a hawk. She therefore had a rotating schedule of staff on which to practice. In between tolerance classes Sue conversed with any staff members who would talk to her and read the Bible aloud to the ones who wouldn't.

CHAPTER 17

JANUARY 28

to: josh@shoopshoop.net
from: shaw@salmonaise.com

Josh,

I used the encryption software you gave me so I hope you can read this. You won't believe it, but the FBI already had official files on all 10,000 MPA offenders. I thought we'd be slogging through background checks for the next month and I told my supervisor Bob we'd be hard pressed to find the 100 that the President wants to roll over by the deadline. He must have passed that information up the chain because, lo and behold, we get a huge delivery this morning from the AG's office. I don't know if you're aware, but 10,000 files takes up a lot of space. I just spent an hour perusing them, we're not talking the quick check we do for someone who wants to be an airport screener. These are serious FBI files, not something you could just churn out overnight. These people have been tracked for awhile, some as far back as 10 years. And it looks like they weren't planning to let us know about the files either, until Bob let it be known to the Director that we wouldn't be able to start the "rescues" on time. I had a big talk with Bob this morning over a coffee break. Had to use my ditzy underling personality which is always difficult to stomach, but the results were worthwhile. First of all, I found out that the AG's office provided the list of 10,000 with no explanation as to why they were picked. He did, however, accidentally or on purpose receive a disk with the list that, when popped into his trusty government-issued pc, launched a fairly unsophisticated selection program. Couple wink-winks and eyelash flutters later and he took me to his office and showed me.

The criteria entered was a list from the IRS of people who file for the pastor's deduction as well as a list of people who claim deductions of 10% or more given to churches on their income taxes. Then there were the people who graduated from Bible colleges and seminaries, and not just any liberal arts school that claims Christian roots, but real solid Bible schools – no liberal theology here. Somehow they got hold of a list of volunteers for the Women's Resource Center. They had every mom in America who home schools. I'm not sure where it came from, but they got a list of every group of five or more that left the country for short term mission projects in the last 10 years. They even had a list from Israeli immigration of groups registering for an Evangelical Christian tour. There was a list of students attending private school. Also the attendance lists for the last ten Youth Specialties conferences. You know, the ones who train youth workers? There was also a rather large untitled list that didn't specify where it had come from.

Select all those lists, press the enter key to cross-reference and Bing Bang Boom, you have a registry of 10,000 solid "true believer" Christians. They did such a good job I'm not sure who to give for the first 100 who are supposed to just roll over and sign the Oath. There's not one hardened criminal among them that we can find by the way. Out of 10,000 only about 100 of them have been cited for the first two strikes of the RFA. All that to say, they can't technically be called wackos.

The second thing I learned from Bob is about the first 50. I was trying to feel him out about why they chose who they did, turns out they didn't choose at all. The AG's office provided that list as well and some pretty thick background files like the ones we received today.

Josh, the FBI has files on hundreds of quacks that could have been named with no problem, people who are doing all kinds of really heinous things in the name of religion. Now why do you think the President would direct the guys this way?

I mean, this used to be my job and most of the really terrible antiabortion criminals are on the loose. We sent a couple guys to jail in the last few years but a lot of the job was trying to track people down, and even at that, we didn't have huge rosters by any stretch of the imagination. Now my buddies over in Hate Crimes, if called upon, could have given up a boatload of big names for the first 50 – serious crazies with all kinds of religious motivations. People with a much higher "quack" factor who would have played great on the evening news. VNs would have skyrocketed. But no, the AG didn't ask any of our departments, he sent the list over himself. Once again I have to ask, what the heck is the AG's office doing keeping track of 10,000 fairly solid citizens whose only crime is that they take their Christianity seriously? And is 10,000 the end of it or is there some master list hidden in Franklin's safe that he's going to divvy out a little at a time?

Anyway, I better get back to work. Just thought you'd be interested in those few tidbits. I should be publishing the first 100 we talked about next week.

One interesting note to close, Dee Tell's name is on this list. She would have been swept up in this group even if she didn't take her stand. Go figure.

Sam

p.s. I don't know if you have this already, but I've attached a copy of the Tolerance Contract. It's quite a bit stiffer than old Farmer said. I thought maybe you could pass it along to someone with a bigger voice than mine.

Sam sat back after rereading her e-mail and hit send. She knew she should be happier than she was. In the great scheme of things she was finally on the right side and doing some quantifiably good work to make up for her past deeds. She should be satisfied. She should be content.

So why aren't I? It was not an easy question for self-reliant, capable Sam Hawthorne, FBI. After a lifetime of practice she was used to living alone and providing for herself. She had good friends. Her work had been, and was again, very satisfying. Most significant, the big ball of anxiety and bitterness that had God's name on it for so many years had been replaced by God Himself and she felt genuine peace on that score. So it couldn't be that.

It was him. That stinking, slimy, weasel lawyer who'd wormed his way into her heart and then bailed out with the first harsh word. True, with her little white lie she'd led him to believe she could be irrational and moody, but she was a woman for heaven's sake. Even though she hadn't been irrational and moody at the time, she knew it couldn't hurt to prepare him for a future such occasion.

But no, he'd accepted her apology in their brief phone conversation and never called her back. Never. Not once. Not even when she'd broken down after a week and called to leave a message on his machine.

Sam wasn't sure whom she was more furious with. Of course he deserved some blame, but he was a guy after all and she'd found from bitter experience that guys were very much a different species. He probably didn't even realize it'd been two weeks. He was probably working some big case. Or caught up in some Superbowl World Series something or other. Or working on his golf handicap.

Actually yes, she did know whom she was more furious with. She should have known better than to let a stinking, slimy, weasel lawyer worm his way into her heart so that she couldn't have a peaceful evening at home watching a simple chick flick without reaching for the hankies. Stupid Tom Hanks and Meg Ryan.

Nothing had been wrong with her life before but she couldn't leave well enough alone could she? She should have known from the first time he called and stumbly-fumbly'd his way through that lame dinner invitation. She'd thought it was so cute and endearing at the time. What a dope.

"I'm holding in my hand a copy of the so-called Tolerance Contract. You all know about the Tolerance Oath, pretty nauseating but understandably signable if you have young children. But this contract is terrible. It's immoral. It's so bad that I offered away my scoop to 10 different friends in the mainstream media in hopes they would do a story and get the information to a broader audience. They each refused saying they'd already run stories on the highlights and no one cared. One friend said, 'What's the big deal? They're just asking a parent to show both sides.' What a bunch of baloney!

"Let me just read you some of the highlights:

Number one: Your child can attend two hours of traditional church services a week and one special occasion service a quarter. Good-bye youth group, Awanas, good news club. No children's choir or programs at Christmas because they can't meet to practice.

Number two: You and your child must attend a weekly tolerance education session, both together and separately.

Number three: If your child watches religious videotapes (i.e. Veggie Tales) you must give equal viewing time for tolerance videos (i.e. Bert & Ernie: A Wedding Story) and other religious videos (i.e. Islam: the Religion of Peace).

Number four: If you want your kid to go to Vacation Bible School or church camp they also have to attend Tolerance Camp. By the way, Tolerance Camp is $2,000 a week. Who can afford that? And it gets worse as the children grow older.

Number five: Starting at age 11 and continuing through 18 the child must attend an hour of alternate religious and/or irreligious education classes every week. They can choose to take instruction from Buddhist monks, Muslim clerics, Scientology counselors, Kaballah experts, even Atheist instructors. The list goes on and on.

Number six: Last, and best of all, you must have weekly visits with your Tolerance Counselor who keeps track of you and reports on your progress. In other words, you have to keep toeing the line or your parole officer will turn you in.

"This is not showing both sides folks, this is the systematic destruction of Christianity. Some of you have heard of Luis Palau, he's been called the Spanish Billy Graham. Well, he made a movie years ago called God Has No Grandchildren. It was about the country of Wales, which experienced a nationwide revival in 1904. It was such a huge revival that bars were converted to churches and policemen started wearing white gloves instead of guns. They sent missionaries out all around the world. One in particular led a young Luis to the Lord in Argentina, so he decided to go back to Wales in the 70's to thank them. And what did he find, but that churches were converted back to bars and the country was more in love with rugby than God.

"The movie was about Wales, but it might just as easily have been a prophetic statement about America. Farmer's administration has clearly stated their mission with MPA: they want to get rid of bigotry, hatred and intolerance and the terrorism such ideologies foster in one generation. It sounds great, until you realize their definition of that is anyone who believes that what the Bible says is truth. Cutting through the subterfuge, what they're really saying is that they want to get rid of Christianity in one generation.

"You think I'm being dramatic? Let me ask you, if you were telling your child one thing and the government and the rest of the country was telling your child that you were such a quack you couldn't be trusted to raise them alone, who do you think your child is going to believe in the long run?"

Rick's normally even-tempered voice was rising in fury. "How can this be happening! How can a society which so proudly and loudly touts freedom and tolerance be systematically cutting out a portion of their own citizenry? How can tolerance be shouted from every secular pulpit in America while at the same time calling fundamental Christians every foul name imaginable? I have been called sexist, racist, homophobic – worst of all, intolerant. What is the meaning of tolerance? Let's look in the dictionary shall we.

186

"According to the Merriam-Webster Dictionary I have here in the studio, tolerance is 'sympathy or indulgence for beliefs or practices differing from one's own.' How is the Tolerance Oath telling parents they can't let their kids go to Vacation Bible School and make macaroni necklaces while learning about God being sympathetic or indulgent to their beliefs?

"There are no 'Swiss' Christians, ladies and gentlemen. I'm telling you right now, if you don't stand up and make some noise we will be the last generation of Christianity in America. Pick a side before we go extinct!"

NBC STUDIOS, NEW YORK
10:31 PM

Beth took off her headphones and stared across the newsroom. She'd been covertly listening to Rick's broadcast stream over the Internet while doing research on her computer. She was a subscriber to his website, under a false name of course, so she could listen to his two hour broadcast minus commercials anytime she wanted. Even though few were in the office this late she still looked around to make sure no one was looking before opening the browser window to close the anonymous portal she'd been streaming his site through.

She had an uneasy feeling in the pit of her stomach listening to his words. She had actually been the first friend Rick had called to offer the contract to but she'd refused. Beth didn't tell him it was because she'd already fought with her producer about showing the contract and lost. She told Rick that it was old news. She hated the defeated tone in his voice. It was much more fun to spar with him when he was energized.

She didn't understand her producer's stance. For one thing, she, Mike and pretty much everyone she knew in the media had been decrying the Patriot Act since its inception for giving the FBI too much power to spy on Americans. They had been doing stories off and on for years about Homeland Security and its spying capabilities. Now she found an abrupt turnaround in policy and was uneasy about it. Why it was suddenly ok for the government to use their formerly illegal, unethical, immoral powers since they were hunting Christians, she couldn't figure out.

To her it was illogical. The government oversteps its boundaries in trying to control the citizenry, we report on it. Telling anyone who has not been convicted of a crime that they have to visit a parole officer with their children once a week means the government is out of control. What was the problem with reporting on that? It was no use, though; Mike shut her down every time she pitched a story even remotely anti-government or anti-MPA. She was having a harder time than usual taking his orders lately.

Beth also didn't tell Rick that she was manically investigating the whereabouts of Dee Tell and the first kidnap parents. It had become a calling of sorts in the last few weeks. She had to know why. Mike wanted her gearing up for the next set of "rescues," but she'd had her fill with the first 50. She knew better than to argue that point, though, so she ended up doing her own research late at night. If she found the Tells and Mike or the network honchos wouldn't let her air the story, she'd walk and take the footage with her. Maybe Fox would show it.

DOMINICAN REPUBLIC

Alan and Dee Tell arrived in the Dominican Republic as Bret and Melody Mann traveling with their daughter Brooke thanks to some quick and fancy footwork Tom did on the six hour flight. They had five-year visas and were happily ensconced in a missionary compound within the week. Alan provided much needed assistance in the accounting office and, though Dee hadn't yet finished her teaching credential, she was welcomed with open arms as a teacher in the high school. Anna had been taking Spanish since grade school so she was immediately in her element. They

188

missed Sue but Amanda kept them regularly informed about how well Sue was doing in her mission to convert the entire staff at Folson.

KADOMA, ZIMBABWE

In just a little over a month the exiles had turned 100 acres of dirt spotted here and there with army tents, countless enormous piles of bricks and sketches on paper into a thriving community. The buildings were all complete, the clinic lacked only supplies and patients, the school was set up with four teachers eagerly awaiting the arrival of children and the orphanage was two days from accepting its first occupants who were being bussed from the slums of Harare.

Frank had never been happier. He worked from dawn to dusk organizing his little procurement department. Providing for the physical needs of their large, and soon to grow larger, community had him sending men in trucks to different cities four hours in each direction. His supply warehouse was soon stuffed to the gills with everything from dental floss and duct tape to bed sheets and taco seasoning. He even had an extra toilet stored in back just in case. Frank and his team became masters of their trade and, though it might take some time, were generally able to procure anything put onto their wish list.

Jackie was also having the time of her life helping Sharon get the clinic shipshape. As well as her position as a hospital administrator, Sharon had been on eight medical mission projects over the years to varying Third World countries so she had a pretty good idea about how things needed to be set up. The last project she'd gone on, two years before, had been to an AIDS hospital in Haiti and that experience was proving invaluable as well. Sharon's one failing in her position was that she was deathly afraid of public speaking, defined in her mind as anything over a group of five. And that's where Jackie came in handy. Whenever called upon, she gave lectures to the clinic team from notes Sharon had scribbled on various scraps of paper. She also gave two lectures to the group at large about what they could expect from their incoming AIDS patients.

Frank and Jackie, as well as every other member of the exiled parents' community, fell into bed every evening with a deep sense of peace. Each morning they arose to a new day and a new excitement, and the first announcement of every day was an update of their children's progress across the ocean. When the Federica docked in Beira the energy level tripled. The children were removed from the crates they'd crammed in to be unobtrusively unloaded and put on buses to travel overland for the 50-hour journey. By the time the buses pulled up into the compound the parents had thrown together as much of a party as they could muster and were lined up along the road ready to mob their children.

And it was a mob. There were tears and shouts all around. Frank spotted Sarah before Jackie saw her and started waving frantically. He saw Sarah turn around and point, then come crashing through the crowd with Jessie in tow. In the two months since they'd parted Sarah had grown an inch and Jessie's beautiful long hair had been chopped into a stylish pageboy, but they were still his girls. He couldn't contain his tears when he sank to his knees and got his arms around them.

The children brought along an additional bonus besides themselves. The ship's hull had been packed with 50 crates of medical supplies for the clinic, 30 crates of school supplies and 20 full of personal convenience items some of the women thought they wouldn't see again during their time in Zimbabwe. The customs official had been expecting the supplies from Aid to Africa and Land Rovers for the actress whose representative was currently cooling her heels in his office, but he was more than a little surprised when two large crates supposedly full of her "personal items" were unloaded. Paul eased his concern in the form of a rather large donation to his retirement fund. The supplies arrived at the camp two days behind the children, after taking a more circuitous route.

CHAPTER 18

Beth, as she had for the majority of her adult life, charted the months going by in her footage. February closed with 20 parents signing the Tolerance Oath in front of rolling cameras broadcasting to the nation. Some had tears in their eyes; all had children under five years old. April and May showed more of the same. More tears, more five-year-olds.

June and July's footage was filled with tears also, but for a different reason as 100 parents, one after the other, sent their teens off to the re-education centers. Beth's sense of overall anxiety grew with each story she filed. Each family broken up – or just as bad, a parent forced into signing – she didn't know anymore which was worse. All she did know was that she was sick to death of the MPA. As July came to a close she told Mike she couldn't stomach another rescue. He told her to take a couple days off and get her head on straight or he'd send her to cover the national hog-calling contest in Iowa.

Beth would have no way of knowing, but the spring and summer months had been carefully orchestrated by a small team trying to do the best they could with limited time. Josh, George and Amanda had extensive conversations in a cloaked IRC chat room and decided the best chance for everyone would come if they had more time to plan. Accordingly, when Sam's deadline arrived, Josh directed her to give her supervisor the names of the 100 parents on the master list with the youngest children. The second 100 were the strongest Christians she could find through her research with children 16 and 17 years old.

Farmer had wanted to start slowly and the Task Force was more than happy to oblige him as they were still madly scrambling to try to find the first batch of kidnappers and weren't too excited about diverting members of their team into recovery duty. Farmer knew the country would get tired of the same story repeated over and over so he had no issue when the first 100 parents took almost three months to contact. As predicted, the country was bored to tears and frankly sick of the topic. The media tried to keep the rescues as a top news story but finally had to give up. America was more interested in trying to win a slot on Green Jam, the newest and weirdest in a never-ending stream of new and weird reality TV shows.

But the four-month lull was not in vain. As summer rolled to a close the hours of planning began to take effect. Slowly but surely the Task Force began to find fewer and fewer parents at home. Everything was immaculately planned, down to Sam's ordering of names on the list.

At the end of June the school in Zimbabwe was up and running. The parents George contacted had been more than willing to send their kids age 14 and up to a year of foreign exchange education. Sam spaced out the 100 cases so that no two would be approached in the same month. Josh even created a killer website for the school so the Feds could look and see what all the fuss was about. Sharon's clinic received five top-notch doctors in the first week of July.

Amanda contacted 20 couples on the list who were teachers with young children. They were more than happy to accept a position at a new international school in South Korea. The first two couples were there by mid-July, with the rest to follow over the next two months, spaced at inconspicuous intervals. George and Amanda hoped to place 100 kids in the school by the start of the fall semester.

Josh contacted several universities overseas and talked them into hiring additional professors in exchange for a tidy, anonymous endowment. He also opened an office in Kiev and hired 20 web developers who were spooling through code before the calendar turned to August.

The plotters came up with all kinds of schemes. They were having fun being creative from the simple fact that they were unhampered by monetary concerns. Almost anything they could dream up, they could do. Rick's superfund was turning out to be a boon. His original donors had quietly put the word out and money was pouring into the Swiss account. It wasn't unusual at all in the circles his donors ran in to shoot money around overseas so they were definitely in no danger. And, wa la, the team had seemingly unlimited funds to work with.

The best part of all of these schemes was that none of them were illegal. Jack assured them from his intimate knowledge that, as long as the families legitimately left the country, nothing could be done about it because the MPA Advisory Council hadn't accounted for parents leaving or sending their kids away. Nowhere in the 400-page document could the Task Force find instructions. It was also not mentioned in the wording of the MPA. If it were legit, the tolerance counselors would have to follow because there was no authority to call people home. There were also no clauses dealing with kids in foreign exchange programs. To top it off, because the Council hadn't thought of all these problems they'd only recommended 100 agents, leaving the Task Force severely understaffed and completely stymied. Tempers flared and some recovery teams started getting really ticked off. When they did find someone at home they didn't always act as professionally as they should have.

Another bonus was that each time a recovery team came to an empty house they had to submit a report to the Investigations Unit. The Investigations Unit put the leads on an ever-increasing stack and got to them when they could. They were completely overwhelmed and were grilled weekly by the Director who passed along the newest profanities the President had screamed in his ear for not finding any of the terrorist kidnappers. Understandably, the IU was focused on finding the first kidnappers to the detriment of finding out where so many families were disappearing to.

By the end of August George was arranging to have someone meet with 90% of the names being visited a few weeks before their "appointment" to discuss their options. It was mostly Amanda's doing and George never failed to praise her for it. In just over six months she'd managed to organize a movement across the country. Starting with her leadership database, those women had contacted trusted friends and family one by one until there was at least one contact for Amanda in almost every city across the country.

All she needed was a name and a city and generally she could have the person contacted within a few days. The local contact used their own channels to test the authenticity of the person's faith and then approached them with a list of options and the approximate date they were scheduled for a visit.

It was an amazingly effective system, partly successful based on the organization and mostly because of the nationwide prayer teams Amanda had her women organize. At any given time, 24 hours a day, there were at least 100 men and women on their knees interceding for their fellow Christians and for their country. There was an entire brigade in this army made up of the grandparents of kids who had been taken. Widespread arrests were far from Amanda's mind since the plain truth was that the overwhelming majority of her "troops" had been tax-paying, law-abiding citizens their whole lives and 90% of the prayer warrior team was gray headed. They just weren't the first people who'd be suspected of belonging to a terrorist network.

As the weeks went by fewer and fewer names on the list were being caught at home, and those who were seemed undisturbed by the visit. No screaming or carrying on. They just hugged their children and sent them off to foster parents or re-education centers. The Task Force did not report it openly, but whispers began to revive the great boogeyman, the vast right wing conspiracy. It would have shocked nearly everyone to learn that this vast right wing conspiracy was managed from an old model computer run by a woman just starting to turn gray.

Farmer certainly would have been surprised. He had weekly screaming sessions with the Director of the Task Force, berating their progress or lack thereof. As August came to a close and he saw MPA's one-year anniversary fast approaching and his long-held dream fast diminishing, he prepared to take action of his own.

"With all due respect, sir, are you nuts?" The Attorney General conveyed just the right amount of incredulity in that statement.

"What's wrong with attaching it to the ID cards? It would make things so much simpler for the Task Force if they could just quickly scan people's cards now that we've got so many people they're looking for."

"Mr. President, don't you remember how hard it was to pass the ID cards in the first place? The Christians were all talking about 'the mark' and the end times. I think the only reason it was accepted was because we had a Christian President at the time who convinced mainstream America that it was for their own protection."

Farmer was truly clueless as to what could be upsetting the AG. "Sure, sure, so what's the big deal adding another item..."

"Tony!" For the first time in years, Benjamin Henry interrupted his boss. "Did you sleep through our entire comparative religions class? Making people take this Tolerance Oath is bad enough, but if you have the results posted on their ID cards we'll have a full-scale revolution on our hands. Christians have been preaching for 2,000 years about the end times, you wouldn't believe the number of books on the subject. You think we have death threats or problems enforcing the MPA now, wait until Pastor Fred gets up in his Podunk, North Dakota church and calls you the Antichrist."

"Alright, Ben, I'll agree to hold off for now, but if they're still having as much trouble tracking people down by the anniversary I'm going to mention it again."

"Okay, Tony, that sounds fine." The AG paused for a moment and took a deep breath. "Now I need to talk to you about the VNs." The President's stony expression caused him pause, but he continued nonetheless. "Everyone I know is making cracks about how they must be the only ones in America who don't think the MPA is working out too well. They still believe in the impeachability of VN results but I'm telling you, if things continue to go downhill we're going to have to let the VNs fall below 50%."

"Absolutely not!" Farmer's face had shifted colors so quickly Ben didn't have time to register the change before the yelling continued. "If we let the VNs drop below 50% Congress will think that gives them the right to revoke MPA. There is no way I'm going to let that happen. You do whatever you need to, but get some good news out there. I want the VNs over 65% before the MPA's anniversary or there'll be hell to pay."

When Tony picked up his pen and started madly scratching on a pad of paper, Ben knew he'd been dismissed. He turned and slowly walked out the door, down the hall and started the short walk over to his office, so caught up in his thoughts that he didn't notice his Secret Service contingent falling in behind him.

The plan was unraveling.

Jack had spent the first half of the year, as George liked to refer to it, in rehab. He spent several days a week at the Rochester home helping Amanda with the steps necessary to keep their conspiracy going. He found the dull and repetitive office work therapeutic somehow, like he was doing penance for his great sins. When George got home in the evening they had marathon Bible study sessions. Jack soaked it in. When he wasn't at the Rochester's he spent countless hours walking the beach getting acquainted with God.

In between all the God stuff, he thought of Sam. Six months had passed since he'd heard her voice. Six months since he'd failed to return her last message. Sometimes he couldn't believe it'd been that long, it felt like just yesterday he was joking with her on the phone. Other times it felt like a different lifetime when he thought of all the changes he'd experienced.

He didn't intend to blow her off. Not really. He'd just been so depressed, then so overwhelmed by everything he had to learn. And he'd been ashamed. So ashamed of his actions, even now, that it was difficult to talk about it. He knew in his heart of hearts that God had forgiven him, it was other people Jack had trouble with. How could other people, other believers, forgive him for what he'd done? How could he look a mother and father in the eye when he knew he was the reason they were separated from their child?

And he found it excruciating that Sam was at this very moment helping to enforce his mistakes. He'd led her astray along with everyone else. Sweet Sam. Gentle Sam. You might not think it when you saw her striding along with her badge and gun, but she was sweet and gentle. And she was just. He'd convinced her that this was the right thing for the country, that it meant freedom and safety for all those children. She was doing what he'd asked her to do.

Jack had picked up the phone more times than he could count over the past months, but each time hung up after realizing he had absolutely nothing to say.

When he walked in his door the last day in August he was truly a changed man. The message blinking on his machine was no cause for alarm, yet he felt an odd pulse nonetheless. When he pressed the red button he quickly found out why.

FOLSON RE-EDUCATION CENTER

"What do you mean I can't look at Bibleverses.com? You've got to be kidding me!" Sue practiced her most outraged tone on a new staff member at Folson. Once they'd been around for a while they just ignored her, but the new ones always tried to carefully explain exactly why looking at the Bible online was against the rules.

"Well...what's wrong with this website? I'm looking up a verse I was trying to remember in Romans for my Bible Study this afternoon. If I don't get it right I'm going to look like a big dork. You wouldn't want that, would you?" She gave him a winning smile. "It's not like I'm looking at porn or figuring out how to make a bomb from toothpaste and coat hangers. I'm not researching how to break out of a minimum-security juvenile detention center. What's the big deal?" She sat waiting expectantly, big blue eyes fluttering.

He was only 20 and had taken the job because he needed something part time in the evening where he could do homework. During the day he was slowly earning a Bachelor's in Adolescent

Psychology so he thought this would be the perfect job. The hiring manager made it sound easy, just keep an eye on students surfing the Internet, stroll behind them every fifteen minutes and make sure they aren't doing anything they shouldn't be. When he heard "keep an eye" he thought they meant keep them out of porn sites. It was only five minutes into the job when he saw the list of banned sites and thought he might have gotten himself in a little over his head. The first evening he caught three kids looking at Bible sites through anonymous browser portals more commonly used to view porn at work.

The young man calmly started to explain it the way he had been told. He was patient and clear, speaking in a soothing tone as his textbooks suggested. "Well, it's on the list of banned sites for a reason. You shouldn't be clouding your mind with this narrow-minded information. There is a clear posting beside each computer of what you can view, many fine educational sites that will expand your mind and teach you tolerance. If I catch you looking up verses again I'll have to report you to the Director and I don't want to have to do that." End with a statement that you're on their side. Check. That should do the trick, he thought.

Sue's wink startled him as she saucily replied, "You do that" before heading out the door to meet her Tolerance Counselor, a friend of a friend of Amanda's. The kind old woman had completed a crash course in tolerance training in record time and begun making weekly trips to Folson right after Sue arrived. So far she'd managed to slip in some sort of contraband every visit. The Director wracked his brain but could never figure out where Sue kept getting portable DVD players and sermons to watch on them.

ATTORNEY GENERAL'S OFFICE
SEPTEMBER 2ND
8:02AM, MONDAY

Jack was more nervous now than he had ever been in a courtroom. He was standing outside the Attorney General's door, shuffling from foot to foot as if waiting outside the principal's office. The buzz at the secretary's desk startled him and he heard Ben's voice crackling over the intercom. "Send him in."

He took a deep breath while rearranging his tie, threw up a quick prayer and headed into the lion's den.

"Jack!" exulted the AG as he came around his massive oak desk. "So good to see you again. Thanks for getting here so quickly."

"It was no problem, sir."

"Well come sit down." He pointed at a chair in front of his desk before swinging back around to sit down in his impressive leather chair. "So Jack, what have you been doing with yourself?"

Jack repressed the urge to fiddle with his tie again and said, "Not much, sir, mostly taking some time off."

He was spared having to expand on the topic when the AG cut in, "Fine, fine," signifying small talk was out of the way.

"Jack, what Tony and I need from you is simple. The boys over at the MPA Task Force are just doing a crummy job. They're not catching anyone at home. They haven't made any real progress on finding any of the terrorists in the first kidnapping, let alone finding out who is responsible for warning all the parents. They don't give any good excuses, just request more manpower and more money. Typical FBI nonsense. It was against my better judgment to give them control, but that's in the past now. I don't have to tell you the President is getting pretty tired of it all."

He paused for a moment and seemed to be waiting for a response so Jack nodded understandingly.

"Frankly, we need someone we can trust to go over there and find out what's going on. The President has appointed you as his special liaison to the Task Force and he wants you to do some investigating and give him a full report on what exactly is going on over there. You won't be working for them, you'll report directly to me and have full investigative authority and clearance. Do you think you're up to that?"

Jack nodded again slowly.

"Good. I have to warn you, they'll all think you're some sort of political appointee spy so you'll have your work cut out for you getting to the truth. I thought you'd need a day to get settled into your office so I told them you'd be in tomorrow morning. Don't be surprised if they hook you up with some low level staffer. After that you're on your own and I won't expect to hear from you until you're scheduled to give your report on the 10th. I've made an office down the hall available to you if you need a place to work outside of the Task Force building. That'll be all."

Jack got up and walked dazedly out the door. Oh boy.

BALTIMORE, MARYLAND
10:15PM

Sam walked in the door and collapsed on her couch in a heap. She was a frugal person on the whole, but she'd spent a mint on her couch. She rationalized it to herself by saying it's where she spent the majority of her off-duty time so she might as well be comfortable. And it was indeed comfortable. It molded to her tired body whenever she came home from a long day.

Like today for instance. Another incredibly long, not so incredibly productive day. She was tired of reading background checks on an endless list of people just like her parents. Even though she sent information on to Josh nearly every day, she still felt futility in every cell of her body. Josh was supportive and kept telling her what a valuable job she was doing, but it didn't help. She knew he was doing worthwhile work every day while she went into the lion's den and had to laugh along to an endless stream of profane anti-Christian jokes. He just didn't, couldn't, understand what it was like.

She wanted to just go to bed but knew she should check her email one last time. She sat quietly with her eyes closed, listening to the sounds of her computer connecting and downloading the new email. "God," she sighed aloud as she waited, "I need help, someone who understands. Please, Lord." At the ding signifying new mail she sat up and took a look.

Sam was sorry the minute she opened the e-mail from her boss. The subject line said "new assignment" so she thought she'd better read it. Big mistake. BIG. Jack Stone was coming back to town and she'd been assigned as his liaison because, as her boss put it, she was the only one in the office who'd been unfortunate enough to be stuck with him during the MPA Advisory meetings. He was there to snoop around for Farmer and she'd better be prepared to give him the grand tour.

The headache that had been threatening all night chose that moment to burst into glorious fullness behind her right eye. Perfect.

After six months of what her best friend cattily informed her was pining, she'd finally put Jack Stone behind her. The man had great timing, she had to give him that.

CHAPTER 19

HOOVER BUILDING
MPA TASK FORCE HEADQUARTERS
SEPTEMBER 3RD
10:35AM, TUESDAY

Sam arrived at work even earlier than her usual starting time. She'd tossed and turned most of the night, finally dropping off around 3 in the morning, only to be abruptly woken by the neighbor's yappy Pomeranian at 5:30. Not a good start to any day, let alone a day of anticipated high stress.

Most of the agents in the office had arrived that morning to a bulletin on their desk announcing the VIP who would be visiting them, and that Sam had been appointed his liaison. The wording was definitely a little nicer than her boss' e-mail had been, but everyone knew what the visit meant and most had dropped by her desk that morning "just to chat."

As if she didn't hate her situation enough already, Sam was forced to join in the general belly-aching and concern people were feeling about whether this meant they would all lose their jobs. I should be so lucky, she thought as yet another coworker wandered off.

The ding of the elevator caused her and everyone else in range to whip their heads around but it was another false alarm. Sam felt her nerves fray a little bit further and sent up yet another prayer for strength. Just then she saw the stairwell door swing open and out he came, not even looking winded from the climb to the 5th floor.

Hating herself even as she did it, Sam slunk lower in her chair and hid behind her monitor as she watched him walk into the Director's office. While she was hunkered down she saw the old coffee cup Jack so thoughtfully had the espresso man deliver many moons before. She hadn't yet had the heart to throw it away. Unbelievable, she thought as she angrily knocked it off the prime spot it occupied on her desk and watched it roll across the floor.

You saved a stupid paper coffee cup for six months? Head in hands, she mirthlessly chuckled.

Jack was anxious to get started. He'd felt guilty for so long that the opportunity to help set things right was intoxicating. Plus, he'd always fantasized about being a spy and realized this was probably the only opportunity he'd ever get to play double agent. The only downside, and it was a big one, was that he still hadn't worked up the nerve to call Sam and let her know he was in town. He figured word would spread pretty quickly and promised himself as he was getting dressed that morning that he wouldn't leave the building before phoning her.

The Director had been prattling on for ten minutes about what a heroic job his agents were doing when Jack's wandering mind was brought painfully back on topic. "I'm sorry, who did you say?"

"Sam Hawthorne. Do you remember her? She was one of your liaisons when you were working on the Council."

The Director was looking at him expectantly but Jack just couldn't kick his mind back into gear from the mental stall he'd entered.

"Mr. Stone? Are you alright?"

"Yes, yes. I'm sorry. Yes, I remember Ms. Hawthorne, I just thought she worked in another division."

"Oh, well we brought her on when the Task Force was formed. She's a great asset to the team. Really understands the mindset of the people we're trying to track down. She works longer hours than almost anyone here. In fact, let me get her in here. She's been tasked with answering any questions you have."

Jack couldn't have been more stunned. He literally had no idea what to do. Hiding behind the fake tree in the corner of the office occurred to him, but he couldn't seem to get his legs moving. Before he knew it, he saw Sam bearing down on them.

She could swear she saw the moment when the Director told Jack about her. Sometimes his big office window looking out on the bullpen came in very handy. She watched Jack bolt upright in his chair and was trying to get a good look at his face when her intercom buzzed.

Ok Lord, just like we talked about . In the wee hours of the night she'd finally come to a realization. Yes, she'd allowed herself to have big hopes about Jack but those hopes had finally withered and died. Whatever they'd had was obviously not as meaningful to him as it had been to her and she needed to move on. What mattered now was for her to do whatever necessary to keep her job and keep intrusive eyes away from the Task Force.

As much as she complained about the position she was in, Sam was very aware that her small part played a big role in the larger drama. As far as she knew, Josh didn't have anyone else on the inside. No matter what her personal disappointments had been, she needed to rise above or the entire operation would be put in jeopardy.

With Sam's hand on the doorknob, Jack's mind finally kicked alive again and he almost groaned aloud. It had been hard enough for him when he thought Sam was just working in a division feeding names to the MPA Task Force. Hearing that she was actually an integral part of this team was more than he could stomach. In one blinding flash he understood the real reason he'd never called her back all these months. He didn't want to lie to her. Ever.

Now he'd have to tell her a whole book of whoppers if he was to finish the job he'd been assigned. He felt like his heart actually tore a little. All the dreams he'd had about telling her everything that had happened to him; how he'd slowly convince her that the MPA was wrong, then reveal that he was actually working on the right side now. All of it vanished in the space of her opening the door and walking in.

"Mr. Stone, it's nice to see you again. Sam Hawthorne." Sam wasn't sure how she'd made it through the introductory formalities, but when Jack looked like he was about to say something she'd glanced quickly at the Director and then slightly shook her head. He seemed to have gotten the hint and pretended to barely know her. The Director gave him a slap on the back and shuttled them out the door.

Jack quietly followed her to her desk where she picked up several folders, then on into the conference room she'd reserved for the morning. He watched her take her seat at one end of the long table and stood so long that she indicated the place beside her.

"I've assembled a dossier on the more minute details of our operation, but if you don't mind I'll talk you through the generalities before taking you around for some introductions." As she was saying this Sam took a packet from her folder and slid it across the table to Jack. She tapped her finger on the post-it note attached to the top page. In her clear block lettering it stated: We can't speak freely here so please remember you don't really know me. I'll ask you to lunch in about an hour and we can discuss other things. She gave him a moment to read and at his nod she removed the note and slipped it into her suit pocket before continuing.

"There are 50 agents housed in this office and 50 agents in the field. We're split into five teams that all report to our Director, who reports directly to AG Henry. The Investigations Unit is the biggest team with 25 agents trying to track down the kidnap victims. List Management and Logistics is my department and I have nine agents who work with me. We monitor activity nationwide and compile all MPA paperwork coming in from local law enforcement. We run preliminary background checks and produce a list every Friday of subjects to be approached the next week. The Logistics agents on my team book flights and hotels and make car reservations. They also inform the local field office or local law enforcement of our schedules and request backup at each MPA visit we make. The local Children's Protective Services office is notified and a temporary action plan is created for where to house the children. Accounting has five agents who take care of all the bills and expense reports that come in from the field agents. We have five agents on the Media Relations team who are kept busy with all the various media requests we get. They do a press conference once a week with the highlights of that week's activities. It usually has high attendance, but doesn't always get much airtime. Lately we're not finding a high percentage of subjects at home so we've recently re-tasked five field agents to a Location team. Whenever a field team doesn't accomplish its mission they send the name back to the Location team whose job it is to track the subjects down. If they find them the names go on a separate list but at present nothing happens in the way of follow-up. The last team is Field Recovery and, as I said previously, there are 50 agents working in teams of two. They do the actual MPA visits accompanied by two agents from the local FBI office or local law enforcement, depending on the location and sometimes a Children's Protective Services representative, though not that often lately – the CPS reps don't like wasting their time. The Recovery agents' task is to meet with the subjects and see that they sign the appropriate Tolerance Oath paperwork. If the subjects refuse the agents take custody of the children and move them to the appropriate local housing facility designated by our Logistics team."

Sam felt that she had just given the longest run-on sentence of her career but noticed Jack was still paying close attention and had been taking notes. "That's the overview. Now I'll tell you frankly how we're doing. You'll find when you meet everybody that we're all pretty frustrated. Our snatch teams find about one in three families at home but we've been instructed to keep up the visits, when the truth is IU is completely overwhelmed and could use more help. IU is supposed to be tracking down the kidnappers but they have no travel budget so they can't even leave this office. They work hard but as I'm sure you can imagine it's pretty difficult. We've all suggested to the Director at various times that we move snatch agents into IU, or at least stop visiting altogether so we can catch up. The Director says the President is adamant about keeping the teams going. On top of that, I get a new list from the AG's office every few weeks with more names to work in somehow. Obviously you'll want to talk to each of the agents and team leaders. We've all been instructed to cooperate as much as possible. If you'd like I can take you around right now and introduce you to everyone."

In spite of his earlier turmoil, he'd actually been able to concentrate on what she'd been telling him. It took a minute, though, to catch up and realize she'd asked a question. "Sure, that sounds great."

All eyes had been surreptitiously looking through the window at them and quickly swiveled back to their desks when Sam and Jack emerged from the conference room a moment later. Sam took Jack around to each desk and quickly introduced him to its occupant. The recipient of the introduction did his or her level best to make a good impression on the man they'd been told could send their careers down the tubes. Accordingly, it took almost an hour to get all the way around the room. When they returned to Sam's desk she dropped her folders and casually looked at her watch. "Well, it looks like it's about lunch time, Mr. Stone. If you'd like we can go grab a bite to eat and I can answer any questions you have so far?"

Jack nodded, just as casually, and said, "That sounds great. Do you have any good Mexican food around here?" By mutual consent, neither said a word during the 15-minute walk to Sam's favorite Mexican restaurant. After being seated in a back corner and thanking the waiter for the drinks Jack abruptly started in. "Sam, I'm so sorry. I had no idea you were working at the Task Force. I just flew in two days ago and was planning on calling you today. Not that I have any excuses about that either. It's just, I've been so busy."

He stopped as abruptly as he'd started and Sam thought he had the decency to at least fake looking miserable as he took a big drink of his water. She decided to get them back on track with the speech she'd rehearsed in front of the mirror that morning.

"Jack, obviously you decided you weren't interested in pursuing whatever it was we were doing. And hey, I had a good time while it was going. But I'm realistic enough to realize neither of us is at a point in our lives or careers where we're ready to throw it all away and move across the country. It's really ok. It's been ok for months."

Since he didn't look like he was going to respond Sam continued, "It was just important to me that we set some things straight. My job means a lot to me, Jack. I feel like I'm doing an immense amount of good and it would greatly undermine my credibility if people found out we'd dated. Or whatever it was. I'd just really appreciate if we could be adults about this and put it all behind us."

LINCOLN MONUMENT
5:42PM

She'd looked at him expectantly, and what could he say really? But I don't want to be an adult? I want to cry like a child? She probably wouldn't appreciate such sentiment since she'd obviously put their "dating or whatever" behind her long ago.

And could she be any more blatant about her beliefs regarding her job? How could she have bought the whole thing hook, line and sinker? He'd thought better of her value system. Everyone knew that the MPA was a piece of garbage. If you took the time to look further than the evening news or the VNs, people were screaming about it. MPA Task Force agents were getting booed almost everywhere they showed up. If she really felt this way he knew he'd have to lie with the best of them to keep her off his track.

He'd mumbled something appropriate and they'd both tucked into their food. As quickly as possible they were on their way back and parted ways as soon as they stepped into the building.

He stayed for a couple hours reading through the materials she'd given him and bolted as soon as decently possible. For the last hour he'd been sitting here, mostly staring into space. Yes, he'd have to lie to her. There were too many other lives at stake to tell her the truth at the moment but the second this crappy bill was repealed he'd march over to her apartment and give her the what for. It made him feel slightly better, though he knew he was probably just fantasizing again.

GARDEN OF THE GODS
COLORADO SPRINGS, COLORADO
SEPTEMBER 4TH
6:30PM WEDNESDAY

Beth walked slowly alongside Rick admiring the astounding rock formations. She'd called earlier in the week to say she was doing a story in his neck of the woods and asked if they could get together. They'd been professional rivals for a number of years and this was not the first such meeting. For the first 30 minutes they'd wandered through the park admiring the different formations and engaging in non-combative small talk. However, as Rick looked sideways he saw Beth rhythmically flexing her right hand open and closed, a sign he'd learned over the years meant she was getting ready to do battle.

"Rick, you know I've always respected you, even if I disagreed with most of your right wing, close-minded philosophies."

Beth was slyly grinning out one side of her mouth and Rick flashed a full smile her way. What an understatement, he thought. They'd had furious arguments over the years as both had risen in opposite media camps. "And you know I've always respected you, even if your liberal theories are quacky and illogical."

"Touché," she said, grinning. "Well, I asked you to meet me because I think things are getting really out of control. Can we go way off the record here? I don't want to hear you talking about some unnamed liberal journalist tomorrow."

"Of course we can go off the record," he said. "As long as I get the same courtesy. I'm tired of hearing the propaganda you think of as news stories bashing an unnamed conservative talk radio host."

This was their usual method of barbed conversation so both were still grinning like idiots. It was a battle of wits whenever they got together. After every meeting Beth went away thinking they could really have something if he'd just get a clue politically, while Rick went away reciting the "unequally yoked" verse over and over in his head.

Beth heaved a big sigh and began, "Well, I can't believe I'm saying this, but I think someone might be tampering with the VN numbers." She took a quick glance at Rick to see his expression. It was blank, giving nothing away. "Way off the record, I've quietly talked with several of my colleagues and a good number of them disagree with what the President is doing, especially this last move to expand the Task Force and move them under Homeland Security. I've also done some unofficial polling using one of our consulting firms."

Beth stopped at a particularly interesting formation and scrutinized it. "I figure if myself and a good chunk of my media colleagues aren't all on board then there's no way the 57% VN approval rating can be correct. I've also been doing stories in some small cities and towns lately and the anti-MPA feeling I'm getting from Joe Sixpack is even stronger than that of my colleagues. I mean, contrary to what you might think, Rick, most of us in the media know we're more liberal than the majority of the country. We just think you're all wrong and are trying to educate people into being more open-minded. That's no different from what you do every day, Rick, we're just trying to show a more balanced picture than they get from you. You can't really blame us for that."

She took a quick peak at Rick and tossed off the zinger she'd thought of months before and saved for the perfect occasion, "And it's not our fault that there are so many more of us liberals in the media than you conservatives. Maybe if you all weren't such reactionary pigs you'd get more mainstream jobs." Seeing Rick's smirk she quickly added, "And if you ever repeat any of that I will deny it immediately and vehemently."

Deciding to forgo their standard argument about how he was a talk radio commentator who was supposed to give opinions and she was an NBC journalist who was supposed to give unbiased news Rick's smirk got bigger. "I always knew ya'll weren't that ignorant."

"Anyway, taking all that into account, there's something fishy going on with the VNs and I intend to find out. You've been ranting for years that they were being tampered with and I've always made fun of your conspiracy theories, especially when you've never been able to prove anything. Now I'd like to apologize and say this might just be the first thing we agree on in our long and glorious friendship. I came to you to see if you had any sneaky conservative friends who might be able to help a curious liberal like little ol' me." Rick burst out with surprised laughter when she completed her pitch by fluttering her eyelashes at him.

"Well, muffin, little ol' you surely has more contacts over at the VN than I do, but I might be able to help you out. Us sneaky conservatives like to stick together."

Laughter floated behind them as they finished their walk marveling at the amazing works of Mother Nature or God, depending on which one of them you listened to.

jdog: Rick?

talker: hey josh, I'm here

jdog: how was your meeting with the looker?

talker: very funny, I told you not to call her that

jdog: you know you love her, too bad you can't fix her politics

talker: I'm signing off now

jdog: ahh, come on, admit it – you luuuuuv her! ;)

talker: seriously, sometimes you make me think we're still in freshman year

jdog: some of us still are dude, you should at least ask her out – if you're missionary dating you'll have a much better chance of getting her to see reason :)

talker: if you promise to knock it off I'll continue this conversation

jdog: alright, alright – no more teasing...for the moment

talker: I think she's going to work out

jdog: no comment

talker: let's be serious please. she was dancing around the topic of the VNs and suggesting there might be some tampering going on – she asked if I had any sneaky conservative contacts who might be able to find out about that kind of thing

jdog: and you said?

talker: I said I might be able to help her

jdog: and...

talker: she's already suspicious of farmer so I think she might be the one we've been looking for

jdog: well you know her better than I do so I'll bow to your judgment talker: I know she has crappy politics, but she also manages to tell the truth a good portion of the time – have you seen some of the reports she's been filing lately? She's really getting ticked off at the brutality of some of the task force agents

jdog: yeah, I saw last week's broadcast. she still ended the story positively

talker: I didn't say she was perfect – I just said I think she'd tell the story truthfully if we decided to throw it her way. Let's see how this series she does next week goes, she said I'd be pleased

jdog: okay, okay – I'm just messin which ya. You know her best, if you think it'll work I'll support you

talker: ok

jdog: and it has nothing to do with the fact that she's a looker and you luv her

talker: goodbye josh

jdog: goodbye loverboy

--

From: sam@zoog.com
To: amanda@e-staffing.com

A,

Hey, are you still looking for someone at Atter Construction? I may know someone who could fill that position – they come very highly recommended but would have to know by next week. Let me know.

I got the pictures you sent of John and Lisa – my, my, they're growing up!

s

From: amanda@e-staffing.com
To: susie@yahoo.com

To Whom it May Concern,

I'm contacting you about the job you posted last month for Atter Construction. I have a couple interested in the position and they could move out as soon as next week. If you have not filled the position, please send me an application by overnight mail.

BTW, unrelated, but thought you'd like to know we got John and Lisa placed. Thanks for your help with that!

Amanda e-staffing

CHAPTER 20

HOOVER BUILDING
MPA TASK FORCE HEADQUARTERS
SEPTEMBER 6TH
1:32PM, FRIDAY

Sam had thought after setting the record straight with Jack that things would smooth out. Sure it'd been hard. He'd done a good job of faking and she'd actually started to feel a little guilty about pushing the "let's be adults" thing on him…until she remembered the six months of silence. If she hadn't had those six months as evidence she really might have believed the way he was acting. Like she was breaking up with him and he didn't like it. What a faker.

Walking back to the building she'd started to build up a pretty good head of steam. Luckily he'd left her at the elevator or she might have blown her cover and started berating him right in front of everyone in the office. The rest of the day she hadn't gotten anything but the most mundane tasks accomplished since she was so busy looking in his direction every 10 seconds.

Thursday had been no better. As much as he seemed to be avoiding asking her questions, there were still things he needed to know to do his job. And if she was really going to pull off her professional act she had to stop by every so often to see if he needed anything. It was a long day and she'd gone home relatively early to collapse on her couch for an evening of staring at the boob tube.

So far today he'd only had a couple questions for her. He'd better get cracking though, because she'd made a snap decision at lunch to go visit her parents. She figured an entire weekend in her pajamas being smothered by her mother would be just the ticket to shore up her confidence. She told her boss she'd be leaving early, so all she had to do was swing by her house for the trusty pajamas, and then she'd be on the road by 3:00.

JOE'S ITALIAN GARDENS
8:02PM, FRIDAY

Jack had lived through his share of surprises in the last couple days, but the e-mail he got from Sam just as he was packing up to leave would have to rank at the top of the list. In a carefully worded request, she'd ask him to meet her for dinner at the scene of their first date. He had a sense of déjà vu when he walked in and saw her sitting at the same table in the back. The only difference was that she had obviously gone home and changed.

Her eyes locked onto his and he maintained the eye contact as he walked toward her, only breaking it off when he tripped on a chair. He made it the rest of the way, hopping on one foot.

"I see you're as agile as ever." He could swear she was teasing him. "Yeah well, I've always been athletic."

His toe was throbbing but it seemed a minor inconvenience as he was distracted by the smile she was giving him. Since she didn't seem to feel it was necessary to keep up her end of the conversation he said, "So was there something you wanted to discuss?"

She picked up a piece of paper that had been lying on the table in front of her and slid it over to him. Curious, he began to read. Five seconds later he looked up at her with wide eyes, then looked down again. It took less than a minute to finish, but by then he was in a full panic.

"Listen, Sam, I don't know where you got this, but it's obviously…" he petered out as she held up one finger in the universal signal for "wait a minute" and pulled out a cell phone. She dialed a number and seemed to be waiting for the person to answer while sweat began to pour down his back.

"It's Sam. Yeah, he's right here." She handed him the phone and, not knowing what else to do, he took it.

"Jack Stone."

220

"Jack, it's George."

Jack knew George Rochester's voice, obviously, but his brain was stuck on the problem of how Sam could possibly know him.

"Jack, hey! Wake up!" George's voice held more than a tinge of humor.

"George. Uh, what's going on?"

"So Amanda and I were having our weekly bull session with Josh and lo and behold, he mentions the gal he has working for us over at the MPA is worried about increasing scrutiny in her department because of a watchdog the President has sent over to clean things up and the fact that she has to work with this guy. She's one of our best contacts, shoots us all kinds of information, so Josh is pretty worried. We usually don't mention names, even between the three of us, because we don't want to be forced to rat out anyone extra if we're ever caught. But for some reason he mentions the name of the watchdog and it's none other than Jack Stone. Well, we're happy to inform Josh about your particular allegiance and he thinks it'd be great if his gal knew who you really were because that would expedite the work. So he shoots her an e-mail and gets a frantic call five minutes later. She's pretty darn sure you won't believe her if she tells you herself, so I've been sitting here by the phone the last couple hours waiting for her to call."

Jack's eyes had gotten rounder and his mouth had opened further the longer George went on. Sam was just sitting across the table with a twinkle in her eye, waiting for him to finish.

"Thanks, George, I'll talk to you later." He heard George start to laugh as he hung up, but his attention was only for Sam. "What!"

MOORPARK, CALIFORNIA
SEPTEMBER 9TH
9:00AM, MONDAY

Amanda was waiting anxiously at the door when the FedEx man brought her package. She had already made some preliminary plans for the Atters, but needed more information about them before anything could be solidified. Tearing open the envelope and reading the first page, she soon collapsed on the couch in laughter.

Amanda,

I'm glad you contacted me last month or I would have had no idea what you were talking about with that cryptic e-mail. As requested, I quietly went around trying to find out about John and Lisa Atter. Can I just say right now – PLANT! My sister's hairstylist's children go to the same school with the Atter children and her words, after bursting out laughing and yelling "you've got to be kidding me," were and I quote "John and Lisa Atter being on the MPA hit list is a big bunch of hooey!" To be more specific, Lisa Atter has been pestering the school board for the last four years to let her teach transcendental meditation to the grade school classes. Her husband belongs to the local chapter of the Atheist League. You'd think if they were going to plant somebody on the list they would do a better job! Anyway, that's the scoop so I wouldn't waste too much time trying to help them out – they'll be just fine!
Let me know if and when I can be of more assistance!

Susie

SEPTEMBER 9TH
6:35PM, MONDAY

"This is Beth Billings, bringing you part one of our five part series following MPA Task Force agents as they go about their duties. I was allowed unprecedented access as we near the first anniversary of this controversial law and traveled last week with two Task Force Recovery agents who have spent nearly eight months on snatch duty, as they call it in unguarded moments. We wanted to see how things were going. What is it like being a Task Force Recovery agent? How do they like their jobs? And what does the country think of all this? Some of what I found will surprise you, some will not. But I can promise you it was a fascinating trip and I look forward to bringing it all to you this week."

The picture switched to a view of countryside flying by in the window of a car and Beth's voiceover continued. "We began Monday in Fayetteville, North Carolina. I met the two agents I'd be traveling with when they arrived at the airport after an all night flight from California. Alan and Gary have both been with the FBI for over ten years. Each talked about his love for the job – pre-MPA. Now? They're not so sure."

A large sign passed by the car window proclaiming Wycliffe Bible Translators. "They rented a car and drove to a small community of missionaries. It was a quick trip. The family they were sent to visit went back to Africa where they've been translating the Bible into an obscure native language for the past four years. They were on a year-long furlough, as it is called when missionaries come home to rest and visit their supporters, but decided to cut it short and go back early."

The scene switched again to show one of the agents as he sat on a plane. "We're tired. What can I tell you? My partner and I have been on the road for nearly eight months straight. We go home every other weekend, but other than that we're living out of a suitcase. We got picked because we're both single, but it's a grueling schedule nonetheless. Most of the time we get our best sleep on the plane."

Beth continued, "This is one of the 25 partnerships currently doing MPA Recovery visits. They travel almost non-stop, rarely getting a chance to stay in one city for two days at a time. They're tired. They're weary. And as you will see tomorrow, they're cynical."

They'd ended up closing the restaurant down again. It was one of the best conversations Jack could remember having in his lifetime. He couldn't get out apologies fast enough, but Sam wouldn't listen. She wanted to hear the story of his past six months and he told her in all the detail he'd dreamed of over that time. And she was as interested as he'd hoped. Then she told him what her journey had been.

Around that time they'd finally noticed the evil eye the manager was giving them so they'd started walking the streets. They'd laughed until tears were streaming down their faces when they'd filled each other in on everything they knew about the anti-MPA fight. He knew quite a bit more about the various schemes and she'd been delighted to hear what had happened on the other end.

It really was like the six months hadn't happened, other than the fact that they were both changed in significant ways. They were still talking on a bench when the sun came up and they'd both drifted down memory lane when he bought her a triple espresso at a coffee shop they found. They finally went their separate ways after a long breakfast. He hadn't thought he'd be able to sleep, but after only a couple hours of work at his hotel he'd dropped off and slept through the night.

Sunday he'd gone to church with her and they spent the afternoon working together in companionable silence at her apartment. It was, quite possibly, the best weekend of his life.

CHAPTER 21

SEPTEMBER 10TH
6:35PM, TUESDAY

Beth watched her taped self begin the pre-recorded four and a half minute story. Yesterday's report had slid under the radar since it was sort of light. However, she had a feeling she'd be hearing from someone pretty soon.

"After the fruitless trip to North Carolina, we took a flight to Spokane via Minneapolis. From there we hopped a small commuter and flew into Moscow, Idaho – possibly the smallest airport I've ever flown into. We rented a car and drove over an hour to a picturesque white house along the banks of the Clearwater River. We were a little surprised to find balloons tied to the mailbox where we turned in, but even more surprised when a crowd of people were there to greet us. It seems there was a small administrative snafu back at headquarters. These agents came to visit the parents of a just-turned 18-year-old daughter. They received a rather giddy welcome, considering their mission. My traveling companions refused the offer of cake and sat in the car while I chatted with the family gathered to celebrate this milestone. What I discovered during that hour was an attitude I would see again and again throughout the week all around the country."

The video showed a gray haired old codger speaking loudly, "What'er you gonna do now, Farmer? You can't use your bully law to tell her what to believe. She's an adult and can make decisions of her own. And d'ya know what she's decided, Farmer? She's going to Bible College, then law school, for the express purpose of making sure you and your ilk never get away with this kind of thing again."

"After an hour we had to get back on the road to keep our schedule."

The car window framed Alan's profile. "Well that was something new. We've had snafus before, but nothing quite like this. I'm sure they'll get an earful back at headquarters when you broadcast. At least this wasn't too painful. The family was nice. I'll tell you what they'd have been like if that was her 17th birthday, they would have been a pack of wolves. We'd have had to call the police for backup and cross our fingers that the cops weren't related."

He sighed before continuing, "You know, Ms. Billings, we spend most of the time traveling. Today was a classic example. We went from North Carolina all the way across the country to Podunk, Idaho. Now we're going back to Denver. I don't know why they make our schedules like they do, but we're being run ragged. Like this job isn't hard enough without being dead on our feet from exhaustion."

WHITE HOUSE
8:30PM

Farmer's face was turning several shades of purple as he listened to the reports drone on and on. He hadn't come into the meeting with a good attitude to begin with, owing to the tape Ed had inadvisably showed him of that evening's NBC broadcast. That trollop Beth Billings had talked her way into traveling with a snatch team. They flew to traitorous Idaho where she proceeded to film some pretty inappropriate remarks by the agents. When he'd yelled that he wanted the series stopped Ed told him he'd already talked to the producer and there was nothing to be done. It would be more damaging to their cause to stop it when it was growing so rapidly in popularity.

Now Farmer was stuck hearing about the myriad ways people were getting out of having their children snatched. It was astonishing. The Task Force was having no luck increasing the percentage of children placed in foster homes, but they seemed to be getting better at tracking down, if not stopping, the families leaving the country in droves.

Jack was wrapping up the 15-minute report he'd carefully authored from his time with the Task Force. He'd saved some of his favorite parts for the end.

"This next one will really get you. We already told you about Advocate's International opening a new office in Egypt and staffing it with 10 lawyers who were on our list. Well, now there's a bazillionaire defense attorney in California who up and decided he wanted an office in France. France! Why in the world he would want an office there I have no idea. But anyway, he decides he wants an office and sets about staffing it. And here's the interesting part, what do you know, but that the 50 lawyers he chooses to go in on the deal are all on our list and all have children under ten years of age. This guy hasn't done anything illegal so we can't nab him. All 50 lawyers moved to France within two weeks where they now have a thriving office, before our teams approached even one. They also took with them 25 clerical staff, ten teachers, five security officers, two marketing directors, six PR people, three handymen, two construction workers, one pilot and one company chef. Also all on our list with young children. They've got themselves set up in the French countryside, practically took over the town, and seem to be working happily along. We wouldn't have even caught the connection since they were all scheduled for MPA visits at different intervals over the next six months, but we've asked the State Department to notify us of all large scale citizen movement so they sent this list over. Since they left before we could make contact we can't touch them. If we had enough staff we could send someone over there and they'd all have to go through the Tolerance Education program, but we can't spare anybody. We've asked the French government through channels to lean on this guy and maybe find some reason to close him down. They, of course, refused.

"Next, we've identified two schools that are actively taking children as exchange students. There's one in Zimbabwe that has a hundred students and one in South Korea that just started and already has 45 students, though it looks like they'll end up taking a

227

hundred total. Obviously, all the students are 16 or older, on the list and would have been in our detention centers if we'd gotten to them in time. Also obvious is that the schools are staffed by 20 list couples. Oh, and I should clarify that these are new schools that just opened. There are also numerous long-established schools that have experienced a large increase in their student bodies recently.

"After years of fiscal mismanagement the University of Moscow is suddenly flush and gobbling up professors at an alarming rate. Give them another few months and it's possible that 50% of their staff will be American. The University of Aberdeen has also opened up a new economics department and taken ten professors. There are several Arab universities hiring as well, though they made a practice of never hiring Christian professors in the past. In case anyone is interested, there are several more universities launching new departments but I won't bother to go into them.

"There's also a new kibbutz that just opened in the Galilee last month and already has 212 American members. They are currently expanding their housing situation and plan to offer another hundred or so memberships before Christmas. That's in addition to the over 4,000 student visas the Israeli government has issued in the past two months, up from their usual 350 in the same time frame and somewhat over their quota for the whole year. I think you might want to check again and see if the Prime Minister still agrees with your plan." Jack's attempt at humor was met by silence so he continued.

"We know the list has been leaked and we've been working hard on trying to track that down. The problem is, there are so many people who have daily access. We have agents all across the country who get faxes or e-mails every day about who they should be visiting. Local field offices have the info. The media invariably gets a call. We're leaking like a sieve and we have no idea how to stop the flow owing to the amount of people needed to make this operation work. There just aren't enough agents on the Task Force to handle the workload and they're now running into the problem that local agents and police departments are refusing to lend them personnel.

"Another big concern is that someone seems to know the order we're going in. Like I said, several of these larger groups have all been spaced out well enough on the list that we would not normally have found out about them until they were all safely away. Or, if we did find out where one had gone we wouldn't know who on the list would be headed to the same facility.

"Finally, over the last month our agents have only found 82 children at home, most of whom seemed less than surprised at the visit. Sixty-nine were over the age of 16 so they went to the detention centers, which is a different topic altogether and a good time for the next report."

Jack sat down heavily. He'd never been a great actor. His impressive courtroom appearances had always been bolstered by his beliefs so giving the report in a somber tone diametrically opposed to the hallelujah chorus tone he actually felt had been difficult.

Another suit stood up and began solemnly, "Mr. President, we now house 1,042 teens aged 16 and 17 in three Southern California facilities. They are wreaking havoc on our staff. At least once a week they bust a group huddled around a screen watching theology classes like they were watching porn and we have no idea where they keep getting the portable DVD players from."

Jack stifled his laugh with a coughing fit and reached for a glass of water.

"We have filters on all the computers but we still catch the kids surfing through anonymous portals onto religious websites. Unless someone stands behind each kid every time they're on the Internet we can't stop them. And any punishment we've tried doesn't really work either. The staff is used to punishing delinquents but these kids don't seem to mind being sent to their room because they just have a prayer session. The Directors tell me they have staff in their office every week complaining about having to watch the kids because they get preached at. The kids recite Bible verses and sing religious songs with great enthusiasm. They snicker when the Tolerance teachers hold classes, or worse, so I'm told, is when they start debating the teachers. That's another problem; teachers are quitting in droves. Three new facilities will be ready to come online next week, which is good. We're already stuffed to the rafters with more coming in every day. But staffing continues to be a problem."

The man sat down and all looked at the Attorney General. "All right, Jed, you're up."

Another grim-faced man stood up and began in a defeated tone of voice, "Well, I'm sorry to report that our plant didn't work out too well."

That sentence caught Jack's attention and he sat up a little straighter.

"We followed all the research we have and picked a young couple with two children under the age of five living in a mid-size town we'd not visited before. The kids went to public school, the mom stayed at home. We made a great background file for them, put the husband in charge of one of the bigger anti-MPA rallies a few months ago. Said the wife volunteered at the Women's Resource Center and has been organizing a letter writing campaign to her congressman against MPA. We sent the file over to the Task Force through regular channels and had them expedite the visit which has been done several times before so it shouldn't have raised any flags. And we didn't inform anyone over there in case it got leaked. But it was nothing doing – no contact for two weeks. On top of that, we now have a problem to deal with in that Task Force agents showed up and actually took the children. They didn't believe the story our plants told them and were, so we've been told, a little rough with the wife. We've got all kinds of damage control to do now." He finished and slumped into his chair.

Ed Gonzalez stood and began, "This is somewhat related to our current situation. Ever since that Tell woman fiasco we've had people picketing the StemCon centers. They're very systematic and rotate so that everyone gets two strikes and then they move on.

After their two strikes they stand just outside the 100-yard radius. Hundreds every day. And it hasn't wavered or slowed down like these things usually do.

"It wouldn't be that big of a deal, except I'm told the collection of stem cells has gone way down. The StemCon Directors are all yelling about it. I think we need to take a serious look at this. If we could get some good StemCon news it would pop the VNs up again as well as knock the wind out of these protestors. We've been hovering in the low 50's for a long time but I think we're on the verge of a big crash without some good news. All my focus groups are fed up and ready to revolt. I don't know how the VNs are hanging on, that's a miracle in itself. I think people must just be trying to be supportive of you, Mr. President."

Farmer was still staring out the window, seemingly in another world, when Ed sat down so Ben felt compelled to jump in. "We have got to find a way into this terrorist network. It's obviously well organized, well funded and the people are highly motivated. Gentlemen, you must find a way to turn this situation around or history will harshly judge your inability to protect this nation."

Jack followed the others out the door, his solemn face no longer feigned as he considered the dangers ahead. He was the last one out and heard Farmer say something that chilled his blood just before the door closed. "Ben, maybe it's time for another California distraction to boost the numbers."

Sam waited by the phone all night. She and Jack had taken a long lunch so they could talk about what he should say in his report. It was kind of fun actually, since they still felt it prudent to hide their relationship from the people at the Task Force. They'd left separately and taken different routes before meeting up at a little diner where Sam knew the owners would let them use the back room.

Oddly enough, she was finding the strain of hiding her feelings for Jack at work even more difficult than hiding her true feelings about the MPA had been. As the watchdog, he was still the topic of much discussion among her coworkers and she'd had to bite her tongue several times in the last two days before jumping to his defense. He told her to chill out, that his reputation could handle a little sullying, but she still didn't like it.

The phone ringing jolted her out of yet another valiant defense of him that she was imagining based on something rude Dana had said today.

"Sam Hawthorne," she answered, automatically.

"Jack Stone," he said with humor in his voice.

"Well it sure took you long enough!"

"Sam, I wish you could have been there. Next time we need to investigate taking one of your sneaky FBI hidden cameras with me because it was priceless. Farmer is losing it!"

She smiled at hearing him so excited. "Go on."

"His face went through so many shades of purple I thought he was going to keel over right there. Well, maybe hoped is a more accurate term than thought. But his heart was definitely getting a workout."

"Poor Mr. President."

"Indeed."

"So did you remember to tape Beth's report?"

She could almost see him slapping his forehead. "That's ok. I taped it for you. I watched it already and it's good."

"Thanks, Sam. I still can't believe the Director let a reporter shadow your people."

"I know! It sure seemed like a lame brain idea, especially with how frustrated our guys have been lately. I imagined they might let something inappropriate slip if given the right circumstances - and you know I got them five great families."

"Nicely done."

"Thank you. I still can't believe she got it all filmed without Farmer finding out. He must be really clueless about what's going on out there. I know the VNs are staying fairly steady, but sheesh, from the stories our guys are telling they're practically getting spit on wherever they show up. I've seen four early retirement requests come through just this month."

"Well, the VNs were mentioned briefly but nobody talked too much about the actual reception agents are getting. Mostly it was a blame game about how ya'll aren't gettin' the job done because you're too busy sittin' around on your hind parts. I, of course, wholeheartedly agreed."

"Spoken like a true watchdog."

"Hey, I'm just keeping up appearances."

"Whatever. I can't wait to see the next three reports Beth does. I'm not sure what she's going to say, but I know who she visited and I've heard through the grapevine that it's NOT good. Maybe it'll come out that I told the Director it would force the President to give us more funding if he allowed the reports to happen. Maybe I'll get fired!"

"You're not getting fired. Now what do you mean the grapevine? I never get in on the good stuff."

"That's because you are a SPY, Mr. Stone. No one trusts you. In fact, Dana told a pretty mean joke about you today. Would you like to hear it?"

Sam was right. As the week went on her stock at Task Force headquarters plummeted. Somehow all the blame came to rest on her. Either she should have plotted things out differently or, more to the point, she shouldn't have put a bug in the Director's ear about more funding. He let that little tidbit slip Wednesday morning by the coffee pot and she was very quickly out of the grapevine herself.

Beth had been right also. Tuesday's report hadn't been over for more than ten minutes before Mike got a call from the News Director, who had received a call from Ed Gonzalez. Mike scurried off and she didn't see him again until the next morning. Overnight results showed that her report had doubled in viewership from Monday to Tuesday, and Tuesday pulled a 60% share. The News Director put off Ed one more day to see how Wednesday's show turned out, by then nothing Ed could say would change things.

CHAPTER 22

SEPTEMBER 11TH
6:35PM, WEDNESDAY

"Three days into this intriguing week we finally have an actionable case. They are a young couple in their late 20's with one-year-old twins and they had no idea we were coming. Normally we would black out the faces of the parents and children, but this couple requested that we wouldn't in their case. They said they wanted the whole story told."

The camera showed two babies giggling in their high chairs while their young mother fed them some sort of smashed vegetables from a jar. "When we arrived on their doorstep I watched this woman's face go completely white. She was on her way to the phone to call her husband before Alan even got through the introductions. He arrived 15 minutes later, peeling into the driveway and running up the stairs with sweat pouring down his face."

Alan and Gary sat on a couch facing the young couple seated on the other couch. There was a piece of paper on the table between them. Alan's voice was grim as he explained the procedure and the camera caught every expression that rolled across the faces of all involved. When the father started to speak in an anguished tone the picture zoomed to frame him. "We don't have a choice do we? You think we'll let you take our babies?"

He broke down at that point and his wife continued in a small voice. "We'll sign. My husband is right, we don't have a choice." She trained her eyes on Alan. "I know you're not a monster. You're just trying to do your job. And I know that the majority of Americans aren't monsters either, they've just been deceived into thinking this is a good idea."

"You know, sir, this isn't about fostering terrorism anymore, if it ever was. We have friends who've signed already. They meet with their Tolerance Counselor once a week. She made them pull their boys out of children's choir. Those boys practice six months of the year so they can go around at Christmas and sing in nursing homes. Tell me how that activity teaches them about terrorism. Our friends gave us all their Veggie Tales tapes because their Counselor told them to get rid of them. Veggie Tales! Do you know what those are, sir?"

She didn't wait for a response before continuing, "They're cartoons! Cartoons that tell moral messages from the Bible. How is getting rid of that going to teach our children tolerance? This is not about terrorism, sir. It's not about religious zealotry. Take a moment to think about real religious zealotry when you remember what day it is!"

Suddenly deflated, she leaned forward and signed the paper. Gary watched closely but Alan looked away.

Beth spoke again from a moving car. "Alan and Gary had to stop at the Denver field office for a few hours of paperwork, but now we're headed to the airport to hop a plane to Seattle. For once we'll get a real night's sleep in a hotel by the airport before driving an hour north to Camano Island. After this visit, there was a burning question I had to ask Alan."

The camera recorded his face as Beth voiced her question, "Alan, tell me why those people were on the list? How could that young couple with one-year-old babies be fostering terrorism? How could they possibly have done anything worth our visit?"

Alan was silent for five seconds, an eternity of blank space on the network news. Finally he cleared his throat and spoke softly, "I can't answer that question, Beth. I can't even think about that question and still fulfill my sworn duties. I have given my oath to follow the orders of my superiors in the service of this country and I take that oath very seriously. I was on one of the original teams that went out on MPA when we rescued the first 50. I still don't know why we took those kids. The first kids I took were eight and 12-years-old. Remember the Governor of Virginia who got caught smoking pot with his son? The one who was supposed to be

Farmer's Vice President the first time? Well, the mother of these girls organized the campaign that got him recalled."

There was another long pause from Alan. "That's it. That's all she did, Beth. If you can explain that one to me please do. I can't think about the why's or wherefores or I'll go insane. Especially today," he said angrily. "She was right. Especially today we should take stock of what we're doing. What in the world are we doing?"

Wednesday night's ratings were the biggest yet with an unprecedented number of people hitting the website and calling the network to ask if the show would be rebroadcast. The News Director suggested to Ed Gonzalez that he might go jump off a bridge when the President forced Ed to call and demand the final segments be cancelled. For all his big talk, he did call Beth and her producer in and ask her to tone down the final installments. She told him she would quit if they edited her story and go public with the pressure they'd been receiving from the White House. He decided the better part of valor would be to ride it out and try to repair things with Ed after this all blew over.

He was right. Nearly everyone in America was tuning in. They called their friends and family. They taped the segments and passed them around. If he'd cancelled there would have been a massive outcry.

It was as if the dam was finally breaking. Most people had just had their heads down, trying to go about their lives and not get involved. They'd seen what happened to people who got involved and with the VNs telling them their opinion about the MPA was in the minority they didn't want to risk their own children's safety. But somehow, seeing golden girl Beth Billings so outspoken against the President and the MPA was giving people the first inklings of hope that they were not alone.

George and Amanda had such a smooth system down that they'd pretty much returned to normal life, albeit with a somewhat unusual hobby that took up a portion of each evening. As they sat together watching Beth's reports they couldn't help but pop off the couch and do a little jig. It was what they'd been hoping and praying for during the past year – that someone with a large voice would finally start yelling.

Rick was so proud of that "large voice" that he sent Beth a dozen roses signed "your favorite nutjob." She knew exactly whom they were from but kept mum to all the queries from her fellow reporters.

Her reports were also met with cheers in the recreation center in Zimbabwe. They had one television with a satellite hooked up to a generator so someone taped the program when Amanda e-mailed them a heads-up. It was shown to the whole group after dinner and the cheers were especially loud when Frank and Jackie were mentioned. Everyone knew each other's stories by now since they'd been working and living together so long. There was a lot of free time for chatting when the sun went down.

SEPTEMBER 12TH
6:35PM, THURSDAY

Beth looked a little less than her usual perky self as she reported from the backyard of a beautiful home overlooking the Puget Sound. "I'm standing on Camano Island, a community of 15,000 about an hour northwest of Seattle. We arrived at our destination at 10:00 this morning to find the family vanished. There's a Lexus parked in the garage but the minivan is missing. The neighbors won't say anything more than that they left three days ago. Alan says this is not that uncommon. Families get a whiff that they're about to be visited and leave in the middle of the night. The father is a lawyer, the mother a teacher, and they have three children aged 12 and under. I walked through the house with the agents and it looked for all the world as if the family merely left for a brief vacation."

Beth paused and looked sideways for a moment before continuing, "I can't explain what it was like to walk through that house. A beautiful house, filled with beautiful things. This family

238

apparently chose to flee and leave all those beautiful and expensive things behind, rather than be forced to make the decision whether to sign the Tolerance Oath or not. I guess what they've done is a decision in itself."

The camera cut to Alan, looking out at the water with a breeze running over his tired features. "Sometimes I think it's better this way, Beth. There's no tearful scene where the outcome is a no win situation. We're not the bad guy. We send their name along to IU or Locations and move on to our next visit."

Beth's voiceover explained, "The IU is the Investigations Unit of the Task Force. Twenty-five agents absolutely swamped with the duty of tracking down the first kidnappings, as well as trying to find out what has happened to all these families who've disappeared. In fact, so many families have disappeared that a Locations team has branched from the original Investigations Unit just to try and track them down. They've repeatedly requested additional agents to help them, but to no avail. What that all boils down to for this family is that they're going to have a really good head start."

From the front passenger seat Beth filmed Gary while he drove. "Gary, this situation reminds me of a question I wanted to ask you earlier. You're not always finding families gone and there are rumors circulating that Task Force agents have been known to use unnecessary force in the pursuit of their duties. What can you tell me about that?"

Gary sighed and took a deep breath. "They're not rumors. I don't know what to tell you, Beth, or any of you watching. We're all professionals here. We've all been agents for a number of years. But the hours we're being forced to keep combined with the incredibly high stress of the job we're performing is causing some people to lose it. We've had incidents and been forced to reassign some field agents. But we're getting spit on Beth. We're getting threatened with bodily harm. Two weeks ago we were in a tiny town in Oklahoma and an 80-year-old woman came up to me weeping, begging me not to force her grandchildren into signing the Oath. We've had agents attacked by mobs. I'm surprised more of our guys haven't cracked under the pressure. All I know is that I loved my job before this assignment, now I'm thinking seriously about a career change."

SEPTEMBER 13TH
6:35PM, FRIDAY

"We battled traffic for two hours to get from the airport to our destination in a very upscale neighborhood of Westlake Village, California. In this area, a million dollar home is a fixer-upper." The camera recorded the truth of her words as they drove slowly along looking for the correct address.

"I find it interesting that on this final day we're so close to where the path of the MPA began. The Jessups and Jack Stone both live two towns over and the Ventura Courthouse where that most historic decision came down a year ago is just 45 minutes up the freeway. I can't say I'm going to be sorry to see the end of this trip. It's been a fascinating look into the daily ups and downs of the Task Force, but it's been tiring and heart wrenching also. We found the family at home and they also wanted their faces shown to the world rather than hide behind a black dot."

Alan and Gary sat again on a couch opposite the parents, a single piece of paper on the coffee table. There was no mistaking the anguish on their faces. Their 14-year-old only daughter was home from school with the flu so she'd seen the agents before her father asked her to go back to her room.

Alan was giving the parents plenty of time to make their decision when the girl returned holding a suitcase. Her father started to tell her to go back to her room, but she broke in over the top of him and the camera caught it all. "Mom and Dad, I'm going with them. You've taught me God's truth all my life and now it's time for us to stand up for it. You don't have to worry; God will take care of me. But you can't choose to protect me at the cost of your faith. I won't let you."

Beth's voiceover asked a final question of the mother. "How can you allow your daughter to be taken from your home when all you have to do is sign a simple document?"

The mother answered with great difficulty, "We raised her with the knowledge that nothing is more important than our relationship with God. How could we look her in the eye if we signed such an appalling document as your so-called Tolerance Oath or that wretched contract? How could we look God in the eye? We're going to fight this now the only way we can, through the courts, and we only pray that we will get our daughter back as soon as possible."

Beth appeared in front of the NBC backdrop to finish her series with a live feed. "We completed the visit by taking that brave girl to the local CPS office where she waited about an hour for her foster parents to come pick her up. She'll have to live with them for the next four years until she comes of age. This being the end of the series, I'm supposed to tell you what I learned, what my conclusions were. I have none. I left Alan and Gary at the airport in Los Angeles, sick to my stomach and sick at heart. The only thing I came away with was a conviction that I need to do some serious thinking. I can tell you, I consider myself a good judge of the pulse of America, and the fact that I am so out of step with my impressions this time around is a bitter pill to swallow. VN approval for MPA remains steady, as it has all summer, hovering at 51%.

"As an update, Alan called me this morning. After last night's broadcast he and Gary were called into headquarters to give an accounting of their words and actions. In explanation they handed in their resignations. Alan told me he hasn't felt so free since this whole thing began. One more casualty in this MPA war."

CHAPTER 23

"What was that! You never ran that last paragraph by me!" Mike was ready to pop.

Beth tried to calm him. "Mike, Alan only called me this morning. I thought it was important to the story to add that bit in."

"You thought it was important!" He paused to mentally tick through the 42 swear words he wanted to say to her. "If you hadn't just pulled in the highest ratings we've had in five years you would be out on your backside in about two seconds. Even with those ratings you won't be able to work in Washington again until there's a conservative in office. You did a great story, Beth, but you've used all your get out of jail free cards. You not only turned in the most damaging press MPA has ever received, but you basically told America they were wrong in supporting it. Now, knowing what I know it sounded to me like you were subtly questioning VN integrity, but I'll give you the benefit of the doubt and assume you wouldn't do anything quite so stupid without the proof to back it up. How many times have I told you that you tell the stories that need telling, as long as you're still on the air in the morning."

"Come on, Mike, it's not that bad." His stony silence was the only response so she brought up what she thought was a different subject. "Well, did you at least get a chance to look at the story I brought in today?" She had been forwarded a clip from an affiliate in Houston of another MPA parent caught at home unaware. The footage clearly showed the bloody pulp the Task Force had beat him into. The children could be heard screaming though they were only shown for the briefest of seconds before being shoved into a towncar. "Some of these Task Force guys are beating the crap out of the parents they find. Don't you think that's news?"

She saw him take another calming breath. "Beth, you are done with MPA. You hear me? Done. Finished. Finito. You blew our last chance with your series. I have the word of Ed Gonzalez himself that if we do another story negative to MPA or Farmer we lose access to the President." He paused dramatically, "for the duration of his term! If you pitch me another story that even mentions the letters M, P or A I'll send you to cover the high school pep rally in my hometown."

She tried a different tack, "Ok, well, what about my request to go to France or South Korea to interview some of the parents who have skipped town?"

"I don't believe this!" At last her pushing had broken through his anger and he saw some humor in his brash reporter's unwillingness to give in. "Are you hearing me? No. Absolutely, completely and finally no. Why don't you find some happy news and stop crusading? You're not doing your career any favors with this nonsense."

"Alright, then I want to pursue the story I pitched you about the VNs misrepresenting middle America. I've been talking to people all over the country. You're here all day, every day in stuffy New York. I can't tell you the last time I ran into someone outside of New York or LA who agreed anymore. They'll talk to me all day long while the camera is off, but the second I turn it on it's a different story. They're all afraid to say anything for fear they'll be next. Everyone saw how Farmer went after Dee Tell after she spoke out against StemCon. I told you Americans were smart enough to see through that line of hooha you made me report that said Dee had already been on the list for months."

Beth saw Mike's eyes begin to glaze over and she knew it would be wise to just stop and cut her losses, but the months of stress and frustration got the better of her. "I mean, I realize you've totally sold out. Last year you thought the Homeland Security agents worked for the devil, now you're so supportive of the Task Force agents who are beating the crap out of people at every turn that you can't see the inconsistency of your position. But you should at least see that there are people out there who disagree with you and their stories deserve to be heard."

Mike's brief bout of humor had indeed vanished. "Beth, don't say another word you're going to regret. In fact, I think you should take a week off. Leave town. I don't want to hear from you. I don't want to see you until next Friday. Don't even take your phone. I'm going to call you and you darn well better not answer it." His cell phone rang and he answered it as he turned, waving her dismissively away.

Beth stormed off. Fat lot of good her fantastic ratings had done her. She knew the affiliate story was a good one. It was a story that needed to be told and she was furious it got nixed. No matter how many times they'd covered it, if this kind of injustice was still going on, it needed to be highlighted until something was changed. This was the reason she'd become a journalist, to bring hidden things into the light, to pursue truth.

She was also ticked about Mike not approving her trip request. What could be more newsworthy? At least it would be worth a good Dateline, exploring the reasons people felt the need to leave their home and move to another country. She found herself wishing, not for the first time, that she had a job like Rick's. He seemed to cover whatever he wanted and didn't have anyone censoring him.

When she got back to her desk she found a sealed envelope with no writing on the outside except her name in big, bold letters. Looking quickly around the newsroom she didn't notice anyone out of the ordinary. She sat down and carefully considered. The procedure for anonymous mail was very clear: call Security, they called the bomb squad, you didn't get your letter back for days, or even weeks. Figuring it was probably just another joke circulating around the newsroom she decided to throw caution to the wind and tore it open.

To Beth Billings:

Do you still want to interview Alan and Dee Tell? If so, be at the rest stop at exit 21B on the Beltway at 6:00am on the 18th.

No recording devices. You will be provided with a video tape of the interview upon completion and will be returned that evening in time to broadcast.

If you're worried about your safety, consider who we are - a bunch of Christians who have done nothing but run in the face of our children being taken away. You have nothing to fear.

It was one in the morning before Sam got back to her apartment. She'd met Jack for dinner at another favorite restaurant of hers and they'd managed to close that one down as well. They laughed for ten minutes straight when recalling the old codger in Idaho from Beth's report, each trying to repeat his speech with correct intonation.

Other than talking about the reports they'd avoided anything MPA-related. That self-imposed blackout hadn't stunted the conversation, though, and they talked non-stop for three hours. She could hardly believe it had only been a week since they'd set things straight. Sam felt like she was walking through one of those dorky Hallmark commercials, with hearts and flowers following her wherever she went.

Several times this week she'd found herself daydreaming at work and only jolted back to reality when her next-door neighbor would throw a paperclip or something similar at her. It was getting to be a little embarrassing.

SEPTEMBER 16TH
8:15AM, MONDAY

The ringing phone broke Amanda's concentration. She'd been trying to come up with a better organizational system for her contact database. She sometimes laughed at how completely she could lose herself in org charts and five year plans. She heard George pick up the phone and say hello, then there was a long silence with George occasionally making noises like he was listening. A few minutes later she heard him quietly say goodbye and hang up. His footsteps were heavy as he walked down the hall from his office and came to the door of hers.

She looked up in time to see his pale face appear. "What's wrong?" George came in and slumped into the spare chair. "That was Nate at the prison. Some Task Force guys came in this afternoon and questioned him again about the day Nick escaped. He was really disturbed. He was so surprised by their visit that he thinks they saw through him. He's really freaked out about his kids, you know he's got three under five-years-old."

Amanda grabbed George's hand in a small attempt at comfort and said, "What do you think? Should we try to get him out?"

George bent over and put his head in his free hand. "This is why I didn't want anyone with kids helping us. I feel so responsible. I know he made the decision on his own, but that doesn't help me feel any less guilty."

"Well that settles it. Why don't I check with Sam and see if she's heard anything about him. Meanwhile we'll start making plans to get him and his family out." She tugged on his hand to get his attention. When he looked up she gave him a beguiling smile and said, "I have just the spot for him."

George smiled tiredly, stood up and headed back out the door.

It took Amanda a minute to compose a note in the appropriate format. Even with Josh's system it was important to be as obscure as possible when writing Sam during work hours.

From: aroch@flazinker.net
To: sam@shonday.com

Sam,

Hey, thought you'd like to know Nate got that job he applied for. He's going to be working for Kopp Construction. Do you want to go in on a congratulations gift for him?

Amanda

When she checked her e-mail an hour later she found a new message from Sam.

From: sam@az3ult1si.com
To: amanda@bingo.org

That's great! Tell Nate congratulations for me – I'll definitely go in on the gift. Is 3 dollars enough? ; -)

Sam

Amanda took the note into George's office where he had given up planning for a while and was reading his Bible. "Well, it looks like Nate's instincts were right. Sam says they're moving on him in three days. We'd better get cracking."

ATTORNEY GENERAL'S OFFICE
SEPTEMBER 17TH
2:15AM

Jack was sweating as his heart pounded nearly out of his chest. He whispered over the cell phone connection to Josh. "Ok, I typed in the url you gave me. Now I'm looking at a website for Tawanda's Washington Flower Shop."

Jack was sweating for good reason. He was currently sitting in the Attorney General's leather chair, breaking more laws than his legal mind could catalog. He'd decided he had to know the whole story, no matter the risk, so he'd stayed in his temporary office down the hall until everyone had gone home, then waited another two hours for good measure. The darkness did nothing to hide the look of terror on his face but his hands remained steady as he followed every command Josh had given him.

"Ok, now you just need to wait for a minute while I find the files we want. Since you accessed my website through the backdoor port that circumvents the firewall I should be able to connect directly to Franklin's computer. My hacker friend informs me that every IT geek in the world leaves one door open so they can play with unauthorized software and video games. I'm going to download the contents of the hard drive. Everything's probably encrypted but we can deal with that later. Once I'm sure I have everything we'll get out and erase our little field trip." Josh's voice was also betraying anxiety but he managed to keep to the task at hand.

"Alright. I'll just sit here and wait for security to come breaking through the door." Jack had been relatively fine, other than the sweating problem, as long as he was following Josh's commands, but now as he waited in silence he had time to think about what he was doing and was overcome with waves of dread.

Five minutes later, which seemed a literal eternity to Jack, Josh harrumphed over the line and said, "We got it!"

"Great! Now how do I get out of here?"

Fifteen laborious minutes later Josh had led Jack through the numerous steps necessary to erase his entry from the computer. Jack quickly shut it down, mopped the chair from all his perspiration and sprayed the entire area with the fingerprint-wiping chemical Josh had him buy. He was out the door and in a taxi roaring toward his hotel four minutes later.

While Jack was presumably taking a shower and trying to postpone a heart attack Josh had been attacking the encrypted files. The AG's e-mail had been fairly easy to crack and he shot the archives off to Jack within 15 minutes, but he soon realized the rest of the files would take some time. Josh was not a hacker by nature. He preferred to stay within the law. But when Jack called him and told him what he planned to do Josh got in touch with an old friend for some down and dirty tutorials.

He was confident they had gotten away clean. Well, mostly confident.

"You moron!"

Jack had been fairly certain Sam wouldn't be too keen on his early morning foray into espionage. Now he was completely certain.

"What were you thinking? You could have been shot, for one thing, if the guards had caught you in there. And now I'm going to have to visit you in prison for the next 40 years."

Jack silently congratulated himself on his decision to simply call her from a taxi on his way to the airport, rather than having her drive him as he'd first planned. "You mean you'd visit me in prison? I'm touched."

She could hear the grin in his voice and it infuriated her even further. "You are touched – in the head! I should have you committed."

"Come on, Sam, Josh had it all worked out. You know what a genius he is, there's going to be no problems."

"You hope not."

"Well," he paused for a minute to consider how odd his next words would have sounded coming out of his mouth only a year ago, "I did pray about it, Sam. I felt a real peace that it was the right decision. That's not to say that I didn't lose four gallons of sweat during the process, but that's beside the point. And it got us this lead which we didn't have before."

She seemed to be calming down a bit, displayed by the fact that she didn't jump down his throat at his first pause. "Now listen, I've got this flight at 8:00. You'll call ahead and make the appointment at the prison for me and I'll be returning on the red-eye at 10:00, hopefully with some great news. Can you pick me up in the morning?"

"Alright. I'll be there. But please promise me you won't do something as incredibly stupid as this for at least a month."

"I promise."

CHAPTER 24

LAX
10:00PM

Just as Jack was reaching to turn off his phone, it vibrated in his hand. "Jack Stone."

"It's me. Where are you?"

Jack grinned at her greeting and stopped in the jet way, much to the consternation of the man barreling behind him. He loved that Sam assumed he would recognize her voice. It made him feel good. He didn't examine that feeling of course, he just felt it and moved on. "Hey! I'm at LAX, just getting ready to board my plane. Why are you up so late?"

She made some sort of shushing noise that sounded a bit like "meeting," then asked, "Well, did you get it?" The excitement caused her voice to fairly buzz in his ear, leaving him with a warm feeling of well being he couldn't quite place.

"Yeah, I got it. We were right, though I still can't quite believe it. He's prepared to testify in exchange for immunity."

"I can't believe that! I just can't believe they would go that far!"

"I know, I was thinking about that on the drive back to the airport. The lengths they've been willing to go. I think we're going to need to be even more careful not to get ourselves knocked off."

She was indignant, "I'm always careful! It's you that has the danger streak running right through you. Skulking around other people's offices. Sneaking through their files."

His grin was back, "I have no idea what you're talking about, but the stewardess is giving me the evil eye to turn my phone off. Are you still picking me up?"

"I'll be there."

Jack split the trip equally between sleeping and staring into space with a dopey grin on his face.

--

Beth was calling herself all kinds of fool. A woman with a kind voice emanating from behind a surgical mask and sunglasses had met her at a deserted rest stop. The woman asked her to leave her watch in the car, then led her to the back of a van and blindfolded her. Beth rode inside for an hour or so, not that she could say exactly as she'd always been horrible at guesstimating times without the trusty Tudor her parents had given her in college.

When the van stopped the woman led her carefully up the stairs of a plane, sat her down and buckled her in. The blindfold came off as soon as Beth heard the door close and she found herself in the cabin of a luxury private plane. The only obvious difference being that the windows were blacked out so that she couldn't see anything and there was no private stewardess offering her a moist towelette.

However, the person who arranged this had thoughtfully set out drinks and snacks, as well as paper and pens. The flight was long but Beth wasn't sure if it was three hours or six. She jotted ideas for questions in between cat-naps.

When they landed another woman came onboard and put the blindfold back on. Maybe an hour more of bouncing in the back of a van brought her to her destination. She was led inside a building and when she took off the blindfold she saw a very dull room and a camera pointed at the Tells, sitting calmly on a plain couch. Alan stood up and extended a hand, "Ms. Billings, so nice to meet you." Dee stood up as well and they shook. Both looked completely comfortable, diametrically opposed to the furor of emotions running amuck inside Beth.

REAGAN INTERNATIONAL AIRPORT
WASHINGTON DC
SEPTEMBER 18TH
7:30AM, WEDNESDAY

Jack came out of the airport doors looking for Sam's nondescript fed car. He didn't have to wait long as she came peeling up in the dawn light and flashed her lights at him. He stowed his carry-on in the back seat and then slid into the passenger side with a big grin before he noticed the grim set of her jaw. "What's wrong?"

"Farmer just had a big meeting. I think something's up."

"What do you mean? What something?"

Sam stopped looking grim at that and smirked in his direction.

"Nice follow-up Counsel, what something?" His grin was back momentarily, and he said, "Hey, I just took the red-eye, I think I deserve a little credit for being able to string two words together, even if they don't make sense. Now start over."

He took the opportunity of her driving concentration to stare at her a little longer than was seemly while he made great efforts to follow what she was saying.

"Ok. Farmer held a meeting til the wee hours last night with Henry, his top advisors and the Task Force department heads. I talked to a friend this morning and the office gossip is that they've found a way to crack the terrorist ring, as we are affectionately known. We have got to find out what went on in that meeting!"

Jack was paying attention now. "Sam, we have got to find out what went on in that meeting!" Only after he spit it out did he realize he'd mimicked her exactly. Luckily she was taking his words about the red-eye to heart and only smiled.

He tried again saying, "Well, what do you think we should do?" She threw a big smile in his direction and said, "Well, I don't know what you're going to do, but I'm going home to take a nap."

"A nap? You haven't taken a nap since I met you. Are you feeling alright?" His look of concern lightened her spirits even further.

"I feel great, Jack, but I have news too. I told you I was in a meeting last night?" She looked for his affirmative nod before dropping her bombshell. "I'm fired."

"You're what!" He was sitting up straight once again.

"As my supervisor put it, I had to 'take one for the team,' which I told him I was more than happy to do. He just didn't realize which team I was talking about. Someone had to go for that debacle over at NBC and it sure wasn't going to be the Director. He had to have someone's head on a platter when he showed up at Farmer's big meeting. Therefore," she slipped into a perfect imitation of her straight-laced supervisor's voice, "I should have known better than to schedule the families I scheduled that week and I have been placed on unspecified administrative leave."

"But that's not fired, fired, is it?"

"In Bureau speak, my career is over. I could come back in a few months and try to work my way up to file clerk if I was so inclined. Since I'm not, I've decided to look about for a new career."

Her voice was so joyful Jack was having a hard time thinking this was a bad thing. "Well, in that case, congratulations are in order! Would you like to celebrate in the unspecified future when we figure out how to get our butts out of the frying pan? That is, if we figure it out and don't end up meeting once a day in the yard at San Quentin."

"Jack, don't be silly. They only send murderers and men to San Quentin. We'll get Maxwell for sure. I hear it's practically like summer camp."

Her enthusiasm was infectious and he found himself thinking there just might be a way out of this after all. Meanwhile, she'd just pulled up at his hotel and it was time for him to make an exit. "Enjoy your nap Sam. I'll call you tonight."

"I will, Counselor. Talk to you then." She peeled out and was gone.

DOMINICAN REPUBLIC

George had spoken with the Director of the Christian Legal Defense Fund months before and got him to send their best legal arguments against MPA for such a time as this. When Beth asked why they, normally law-abiding citizens, would flee the country, Alan was ready.

"Ms. Billings, if it's alright with you I'd like to quote the Establishment Clause of the Constitution that my friends at the ACLU are so fond of: 'Congress shall make no law respecting an establishment of religion, or prohibiting the free exercise thereof.' The Minor Protection Act is in violation of this Constitutional provision. What MPA had done is make the free exercise of Christianity, in its most fundamental form, untenable. Dee and I feel that the MPA goes against the most basic principles this country was founded upon. Under normal circumstances we would have stayed and fought it through the court system, but when our children were threatened we decided leaving the country was the only option left available to us."

Beth appreciated Alan's legal argument and thought it was a valuable part of the interview, but she knew she needed something more, something that would grab people's attention. She decided to try Dee. "Dee, nearly everyone in America has seen the response you gave to the Sheriff's question in Boise. Do you still feel the same way, seven months later, now that you're in hiding with the most powerful nation in the world hunting you down?"

When Dee finished talking Beth knew she had both the answer she'd been searching for and the ending to her story.

5:45PM EST

Sam's cell-phone's vibrating on her night-stand woke her from a much-needed nap. "Hello?"

"Hey are you still sleeping? I'm sorry." Jack's voice came through contritely.

Sam sat up and quietly cleared her throat as she blearily looked at the clock. "No, no. It's ok. I was just about to get up anyway."

"Well I've got something I think will wake you right up. I had to show my face at the office this morning, but when I got back after lunch I found a FedEx from Josh with some more decrypted files, mostly correspondence. I've been reading through them for the last five hours and I've just seen a memo that Henry sent Farmer two days ago. Henry referenced a 'Convert Project' and said, in effect, that the mole is in place and the terrorist situation is about to be resolved satisfactorily, most likely today."

Sam bolted out of bed at his words and, for no reason in particular, started searching for her shoes. "What does that mean? Who could they be talking about?"

"I have no idea Sam, but we really need to get ahold of Josh. Have you talked to him lately?"

"I was on with him two nights ago for a few minutes, but he had to run. He said he had to talk to George and Amanda about a new project before an important appointment. I assume he was talking about meeting you for a little B&E."

Jack snorted at that not-so-subtle dig and wondered if she'd ever let it go. "Yeah, yeah. Do you have any idea what he was working on with George and Amanda?"

"Let me think. The last e-mail I got from Amanda was asking about a Nate Kopp. I checked the list and saw he was scheduled for a rush job, which was a little weird because I never put him on the list. I just assumed he was someone special and forwarded that and the usual update to Josh on Monday. That's why the other night was so brief, there just wasn't much happening."

"Well, something is definitely going on. We need to get either Josh or George on the line immediately and warn them to stop all their current projects."

Beth couldn't help but laugh, despite the circumstances. When she'd gotten back on the plane with her videotape there was a portable editing bay and a satellite phone left for her to use. She decided to check her messages before editing the interview footage and giving Mike a call. However, he had apparently already been trying to reach her. The first message was a simple "Call me now," followed thirty minutes later by "if you're such a moron that you didn't take your phone with you on vacation then I can't be responsible for giving this story to someone else." She listened through several more before she got to the "you're fired" finale.

She decided to call in anyway and when Mike heard where she'd been and what story she was bringing he offered her a raise and promised to save the 4 1/2 minutes she requested on that night's broadcast. He began running promos five minutes after getting off the phone with her.

6:00PM EST

"What do you mean he's already left?" Josh was fairly shouting through the phone line.

"I mean," said Amanda, "he's already left on that assignment we talked about last night. What's the big deal?"

Josh's heart was beating unsteadily as he started to sweat, "Amanda, Jack found a memo that said they placed a mole in our group. They have someone who is going to bring us down today and this is the only assignment we're working on today. To me that means Nate is the mole."

"You can't be serious Josh, you just don't know Nate. George has been his mentor for years. And I heard his voice Josh, Nate was really scared for his children."

MEXICAN BORDER
6:30PM EST

The car was silent as George approached the border. Nate, his wife and children were in the back of the truck covered by stacks of blankets. Not a great hiding spot, but George felt no fear as he spotted the line his contact was manning.

George was idling five cars back when he caught the frantic look his contact shot in his direction. His hands tightly gripped the steering wheel while he casually glanced around trying to spot anything out of the ordinary. It was then that he saw a swarm of agents coming at him, guns drawn. He and Josh had set up an emergency number months before in the event one of them was caught and he knew if he could just get his phone out and dial, Josh would take care of everything.

Unfortunately, the Task Force agents had been briefed so often on the "armed and dangerous terrorists" that when they saw him reaching into his coat pocket they reacted immediately. Four shots went through the open window and hit him center mass before he could even pull the cell phone out.

As he lay there in his seat George knew he was dying. He could feel the blood pumping out with each heartbeat. He wished he could say goodbye to Amanda, but felt peace that he would see her again. Just as he started to close his eyes he heard Nate shouting in the distance. There was a sound of scuffling, and then Nate's face appeared through the window. He was crying, "George! George, I didn't mean it. They were gonna take my kids! They said they wouldn't hurt you. I'm so sorry George."

George put all his energy into lifting his hand and lightly touched Nate's shoulder. "It's ok, Nate. I understand." He paused to pull in one more difficult breath. "I forgive you, Nate." And with that his hand fell back to the seat and a slow smile spread across his face as his eyes closed.

CHAPTER 25

NBC STUDIOS
6:35PM

Beth arrived with only a few minutes to spare. The broadcast was about to begin and she was the second story. She dashed through makeup, threw her video at Mike and made it to her seat exactly three seconds before the anchor introduced her.

"Good evening. Tonight I have a fantastic story to share with you. Ever since Dee Tell made her incredible stand outside the Boise, Idaho StemCon center I have been intrigued by her. I've wanted to know what would make such a normal, level-headed housewife put her children at risk by doing something as ineffective as blocking the entrance to a building.

"I've been trying as diligently as our government to find the Tells since about five minutes after their disappearance. I have to confess though, that all of my efforts proved in vain. Then out of nowhere, five days ago I received an anonymous envelope on my desk here at NBC asking me if I wanted to interview them. I was told to go to a rest stop outside New York where I was met by a woman with a mask over her face who told me to leave my watch in the car. I was blindfolded and rode in a van for an uncertain amount of time before being transferred to a jet whose windows were covered so that I couldn't see where we were going. Several hours later we touched down, again I don't know how long as I am terrible at telling time without a watch. I was blindfolded once more for another van ride.

"When my blindfold was taken off I found myself in a room with the Tells. They were sitting on a beat up couch and the only other furniture was a chair for me and a camera operated by another man in a mask. I spent two hours with them and came away incredibly enlightened. Of course there is no time in this format to show you the whole interview. I've had to cut it down to the usual 41/2 minutes, which was difficult in the extreme, I can assure you. I've included one question and answer from both Alan and Dee."

At her signal the technician started her tape. The first thirty seconds was taken up by her question of Alan and his response. The second thirty seconds showed the now infamous clip of Dee talking to the Sheriff at StemCon that Beth had instructed the techie to insert. Then the tape switched again to her question for Dee.

"Your question tells me that you think I had a choice in the matter, Beth. I didn't. I've believed that embryonic stem cell research was immoral since I had to do research for a debate class I was in five years ago. It was that class that started me on this path. I began to get involved in politics somewhat and when one of our local senators introduced a bill banning that kind of research in our state I fully supported it. Against my personal feelings of inadequacy I campaigned for all I was worth. I spoke in front of the congressional panel considering the bill and held three different press conferences.

"I tell you all that, Beth, to explain. I have never been interested in being the center of attention. Everything I did in service of that bill was difficult for me, but I felt it was a duty God had set before me so I held my breath and jumped in. And that's why, when my daughter Sue confronted me about not doing anything to stop StemCon, I was so convicted. She was right. I had let the MPA bully me into not following God's commands.

"The problem here, Beth, is that you believe, like most non-Christians, that Christianity is a lifestyle. I'm here to tell you it's not. Christianity is a life preserver. The Bible says that God is holy and that men are sinful. Without accepting the sacrifice of Christ's death for your sins, you'll go to hell. That's it. It's not pretty. It's not complicated. It's just the plain truth. Anyone who tries to make Christianity any more or any less is not being faithful to the Word of God. Let me ask you, Beth, do you think a lifestyle would be worth dying for? I'll tell you what; if Christianity was just a lifestyle the first apostles would have given it up instead of being martyred en masse. The first Christians in Rome would have given it up when they were being hunted by Nero. All he asked was that they deny their God. They didn't and he slaughtered them by the thousands. He set them ablaze and used them as human torches for his parties. He filled the Coliseum with them and had them torn apart by wild animals in front of the screaming masses. Can you actually believe that if Christianity was just a lifestyle any one of those men and women would have let themselves be torched? I could go on and on, Beth, because the history of Christianity is filled with the blood of martyrs who chose death rather than denying their Lord. "If I had been raised in Indonesia instead of America God might have asked me to try and protect my Christian brothers and sisters from the Muslims who come to kill them every few months. If I had been raised in China I would have had to decide whether to break the law by telling my children about Christ. God asking me to hold a sign in front of a building seems pretty small in light of what's going on around the world to this very day.

"So you see, Beth, I didn't really have a choice. I believe that what the Bible says is true. I believe that there is a God above who will judge everyone at the end of their life for the deeds they have done. And I believe there is such a thing as clear right and wrong, truth and lies. Do you think I would have made such a decision if I had any choice at all? True, it was a choice I made, but it was only the choice between living and dying, and that's not really a choice, is it?"

The tape ran out at four minutes. Mike felt a pinprick of sweat break out on his forehead when Beth's tape finished a full thirty seconds early, but he had no choice other than to bring the camera back onto her.

"The Tells are in hiding. They don't know if or when they will be able to return to America. They don't know if or when they'll be able to see their oldest daughter again. She's currently being held in the Folson Re-education Center in California. Alan told me that their daughter had the chance to escape with them and refused.

Apparently she takes after her parents because she told them it was her duty to make sure the teens at Folson heard the truth among the bunkum.

"And the Tells are not alone. There are currently thousands of Americans who have chosen exile rather than stay in a country in the business of legislating religion. I, for one, believe that the Minor Protection Act is wrong. I believe this government of ours has lost control and is hunting Christians for no other reason than the fact that they are Christians. I don't know what the real motive is, but I do know it has nothing to do with the lies we were told. It has nothing to do with religious zealotry or the fostering of terrorism. The only zealotry I see these days is coming out of the White House.

"In closing I'd like to say that I believe I am not alone. Though the VNs currently show an MPA approval rating of 51%, I believe that is an inaccurate measurement of the actual feeling of you, my fellow Americans. Whether that percentage is a reflection of the fear we're all feeling, that if we speak out our names will be added to the MPA rosters, or whether it reflects something far more sinister, I promise you I will get to the bottom of it."

When the camera blinked off signifying they'd gone to a commercial break Beth slowly unclipped her microphone and gathered her notes. Her favorite cameraman was grimacing and giving her the slit-throat sign. She could see Mike in the control room talking on his cell phone and violently shaking his head in denial. She walked slowly back to her desk and started packing.

MOORPARK, CALIFORNIA
7:15PM EST

Amanda was waiting to hear from George, certain that he would call the minute he had seen Nate and his family safely away. That should have been an hour ago but a lifetime of being married to a cop meant she wasn't inordinately worried. She just couldn't suspect Nate of turning on George. She was sitting quietly on her couch in the darkened living room when her front door burst open.

LAS VEGAS, NEVADA
8:30PM EST

Josh was silent in his leather chair, swinging slowly back and forth as he stared at the blank screen before him. It was the first instance in years that he'd sat for any length of time without the gentle humming of electronics to lull him. It was strangely disquieting, the only sound reaching his ears the little tick tock, tick tock of the clock on the wall. He'd just finished a bout of frantic activity set off by a quick phone call from Jack. He was surprised to have gotten a little choked up while running the large magnet over his hard drives. The microwave dinged softly from the kitchen after completing its task of frying almost 100 cd's. "Well, that's that," he said, just because he felt it was a moment when something needed to be said. Not a minute later he heard them coming and quietly bowed his head.

SPECIAL REPORT
8:45PM EST

"My fellow Americans, I'm pleased to report tonight that, after a long and difficult investigation, the MPA Task Force has apprehended the main cell of terrorists responsible for last year's kidnappings. Unfortunately the leader, a George Rochester of California, was killed while trying to evade capture. However, we have the rest of the cell in custody, including Mr. Rochester's wife and nephew. The Task Force expects to make additional arrests in the coming days as more information becomes available. I'd like to take a moment now to applaud the diligent efforts of the Task

Force. I trust that MPA enforcement will continue at an easier pace from now on."

When Beth walked into her apartment much later she had a message on her home phone from Rick. His familiar, steady voice coming through her machine caused the tears that had been hovering at the edge of her throat to come through full force. "Hey, lady. I saw your story tonight. I've never been prouder to know you and I just wanted to make sure you knew it. I'm guessing that with that closing commentary you're going to have some free time coming up. As a way of a bonus, one sneaky conservative to another, I've got someone for you to meet when you feel up to it. He just called me tonight with his decision to go on record about the President tampering with the VNs."

Jack spent the evening at Sam's as they talked quietly about what to do. Josh had assured Jack over the phone that there was nothing in Amanda's computer that would link either him or Sam to the plot and Josh had fried his computers. The only thing he thought Amanda had on her computer was her database information, which was obviously bad enough. But all communication between Amanda and Sam had been through the anonymous e-mail accounts. Josh closed all those accounts before turning his computer into scrap metal.

Jack and Sam were obviously relieved that they didn't need to worry about themselves for the moment, but they were sick at heart over George's death and the arrests. They sat on Sam's couch in silence most of the evening; the only contact their clasped hands between them. There just wasn't much to say and they tacitly agreed to plan for the future in the morning.

SEPTEMBER 20TH
2:00PM, FRIDAY

Jack stood tall before the phalanx of press shoving microphones in his face. He scanned the crowd for Sam and nodded slightly when he saw her toward the back before clearing his throat and beginning. "Thank you all for coming. I'd like to make a quick announcement and then I'll take a few questions. First of all, I've tendered my resignation to the Attorney General and will no longer be working for the MPA Task Force. Second, I have agreed to represent Amanda Rochester and Joshua Naylor. I believe they have been wrongly accused and I will do whatever is necessary to clear their good names. Now are there any questions?"

The audience exploded and Jack called on one face he recognized, "Bill?"

"Bill Fredrickson, CNN. Why have you switched sides?"

"That's a very good question, Bill. The short answer is that I have come to believe the Minor Protection Act is the single most harmful piece of legislation to be enacted in our country's history. Since I take full responsibility for its passage I feel the necessity of defending the honest citizens who have been snared by my hand. Ned?"

"Thanks. Ned Anderson, Fox News. Jack, don't you think it's a little late to be saying this? The Minor Protection Act is the law of the land. The MPA Task Force employs 100 full time agents and the President has submitted a request to Congress to fund an additional 300. There have already been almost two thousand children placed in new foster families and re-education centers. What good can you do?"

"Ned, I don't know yet. But this is my mess and I intend to do all I can to clean it up, starting with this. Thank you all for coming, I'm sure we'll talk again in the future."

Time was planning to run a cover photo of George and Amanda's wedding picture and Newsweek had gotten a hold of an old family photo with George, Amanda and Josh at a barbecue but when Jack held his press conference they scrapped those ideas and put him on instead. He spent most of the next week giving interviews at the same frantic pace he'd given them following the Jessup trial. He didn't have a lot of free time, but what he did have he spent holed up with Sam in her apartment, talking about almost anything but the trial before dragging himself away to spend the night at his hotel.

He also spent hours at the federal penitentiary where Amanda and Josh were being held until trial since they had been denied bail. He tried to get through to them that their chances of getting away scot-free were slim to none since the government had them cold with the data they'd found on Amanda's computer. For some reason they didn't seem to mind.

Beth was working just as frantically. She knew it was only a matter of time before Rick was arrested owing to his involvement with Josh and her peers' longstanding history of following the money. She was doing everything in her power to get the story before that happened. Rick had given her his VN contact information and passed along what scraps Jack knew. She had to get the dirt on Farmer before it was too late. She figured her name was mud in Washington anyway, so she might as well call in all the favors she'd accumulated on her rise to the top. Favors were always good in this business, even when you were unemployed.

CHAPTER 26

Sam was startled from her Internet job search by the trill of her cell phone. "Hello?"

"Samantha!"

"I told you, if you keep calling me that I'm going to keep hanging up on you." The smile on her face belied the words she used.

"Ok, ok. Sam. Greetings."

"Aren't you supposed to be working? Closeted? No interruptions?"

"Yeah, yeah. But I have something to tell you." His voice sounded exactly like a little boy who'd just found out he was getting what he wanted for Christmas.

She closed her browser window, as the search had been fruitless so far anyway. "I'm all ears."

"Well, you'll never guess who called me just now…"

She remained quiet.

"Aren't you going to guess?"

"You just told me I'd never guess so I'm waiting for you to deem me worthy of that knowledge."

"You are one tough cookie. You know that, don't you?"

"It comes from years of interrogating criminals like you. I have to be tough."

"Alright, I'll tell you who called. Roselyn Jessup. I just hung up with her before I called you."

She sat up straight. "The Roselyn Jessup? Your old client Roselyn Jessup?"

"One and the same."

"Well, what did she want?"

"I can't tell you, it was a protected conversation."

She could hear the grin in his voice so she wasn't as ticked as she might normally have been. "Excuse me? Then why did you call?"

"I just had a very enlightening conversation that is going to be extremely helpful to my case and I wanted to share it with you. That's all."

"Well thanks for sharing Jack, I'm happy for you."

"No…thank you Samantha. I appreciate your…"

Click.

"Sam…Sam?"

FEDERAL COURTHOUSE
SEPTEMBER 29TH
4:30PM

Jack was midstream through his opening statement. He'd decided the only chance of getting Amanda and Josh off, slim as it was, would be to prove that MPA was illegal. Of course, he couldn't actually prove it since MPA was the law, but he could sure blast every gun he had and hope for a public outcry.

"The Minor Protection Act was begun as a noble idea with noble intentions, but even noble intentions can be wrong. Trust me, they were my noble intentions. But I don't believe America would have supported the MPA in the first place if they'd known how far President Farmer was going to push it. I know I certainly wouldn't have. Rooting out terrorism in theory is one thing, but in practice MPA has become something else entirely. I believe more Americans would be speaking against this right now, but they're afraid Farmer will sick the Task Force on them.

"Ladies and gentlemen of the jury, you are going to have the chance to right a great wrong, a wrong that was begun with a lie. This whole business started because of the journals left behind by a tortured young girl, Jayla Jessup. You should all be familiar with those journals, but she wrote one final chapter that has yet to be read. Roselyn Jessup contacted me three days ago - she'd finally worked up the courage to clean out her daughter's room. Roselyn found Jayla's final words, recorded in a journal that was missed when Jayla died because it was stuffed under her bed. In closing I'd like to read it to you:

Journal of Jayla Jessup

1:12am, January 1, 2007 I'm beginning my new life in this new journal. I'm only halfway through my old one, but I feel the need for a symbolic new beginning. I finally did it! I spent all night locked in my room reading through my journals and Nick's letters, thinking about things he's said all year. Around midnight it all began to make sense. It took all my courage, but I got on my knees, put my face to the ground and asked God to forgive my sins and come into my heart, repeating the words Nick has said so many times. There was the most incredible warmth that encircled me, almost like someone hugging me. I actually brought my head up to see if mom had snuck in without me hearing her. But there was no one there! I had the greatest sense of peace I have ever known. It still hasn't left actually.

I can't wait to tell Nick. He was right! I can't believe he was actually right! All this time, all these questions, all this pain I've endured - it was unnecessary. Well, maybe it was necessary because it brought me to this place. What an incredible place!

I wonder what my parents will think. That was my first actual prayer, if you can call it that. "God, help me tell my parents." After that, what do I tell my friends at school? What do I tell Ms. Jacobs? Even with all those questions still swirling around in my head, I know I've made the right decision. I feel, well, RIGHT, for the first time in SOOO long. And clean. I can't remember the last time I didn't feel just filthy. That's all gone tonight! I feel joy and I don't know as I've ever felt that before. It's like I'm a new person! I can't wait for tomorrow.

As the finale on my old life I poured out an old bottle of vodka I had hidden under the bed and flushed all those stupid anti-depressants down the toilet. I'll talk to mom about it tomorrow but I'm tired of all the side effects. Today my chest felt like it was going to explode after our flag football game. I asked God to heal me of the depression so I don't have to take the pills anymore and I think He already has. I feel great!

Jack walked back to his table and set the journal down. He stared at it for a few seconds before turning to face the jury. "Jayla Jessup did not commit suicide. Her death was ruled a suicide because of the wealth of circumstantial evidence. The combination of large amounts of anti-depressants and alcohol leads to respiratory depression. In combination with the apparent suicidal thoughts she'd been having as represented by her journals, no autopsy was done. However, after finding this last journal Roselyn Jessup had her daughter's body exhumed. I will call to the stand the pathologist who performed the autopsy and identified the ruptured aortic arch that proves Jayla suffered from Marfan's syndrome. She died from a hereditary disease that also struck two other members of her extended family with no warning. It was tragic, yes, but it was not suicide. Therefore, the string of injustice that runs from Nick Rodman, to his parents, to Amanda Rochester and Joshua Naylor must be broken."

He had to stop and catch his breath before continuing. "I was right when I came before you and said we are living in a culture of hatred. I was right when I said we are living in a culture of intolerance. But I was wrong when I made you believe that we would solve this by acting in a hateful and intolerant manner toward Christians raising their children to believe in the principals our forefathers founded this country upon.

"Terrible things have been done in the name of Christ and Christians. But to blame all Christianity for what one person or a group of fringe extremists do is like blaming all Arabs for the atrocities done by the PLO. It's like painting all Germans with the hatred of Hitler. Or punishing all Iraqis for the evil actions of Saddam Hussein. It's wrong. I was wrong."

This time the pause was longer as he tried to swallow the lump growing in his throat. "Every day in America people preach about what they believe. From things as simple as trying to persuade someone your football team is tougher, to huge ideologies like

270

Democracy that we advertise to the rest of the world. America is about beliefs. The very idea of tolerance is putting up with a belief with which you disagree. Putting up with someone even though you think they're a kook. America has never been about punishing someone because they teach their children a different path.

"The MPA is a lie. It was based on a lie and its enforcement has been the biggest lie of all. You must not find Amanda Rochester or Joshua Naylor guilty for doing what they could to show the truth."

NBC STUDIOS
6:35PM

Beth was back for one more story. That was the deal. She had been fired after her last one, of course, but when she approached Mike with what she intended to report he'd agreed to give her the airtime. It was very generous of him, considering she would be pulling in 99% market share by the time he'd run promos for two days.

Josh's hacker friend had come through with the decryption, but when Josh was arrested he hadn't known what to do with it. The second he saw Jack's press conference he bundled everything up and sent it Federal Express. Jack received the package, glanced through it and immediately went to visit Josh. The suggestion was to send it all to Beth, who had more than proven Rick correct in his estimation of her. So it got bundled again and forwarded on to her.

The documentation only helped nail the lid on the coffin for Farmer and the Attorney General. She already had Rick's VN contact on tape saying he'd seen internal memos ordering the VN Director to misrepresent the numbers. Now she had the memos between Farmer and Franklin discussing it. She also had Franklin's list of 2.4 million Christians who they were intending to target if they could make it that far. Thanks to the diligent efforts of Mr. Hacker she also had a whole file full of "ideas" that Farmer had forwarded onto Franklin. It would seem that the Attorney General had been the levelheaded one of the two.

Jack had already sent her the information about the California teen Franklin paid off to pretend he was going to mow down his entire basketball team because of their religious bullying on the day Farmer introduced the Tolerance Oath. The teen got released from prison one year early in exchange for his interview with Beth. The court even allowed him to keep half of the $250,000 dollars he'd received from Franklin, provided he use the money to pay for college.

FEDERAL COURTHOUSE
SEPTEMBER 30TH
7:59AM

Jack was shuffling through the papers in his briefcase trying to get energized about presenting his case when the federal prosecutor came strolling in and winked at him. Taken aback, Jack wondered what the man could have up his sleeve. He didn't have to wonder long. The judge entered just then and, once seated, asked if there were any new motions. The prosecutor immediately stood up.

"Your Honor, I have just been informed that a special joint session of Congress met early this morning for the purpose of voting to impeach the President and repeal the Minor Protection Act. Owing to their actions, the government feels it is in the best interest of the country to drop all charges against Amanda Rochester and Joshua Naylor."

It was September 30th, a day America would never forget.

EPILOGUE

Beth saw the winter whiz by from her new position as an anchor at Fox News Channel. There were plenty of interviews to do with returning families and she even got to do her first international series. The first week was spent at the Zimbabwe compound. Everyone there had decided to stay and her coverage actually brought in a few more volunteers. She spent the second week helping build houses in the Dominican Republic with the Tells, who had also decided to stay. She was there with her camera crew when Sue got off the plane and was reunited with her family.

Her interview with the Rodmans was one of the most watched programs of the winter. No one could believe that they were returning since Nick's conviction was still in effect, but she was there with camera rolling when he explained that he had to go back and finish his legally delivered sentence now that he knew his sister would be safe. She was also there a month later when Nick's conviction was overturned due to Jack's legal maneuvering about the real cause of Jayla's death.

Beth tried to keep America focused by doing a series on the teens coming out of the re-education centers, 95% of whom headed either to Bible College or law school, but America quickly lost interest. It seemed a chapter everyone wanted to forget as quickly as possible.

Since she'd watched a lot of the C-SPAN coverage of the impeachment trial she wasn't surprised when the vote fell along party lines and Farmer kept his job by the skin of his teeth. He was a severely chastened man and limped through the rest of his two years in office, never again sitting in his Talk anchor chair.

AG Franklin was not so lucky. He ended up taking the brunt of the blame for their schemes and was sentenced to five years at Maxwell Prison.

LOS ANGELES AIRPORT

Sam had never been so happy to leave a job. She'd been called back from her unspecified leave to help the Task Force disband and the paperwork needed to clean up their mess had taken over a month. After finishing her assignment she'd requested a transfer to the Ventura Field Office and because of her excellent record preMPA it was approved. She was looking forward to a more casual work environment.

Among other things, she smiled to herself as she walked through the security gate. Eyes roving from right to left, she methodically searched the room as she'd been taught. A big grin slid across her face when she saw Jack pop out from behind a pillar with a huge bouquet of flowers in hand.

THE END

ACKNOWLEDGEMENTS

It's a miracle that I'm sitting here at 11 o'clock at night trying to figure out what to put in my "acknowledgements" before sending this off for typesetting. The miracle, of course, is not that I'm doing this at the last minute – anyone who knows me knows that this is per usual. No, the miracle is that this five year labor of love is actually going to print. That's something I still have trouble believing.

The truth is, this book probably would never have been finished, or if finished, would never have moved beyond my desk drawer were it not for a few stubborn people. Foremost among them are my number one cheerleaders – Mom and Dad. Thanks for being typo-checkers and unpaid research assistants answering countless telephone calls and e-mails. "How fast does a Lear fly?" "What's the name of that guy in that story you were telling me about last year?" "Are you sure this isn't the stupidest idea I've ever had?" All my life you've given me unflagging support which, at times, seems wildly misplaced. I will never be able to fully express my gratitude.

Mel-OD: couldn't have done it without your friendship, eternal optimism and continual kicks in the rear. The guinea pigs (Grandma, Jill, Gail, Ryan, Sheryl, Pami, Prudence and Kim): thanks for reading, commenting and being so supportive. Mike and Sue: thanks for giving me more than just a roof over my head while I wrote. John, thanks for the great flight plan and international flying info. David, thanks for the last minute medical intervention so that I didn't sound like a complete idiot. And to the family and friends (Cole STMC!) who answered my frantic email, thanks for your last minute prayers during the final editing phase, as well as your support throughout the entire process.

Finally, to Him in whom I live and move and have my being. The original Author. No words do You justice. Psalm 69:6

Jodi Cowles

October 17, 2005, Boise, Idaho

Made in the USA
Coppell, TX
17 February 2023

13013039R00163